Other books by Bill Norris

Dagger Four Is OK

FLYING INTO THE STORM

By

BILL NORRIS

ISBN 13: 978-0-9915409-5-2

Library of Congress Control Number: 2014904437

Published by Nekko Books LLC
www.nekkobooks.com
Email: info@nekkobooks.com

Edited by C. E. Wertheimer

Cover Art By:
Sheila Norris
Nekko Books, LLC

What's being said about

FLYING INTO THE STORM

"This book gives real hope for the true healing of the ghastly and despicable cries against humanity on both sides of a war…and all the stuff in-between."

Father Ron Camarda, author of Tear in the Desert, Roman Catholic priest and Navy chaplain (ret)

"This book took me back so vividly that I could only read for a short time. I really related to the descriptions of the people, the terrain, the heat and the monsoons…no self-proclaimed heroes, no heroic battles, just the way things really were. Best Vietnam book I have read. Surfaced so many memories for me that I thought I had buried."

Bob Short, Vietnam veteran, Army helicopter door gunner in 1968, international textile business owner

"From the moment I started reading, I could not put it down. The account of "Jared" from beginning to end showed everything in an American soldier: bravery, heroism, compassion, the ability to lead men in combat. It was a book written so well that it gives us a unique understanding of the heart of the American soldier. Absolutely heartwarming."

Howard Levine, owner, United Van Lines Agency

"I really liked the book. It was well written and held my attention. What makes this story so compelling, it was told by a fine leader and courageous infantry soldier."

Colonel Jim Franklin, Vietnam veteran 1968, U.S. Army Infantry Retired (Hon)

"Seldom does a historical fiction book read so accurate and true that one senses it is not fiction but rather in this case a true memoir of combat. Bill Norris undoubtedly has put his personal experience into this remarkable work."

Richard C. Geschke, Military Writers Society of America

"Each page evokes memories and an emotional response to that memory. It is a great book and I can really sink into it and forget the passage of time."

> *Larry Eckels, Vietnam veteran, Sergeant Army Infantry, businessman*

"These are sacred stories of men doing things a soldier in a soldier's world must. The stories make the experience real and immediate and humbles even one who shared a part of the journey. Stories like this that are told well enough and that are powerful enough of people acting well in the worst of times can inspire and even transform the possibilities for all."

> *Terry Maloney, Army officer severely wounded in Vietnam, writer, businessman*

"It was fascinating to see how Jared was forced to essentially ignore his humanist feelings after befriending children of the area and having to become a soldier following orders again. This would be an important read for anyone who wants a better and more personal, intimate look at the everyday horrors of war as seen through the eyes of a very perceptive soldier."

> *Joshua Reyes, musician, business manager*

"This book is packed with wisdom, warmth, horror and the realities of war with all its blood, guts and human emotions. It flows, it excites, it moves, it scares, it's heartfelt. Couldn't put it down, riveted to it! One of the best books I have ever read."

> *Lieutenant Colonel Jerome Domask, Vietnam veteran, U.S. Army Retired (Hon), artist and businessman*

"This story is great! So interesting and told in such a way that it makes me feel that I was there…feel the pain and the struggles encountered. Once I started, I could not wait to finish it."

> *Larry Stone, retired President, Lowe's*

"I found myself flooded with so many emotions that at times I had to lay the book down to recover. No fancy glorious stories here; just the truth which is much more powerful. The book made a powerful impression on me."

> *Bruce Evors*

Acknowledgements

To Larry Eckels, aka Lenny Enson. Lifelong friend, advisor and comrade in war. We created the memories. You patiently helped me to bring them back.

To Lieutenant Colonel Jerry Domask and wife Mary. Your proof reading as I was writing kept me on path as the story evolved. Your enthusiastic encouragement saw me through to the finish.

To Charley Wertheimer, editor. Your personal Vietnam knowledge and experience together with your editorial professionalism helped me to effectively bring the story to life.

To my wonderful wife Sheila, my 24/7 partner in life and business, my technical support group of one, my old soul companion and lover and my inspiration to achieve. You give reason to my existence.

For
Franny and Gerry

Adieu sacred friends.
We flew together, over the horizon and beyond,
where eagles soar.
We'll meet once again,
in the mystical glow as the sun sets,
and share tall tales of war.

Chapter 1

The airplane banked left to begin its descent into Cam Ranh Bay. I was seated by the window, in row eighteen on the left side of the plane, and had a bird's eye view of the coast of South Vietnam.

Bobby Dow was sitting beside me. We were in the same training company at Fort Jackson. After graduation, just before Christmas, we were granted a three week leave to go home and say goodbye before heading to war.

We processed through the army's demarcation center at Fort Lewis and boarded the Northwest Orient flight in Seattle. They were moving so many of us through the processing center for Vietnam bound replacements that I wondered how they could keep track of us. It seemed miraculous to me that I could end up nearly three thousand miles across the country seated beside somebody I had gotten to know in training. The majority of the half million Americans deployed to Vietnam had to be replaced each year, so that averaged about twenty-eight hundred soldiers moving in and out of country every day, fourteen hundred in and the same number out.

Every passenger on board was headed for war. The twenty-three hours we were on board passed too quickly.

We landed to refuel in Tokyo but were not allowed to deplane, probably for fear we might disappear. Based on the silent tension that filled the flight they were probably right.

"There's Cam Ranh Bay airport," Bobby pointed out, leaning over the armrest between us to get a better view. Those were the first words he had spoken since we left Japan hours earlier.

The pilot banked the airplane more severely and began a steep descent. We were nearing the runway up ahead and to the left.   I felt a jolt from the undercarriage as the landing gear was lowered. The aircraft slowed so quickly it pitched me forward and increased the pressure of my seat belt across my waist.

I was a nervous and inexperienced passenger. My first flight was three days earlier when I boarded the Seattle bound flight in Charlotte.   The creaks, bangs and clumping noises, probably routine to experienced flyers, all made me cringe and hold on tighter to the arm rests. At the same time, flying was becoming a fascinating adventure to me, one I knew I would want more of in the future.

I looked out the porthole, my head now ear to ear with Bobby as we tried to share the view. The white cumulous clouds floated around us like big fluffy pillows suspended from the vast blue sky. The military base at Cam Ranh below us was distinguishable by its rows of canvas roofed wooden barracks surrounded by dirty sand roads that led out from center like the tentacles of an octopus.   That combined with a lack of green foliage were distinct signs of destroyed terrain that comes with military occupation.

The pilot pivoted the aircraft onto its final approach. It felt like someone was putting on the brakes as we slowed some more when he adjusted throttle to landing speed. Suddenly the engines roared to life and the airplane changed attitude to nose high, the landing gear banged and bumped back into the airplane's belly followed by the hydraulic groaning as the flaps were withdrawn.

"It sure would be ironic to fly all the way to Vietnam and get killed before we ever got to war," Bobby said.

"Maybe there's something wrong with the plane or maybe the pilot just decided to take us all home with him." I was trying not to let how scared I was show.

We passed over the shoreline heading east out over the South China Sea. Once over open water the pilot turned south and seemed to be maintaining level flight and airspeed. Lying offshore beneath us was an American aircraft carrier and the fleet of destroyers, battleships and other Navy vessels that supported the carrier group. Sampan fishing boats surrounded the fleet keeping a required safe distance from the ships. As we cruised above them I could see their nets making wakes as they dragged along behind the small crafts.

"Sorry to disappoint all you guys," the pilot's voice boomed over the airplane's intercom. "I know you are all anxious to get out to the boonies but the tower told us to circle around and wait a while. It seems the base at Cam Ranh is under an enemy mortar attack although no action has been reported at the airport. It's likely just a precaution. Please stay seated with your seatbelts fastened. When they give us the all clear we will need to get in, unload and reload as quickly as possible. So, once we're on the ground and the flight crew gives you the signal, please double time the unloading process and be prepared to follow directions from the officers on the tarmac. We'll do our best to get you down there ASAP so you can go give our regards to Charlie."

The captain's humor broke the tension and the cabin exploded in cheers and applause.

"I've always thought you looked like a good candidate for NCO school," I admitted to Bobby. I felt a nervous need for conversation. Bobby had this look about him like he was always about to break into a big smile. He had a kind sparkle to his hazel eyes that made him approachable. He took a lot of harassment from drill instructors during training because his toes pointed outward severely when he walked making his head bob up and down. The sergeants thought he smiled at them when they were dressing him down for one infraction or another. However, he was a good soldier who always did what he was told and was good at taking the grief in stride.

"Yeah, right," he responded sarcastically. "If I was interested in going to school, I would have stayed in college. Right now that is what I'm wishing I had done," he added, thoughtfully stroking his heavily bearded chin. His facial hair was so thick I imagined he needed to shave twice a day.

"So how did you end up here?" I asked. "You strike me as the scholarly type. I bet you were an A student."

"Yeah, I pretty much had the grades. I just didn't like all the other garbage that came with the whole college scene, especially the social aspects. I'm pretty shy and I just wasn't up for all the pressure to fit in on campus. Uncle Sam sure didn't mess around. I got my 1-A draft classification less than a month after I dropped out," he finished.

That was the most I had ever heard Bobby talk. I never noticed the slight lisp in his speech emphasized by the way his upper teeth came to a point in the front. His shyness was exacerbated by his five-foot-eight inch stature and his drooping shoulders that seemed to slope forward making it appear he was always looking at the ground, another reason for him to get attention from the drill sergeants. But he had an underlying exuberance for life emphasized by his pleasantly sarcastic attitude.

Bobby pulled away from the window and sat back. The young man sitting in the aisle seat and wearing sergeant's stripes leaned over Bobby and asked if he could take a look. A big yellow First Cavalry patch decorated his uniform shoulder. He had seemed lost in thought the entire flight and had not spoken until now. I pushed back into my seat to give him a better view.

"I like Vietnam much better from up here," he said. "I've already done six months. I'm not feeling real wild about coming back." He went on to explain that he was returning from a bereavement leave. His mother died after a long battle with cancer that began before he enlisted in the army.

We exchanged introductions and made small talk about where we were from and took turns describing our military experience up to now. His name was Colt McCray from Enid, Oklahoma.

"I noticed you were sort of into your own space," Bobby admitted. "That's why I haven't tried to talk to you."

"Yeah, I asked them to end my one-year tour so I could help my father out, but they turned me down, so I've been feeling pretty funky about it."

"I bet you take a lot of grief about your name, I mean being that you are in the First Cav, horse on the insignia and all," I joined in.

"Yeah, I was named after my grandfather who herded cattle back in the old days," he offered. "Colt was his nickname and everyone called him that. My folks wanted to name me after him and decided Colt sounded better than Henry, his given name."

"What is the First Cavalry Division like?" Bobby asked. "I mean, I don't guess they have horses down there," he added, pointing to the port hole.

"We're the original air mobile combat assault division," he explained. "We are still considered infantry but we attack by helicopter. They use helicopter tactical assaults to try to catch Charlie by surprise. Sometimes it works and sometimes we get our asses kicked."

"Do you think we're winning the war?" I asked.

"Hell, they don't even call it a war," he answered sarcastically. "You guys are coming into a real ugly mess that I don't think we can ever win. They call it a policing action since it is not a declared war. There are no lines so you don't know who your enemy is and most of the time you don't know who is shooting at you, man, woman or child. There is a demilitarized zone north of Da Nang that is supposed to mean the North Vietnamese cannot enter or cross from the north to get to the south and the South Vietnamese and their American allies aren't supposed to go north of it or enter it from the south. Problem is, the NVA keep sending their divisions south to fight us in South Vietnam, but except for bombing missions, we do not attack them or cross their borders."

"Don't we have some way to stop them from crossing the DMZ?" I asked.

"It's not that simple," Colt declared. "The North Viets use the Ho Chi Minh trail to move troops and supplies north to south back and forth across the borders of Laos and Cambodia. They have whole divisions of NVA regulars scattered around South Vietnam. On top of them there is a whole other army of Viet Cong soldiers made up of the good citizens who want to overthrow the government in the south."

"Doesn't the south have an army too?" I queried, feeling a little stupid for asking such a dumb question.

"Yeah, there's an army," Colt replied. "Don't expect to depend on them when the battles begin. They are the

Army of the Republic of Vietnam or ARVN. We've killed some of them when we thought we were getting shot at by VC."

Colt was intelligent and seemed to have acquired a lot of savvy about the war. He was regular army which meant that he enlisted for three years as compared to being drafted. He was clean cut and blond and was about six feet tall, I guessed. He looked almost boyish with big dimples in his cheeks that seemed to crease his whole face when he smiled. There was a toughness about him that belied his youthful appearance, a harsh directness that said 'don't question what I tell you because I've been there and know what I'm talking about.'

"When did you join the army?" I asked.

"It will be eighteen months next week," he answered as he unbuttoned his shirt pocket and extracted a folded up paper. Spreading the paper out on the seat tray, he announced "this is my short timers' calendar."

It was a mimeographed drawing of a naked woman with 365 numbered spaces on her body. Number "1" was on the tip of her nose. It was marked through with an "X" followed in sequence by more crossed out numbers. Number 187 near her navel was the first number not crossed out.

"I will have been here 187 days today, just haven't crossed it out yet," Colt declared. "I'm looking forward to number 365," he added, pointing to the number space that was in the woman's pubic hair. "My ETS out of here is July 6th."

"It only took Uncle Sam five months to get me through training and headed for Vietnam," I pointed out. "I guess maybe it was because I am only in for two years."

"That's about right," Colt agreed. "It took me longer to get through NCO school before they shipped me out. That's how I got the sergeant stripes," he added.

The pilot interrupted us to announce that we had been cleared to land with instructions that we remain seated with our seat belts fastened. Bobby and I exchanged a look of dread that was not lost on Colt.

"Relax guys," he instructed. "Cam Ranh Bay is about the safest place in 'Nam. If there was an attack it was probably some Viet Cong soldier firing one rocket propelled grenade on the outskirts of the base and it probably didn't even hit anything. It's Charlie's job to maintain the harassment to keep us on our toes."

Nonetheless, when the airplane taxied to a stop and the stewardess opened the exit door, everybody, including Colt, shouldered their gear and double timed down the steps and trotted across the tarmac to the reception station.

Chapter 2

The end of January was approaching and with it the beginning of the 1968 Vietnamese TET new years' celebrations. I really did not mind finally getting my unit assignment and orders after a week of night perimeter tower guard and daytime busywork details. Like everyone else, I was terrified of going into the field with the prospect of meeting the enemy face to face. We were all just kids, most of us no more than six or seven years out of puberty. I had turned twenty in November, only two months earlier.

After chow I processed through supply to get my field gear which consisted of a rucksack, a poncho, poncho liner, an extra pair of socks and a clean set of jungle fatigue shirt and pants. I already had my utility belt that held two canteens and two ammo pouches capable of holding five twenty-round magazines each for my M-16. Two concussion hand grenades could be attached to each side of the ammo pouches. My black leather boots were replaced with canvas topped jungle boots complete with steel plates in the soles to protect from bungee stakes and small caliber booby traps. The special canvas from ankles up was designed so a snake could not bite through it. The steel helmet and liner with camouflage cover felt like it weighed a ton. I was now a fully equipped combat infantry soldier.

I lugged my gear over to the guard tower to get situated for another night of perimeter watch duty. I would not be returning to the battalion barracks before heading off to my new home on Landing Zone Liz in the morning. As I settled in, I spotted a fatigue clad sergeant holding a cardboard box next to the rolled concertina wire fence. He was shouting something to a village kid on the outside of the fence. The kid threw what appeared to be a rock to the soldier. He examined the small bundle and I could see that he was peeling off and counting American currency. Evidently satisfied with the amount, he picked up the box, backed away from the fence and got a running start to fling the box over. The kid gathered up the box and scampered away.

The box was a sundries pack intended for troops in the field. It contained supplies like candy, cigarettes, tooth brushes, soap, razors and other much appreciated luxuries not otherwise available to the infantry soldiers that had no or limited access to the brigade PX. In short supply, these sundries packs were being sold to villagers on the black market.

During our week of jungle training, we were instructed not to support the black market by buying American products from the locals. The illegally procured goods were marketed by villagers and street vendors all up and down Highway One, we were told. American cigarettes were the most popular contraband and could be found in most roadside store fronts. Village kids would load up their bicycles and hustle them and other items from the sundries packs. It did not matter to the black marketers if the soldiers were American, South Vietnamese (ARVN), Viet Cong (VC) or North Vietnamese Army (NVA). It was all about the money. So the sundries often landed in enemy hands. That didn't make any difference to the sergeant who was profiting from his rear echelon position.

My last night on perimeter guard passed quietly and I was able to get some sleep every two hours when my replacement, a soldier assigned to roving guard duty, came by to relieve me. The roving guard showed up for the last time at five o'clock and I went to the battalion mess for breakfast. I devoured the hot meal of powdered eggs, pancakes and canned peaches, hungry after a long night spent mostly awake staring into darkness. I finished eating and visited the latrine, a line of elevated wood outhouses with half barrels under toilet seats. When you did something to piss off a duty officer, you would get assigned to latrine duty which consisted of removing the barrels and burning the contents in kerosene. That was an odor you would not soon forget.

A deuce-and-a-half supply truck arrived before sunrise, the clunky diesel engine a sharp interruption to the still early morning. I would be accompanied on the trip to Liz by a seasoned looking private first class, the same rank as me since we were all promoted to PFC as soon as we arrived in Vietnam. He was returning to the field from sick call. Along with him, we were joined by a company clerk in pressed fatigues who was delivering the payroll out to the troops on Liz.

We helped load the cases of soda, beer, c-rations, ammunition boxes and mail bags into the canvas covered truck bed then got on board and used the boxes for seats. The driver and his shotgun, a black specialist four from Georgia, climbed into the front and we said farewell to the brigade headquarters called Bronco.

The security gate opened onto the main street of Đức Phổ. I had only seen the street from atop the guard tower where I was posted during the few days it took to get processed and assigned to an infantry platoon. The sun was not awake yet but shared a few strands of light in its skyward rotation from the direction of the South China Sea to the east. The village buildings lining the dirt street started to come into focus, a combination of old French architecture with plain concrete walls among thatched grass roofs and mud walls roughly arranged in rows along the roadsides.

In the predawn quiet, people were moving about their daily chores, lighting cooking fires and gathering water from the town well so they could cook their rice. The foods they cooked, rice, fish, chicken and even water buffalo, created a distinctive odor that clung to your memory. The villagers had no refrigeration so the only certain staple was rice. Meat and fish had to be used the same day it was killed or caught and villagers shared rather than waste anything. Although considered sacred, they would eat water buffalo when one died or was killed in the war or by accident. Villagers would come from miles around to get a slab of the precious meat even though it was mostly used for its flavor. It was too tough to chew and swallow although it made a good flavoring to add to rice. It smelled much better than the sauce they made by fermenting fish heads and entrails in water, a mixture known as nuoc mam.

We turned right heading north away from Đức Phổ and came to an abrupt stop. The mine sweeping crew had just begun their job of scanning the roadway for mines and booby traps. The big diesel smoked, clanged and chugged as we slowly followed along behind the mine sweepers.

The narrow road slicing the village in two parts was the main artery that connected cities to the south and north. Highway One ran from Saigon and Nha Trang in the south to Quảng Ngãi, Chu Lai and Đà Nẵng in the north. I had noticed from the guard tower that the roadway was always jammed with motorized and pedestrian traffic until early evening. No traffic was allowed on the road after curfew during the night. As the day lightened, people and vehicles seemed to come from everywhere as Highway One came alive.

The PFC was rowdy, shouting insults at women toting heavily laden baskets on the ends of poles balanced across their shoulders. He clearly disliked Vietnamese people and I wondered what had happened to make him so bitter towards them.

Occasionally a woman would scurry off to the side of the road down toward a rice paddy, pull one silk leg of her black pajama bottom pants up to the top of her thigh and stoop down to relieve herself, her load never leaving her shoulders. The deed completed, she would stand, drop the pant leg and quickly retake her place in the endless supply line of basket toting villagers.

The young women were slender and attractive, long black hair flowing from beneath their pyramid shaped bamboo hats called mũ lá, meaning leaf hat. The older women had leathery and wrinkled skin. Their teeth were stained with a purple coating from chewing betel nut. It helped to numb against tooth decay and gum infection. Their stride was natural and graceful displaying their strength as they managed the heavy loads of rice, grain, vegetables and other products en route to market.

They stared at the ground to avoid eye contact with the soldiers. I wondered if this was because of their fear of Americans or to avoid suspicion about the loads they carried. The Viet Cong recruited local village women to tote baskets down the Ho Chi Minh Trail from North Vietnam. They moved supplies of explosives, munitions, hand grenades and even heavy rocket propelled grenades following the rugged trail from the north that weaved in and out of Laos and Cambodia, crossing back and forth into and out of South Vietnam. The enemy constantly rerouted the trail to make it hard for Americans to know where to plan B-52 bombing runs.

Our pace was a crawl, the truck driver never shifting beyond second gear and stopping intermittently while the mine clearing team worked to clear the hard packed dirt roadway of enemy handiwork from the night before. Manufactured mines were in short supply so the VC used unexploded artillery rounds, hand grenades and blasting powder packed with glass and nails to craft explosive devices buried in or alongside the roadway. They could be exploded by detonators remotely wired to hiding places, by trip wires or by impact devices with firing pins. Remotely fired booby traps required Charlie (shortened from Victor Charlie for "VC" in military jargon) to hang around so impact devices and trip wires were the most common. The unmanned booby traps were sometimes detonated killing innocent civilians who ventured onto the roadway before it was cleared by the mine clearing teams.

Children followed along begging for food, candy, cigarettes or anything the American soldiers would give up. The private first class pulled out a package of ex-lax, separated the individually wrapped doses and threw them to the kids, who pushed and shoved each other to scrape the foil wrapped pieces from the dirt.

"Why would you do that?" I asked.

"You can't trust these dink kids," he answered. "You got to watch your ass 'cause they'll drop a frag on you while yelling for handouts. You'll learn out in the field," he continued. "When you're humping in the boonies with a five-day pack on your back and you hear some kid yelling 'Joe, souvenir baby san chop-chop', you'll know Charlie's alarm system just went off. I'm hoping he'll take the 'candy' home to papa san who's probably ARVN by day and Charlie by night. I hate all of these people.

You'll see. We all do."

"Why would you hate her?" I asked, pointing to a smiling little girl who was riding her bike along beside the truck, offering candles for sale.

"Just wait. You'll find out what this stinking country does to you," he warned.

"I'm going to get off and buy a candle," I shouted to the driver. "I want to see for myself why I should hate these kids," I told the PFC.

"Get me one, too," the driver shouted back. The column had stopped again most likely so the mine clearing team could disarm another booby trap.

The little girl heard our exchange and stood waiting beside the truck, a big knowing grin revealing even white teeth. What a shame that her pretty smile would someday be purple from betel nut, I thought. She was surrounded by other boys and girls who were carefully attentive to her progress with the soldiers. She appeared to be the honcho among the street vendor kids.

"You buy candle, one dollar," she said, holding a shiny red candle up for my inspection.

"Yes, but first tell me your name." I wanted to learn more about these kids.

"Dam," she answered without hesitation. "What you name?"

I told her my name. Dam was different from the children surrounding her. The other girls had long, silky, black, flowing hair. Dam's hair was black, but short and curly. Her face was square, with more pronounced eyes than the others, whose faces were elongated with lighter folds over their eyes that accentuated their oriental appearance. While the other girls were skinny with delicate features like slim legs and long thin hands and fingers, Dam was short and square shouldered. Her bare feet looked like the toes were all the same length and her hands were short and stubby.

The other girls were prettier, I observed. But there was something special about this one. She had a presence about her, a persona. She looked you in the eye when she talked to you and her eyes sparkled, her life's difficulties hidden behind her outgoing personality. She seemed to have us Americans all figured out and she knew how to befriend us and gain our confidence. When she smiled, it made you feel you had been rewarded, like she had shared a gift with you just for talking to her.

I noticed Dam protectively gripped the left handle of her rusted green bicycle. It was adorned with her wares, two woven bamboo baskets filled with candles, Cokes in eight-ounce bottles, and Winston and Marlboro cigarettes. Even when reaching for the candles I ordered, she held the bike with one hand while extracting the sold items. When I handed her the two dollars for the candles, the money quickly disappeared into the waistband of her black silk pajama pants.

"How old are you," I asked, bewildered by her maturity knowing that it masked her true age.

"Mười ba," she replied. Then realizing I did not speak her language, she raised both hands, palms forward showing me ten fingers, then closed her fists and extended three fingers from her right hand. "How old you?"

"Twenty," I replied then followed by holding up ten fingers, closing my fists and holding them up again.

"Hai mươi ," Dam repeated my age in Vietnamese. Then she explained by holding up ten fingers and proclaiming "mươi", then she held up two fingers and said "hai." She was a good teacher, two times ten is twenty. I had just received my first lesson in Victnamese.

Warming to our conversation, a remarkably pretty girl stepped up beside Dam. "You buy Coke?" she offered. "One dollar."

"This my friend Anh, same-same American Ann," Dam politely made the introduction. "Okay you buy Coke from Anh, not me." I admired that she wanted to help her friend and guessed maybe this was part of the ploy to sell more product. Despite my suspicion, I was unable to refuse and also bought a pack of Marlboro cigarettes, another dollar. I didn't have much money and lived from payday to payday. These kids could have talked me out of all I had if they tried.

Unlike Dam, Anh was shy. Slightly taller than Dam, she was thin with lovely clean olive skin and characteristic long black hair. Her cheek bones were higher than Dam's, highlighting her long slender face. She would not look directly at me, her gaze always toward the ground. I guessed she was more frightened of soldiers, probably because she was pretty and most likely got some verbal abuse and maybe even of a sexual nature. We established that Anh was mười một, or ten plus one in finger counting.

Anh said something in Vietnamese and extended her hand to give something to Dam. I caught sight of the foil wrapped ex-lax that one of the other kids must have shared with her. I patted Dam's hand to get her attention.

"This number ten," I told her. "This make you very sick," I said holding my stomach and making pained expressions to be sure she understood. "Tell the others not to eat it."

Dam shook her head acknowledging she understood my message. She held the ex-lax up to them, raised her voice and spoke authoritatively, giving them instruction as would a parent. She threw the package to the roadway and ground it down with her foot to make sure nobody else would want it.

"Time to go," the driver yelled. Highway One had gotten more crowded while we were stopped, the accumulating vehicle and pedestrian traffic was catching up.

Dam reached out and took my left hand in hers, placing a light weight gold colored bracelet over my fist. Then she produced an ink pen from her basket and wrote "Dam" on my palm.

"You number one," she said. "Now we friend."

I waved goodbye to Dam and her business partners. I no longer viewed them as just street kids. On the truck, I heard Dam announce to her troop, "tôi biết Jared!" I thought she must be saying goodbye.

"That means I know Jared," the PFC informed me. "That gold bracelet she gave you is supposed to mean you did something nice for her."

"Thanks. She wrote her name on my palm and declared us friends," I said rolling my hand over to show him the inscription. "She spells it Dam but pronounces it Dom, like expensive champagne. I bought you a pack of cigarettes from the pretty girl, Anh. I just couldn't resist buying something from her and I quit smoking when I went into basic," I said and handed over the Marlboro's.

My first encounter with local villagers was nothing like the PFC led me to expect. I looked out the back of the truck and watched Dam as the other kids gathered around her, allowing her to brag over her successful sales to the new soldier. Her mũ lá (leaf hat) that she wore hanging from a string on her back reminded me of Dale Evans' cowgirl hat in the old Roy Rogers television series I watched as a kid. Dam slid the hat up onto her head. The coned tip made her look taller and more like a young lady than just a child. She mounted her green bicycle and followed along behind the truck waving and smiling. When the truck was going too fast for her to keep up she stopped and waited for her gang to catch up with her.

I still held the Coke I purchased from Anh. I rolled the bottle around in my hand. Out of habit, I held the bottle up and studied the bottom, curious to see if it would be stamped to show where the bottle was manufactured. During high school, when I worked as a bag boy at a Teeter's Super Market, we had a Coke machine in the back of the store. The store manager would sort through the eight ounce bottles and pick out the ones whose manufacturing imprints were from the most distant cities, then load them back into the Coke machine. At break time all of the stock men, bag boys and the guys from the meat department would gather around the Coke machine to "ride Coke bottles." We would put a dollar each in a pool held by the manager, insert a dime into the machine and pull out a Coke from the vertical dispenser that held one Coke per level. Whoever came up with the Coke with the city name on the bottom that was furthest away would win the pool, usually eight or ten dollars.

I showed the bottle to the PFC and pointed out the imprint on the bottom. In a circle around the rim it read "Coca Cola Bottling Co Atlanta, GA." I told him the story of "riding Coke bottles". I guess it made sense that it came from Atlanta, headquarters for Coca Cola, since that is probably where they would originate their shipments to Vietnam.

I wondered how the folks at Coca Cola and Phillip Morris would feel about their products being sold on the black market. No doubt the products Dam and her friends sold came from soldiers like the one I saw tossing the sundries pack over the fence. Oddly, I did not mind paying Dam and Anh for what we should be getting gratis. It was good to feel like I was helping these poor kids feed their families even though I resented the soldiers who were profiting from their black market activities.

The going was still slow on Highway One, which was

now crowded with foot traffic, bicycles, motorcycles, three wheeled motor carts and overloaded buses. Everyone seemed to be talking to nobody in particular, creating a constant drone of Vietnamese language.

The zing…zing…zing from small arms fire silenced the hordes of pedestrians. Traffic stopped and people flurried to get down off the side of the road abandoning bikes, carts, trucks and basket loads. Our driver shouted for us to take cover as he and his guard fired their weapons on automatic in the general direction of the sniper fire coming from the east. I followed as the two soldiers in the back jumped out and took cover on the left side of the truck shooting their weapons anywhere that looked like it might harbor the unseen enemy.

I instinctively looked back to see if Dam was okay. She and her troop of kids had disappeared among the masses that trailed behind us on the busy highway. I was relieved they had fallen far enough behind to be out of harms' way.

As suddenly as it began, the commotion stopped and everyone silently held their positions, still hunkered down and checking themselves and those around them to see if anyone was wounded. A few minutes passed and the crowd cautiously crept back to the roadway, picked up their loads and remounted their rides. There was no whistle or other all clear signal. They just all seemed to know the threat was over, experienced as they were from these daily wartime interruptions.

Nobody on the roadway was wounded or killed. I

wondered about people in the rice paddy villages where we had directed our barrage of bullets. Did any of our random fire hit the elusive enemy or kill an innocent peasant farmer?

I wondered where Dam's family lived. Were they safe back in Đức Phổ or out in a remote village like the ones scattered among the rice paddies we fired into? It seemed odd that I felt I had someone to worry about after my first opportunity to get to know some local villagers. But Dam put a face of purpose on my cause for being here that had been eluding me since my arrival. Dam proved to me that the normal workaday person in this country was just as human and breathing and feeling as anywhere else in the world. They were just caught up in a war between the north and south of their country. It just happened that it included foreign soldiers like us who did not speak their language or understand their customs, religions, traditions or beliefs. It was a tough situation and I could see that I had a lot to learn.

Our driver inched forward, constantly starting and stopping as traffic resumed its effort northward. The mine sweeping team could not be rushed. They held an onerous responsibility to find and disarm or destroy booby traps that were not selective of their targets. Shortly after the sniper ambush, we heard a loud explosion up ahead. They discovered and blew a mine in the roadway.

"Now we know what the snipers back there were about," the PFC announced. "They were trying to get our driver to pass the mine sweepers so they could blow us away."

A mile or two on up the road our truck stopped again. Looking out the back, we could see that the traffic had halted its forward progress and the people were milling around talking in whispers. Our driver ordered us to dismount the truck and take cover. I jumped down expecting to hear sniper fire and headed around the left side since it proved to be a safe haven the last time. I did not hear the now familiar sound of enemy fire and instead saw ARVN soldiers gathered around the bridge up ahead.

Off to our west, rising from a wide expanse of rice paddies, was a pair of mountains connected in the center by a sway. Sandbag bunkers formed a ring around the top edge of the mountain to the south. A single taller bunker was visible on top of the higher mountain to the north. In between the two mountains I could see a steep footpath that connected them. A one lane road wound down from between the mountains and formed into a dike that rose above the rice paddies and connected to Highway One just beyond the bridge to our front.

Our driver was in front of the truck talking to a visibly excited Vietnamese soldier.

The ARVN waved his rifle about, signaling that he wanted us to get back on the truck and move on. The driver ordered us to mount up as he climbed into the cab and cranked up.

As we moved forward, we saw more ARVN soldiers by the roadside. A few were positioned on guard with their weapons at the ready, all appeared distraught and exhausted. They were dressed in tailored and tight fitting fatigue pants and tapered shirts. The rest of the platoon-sized troop were squatting down, positioned so they appeared to be sitting on their heels, calves tight against thighs, affectionately holding one another with hands on each other's legs and arms. The soldiers were slight, perhaps five and a half feet tall and weighing no more than one hundred and twenty pounds. They struck me as effeminate, certainly not manly.

Further ahead we heard loud wailing and crying but still could not see forward from the canvas-covered truck bed. We felt the road surface change as we mounted the bridge. In a few seconds we were off the bridge and on the smooth dirt surface again. It was a small bridge over a stream and connecting channel between two rice paddies.

We could hear people crying, or more accurately, wailing. The loud sobbing would not be ignored, so I stood and holding on to the canvas covered steel tubing, leaned out to look around toward the front of the truck. Sprawled on the red clay roadway beside the truck was a young girl, her open eyes stared in my direction and her long black hair was a splayed pillow framing her face. I guessed her to be about Dam's age. I was shocked to see that her boyish chest was coated red with blood.

I pounded my fist on the side of the truck and yelled for the driver to stop. I stepped over the tailgate to the tow railing below and jumped to the ground. I ran over to the wounded girl and knelt down on one knee, anxious to do something to help her. I touched her face and made my first contact with the chalky cold stiffness of skin that signaled rigor mortis. I saw that her staring eyes had turned to glass.

I then realized that black pajama clad women, all gasping in desperation, were moving from one bloodied and dismembered body to the next. The dead were mostly women and children. There were some bearded old men among them.

I felt a hand on my shoulder. Our driver was by my side. He told me ARVN soldiers had been on bridge guard. The Viet Cong corralled the village people and forced them to walk in a group toward the guarded bridge, using them as a shield. When the ARVN soldiers commanded them to stop, the VC opened fire towards the bridge. The ARVN soldiers responded and slaughtered their own people.

Chapter 3

On Landing Zone Liz, I was assigned to the first squad of first platoon. My new home, which some referred to as a living-fighting bunker, was a southerly exposed sandbag structure framed by eight-inch wood beams. Four wood bunk beds were built into the back walls two high. Sandbags stacked the eight foot height of the bunker formed a foyer as a shielded entranceway. The uneven dirt floor ensured that boots, fatigues and equipment would never be clean.

The roof was plywood capped by layers of sand bags intended to withstand enemy mortars and rockets. There was a space left for ventilation between the roof and top row of sand bags. During the night, rats the size of cats used this space as a rat run. A rat run can be recognized by the greasy streak along a wall from the rats' fur since they run with their bodies against objects or walls for guidance. We would grow accustomed to their scurrying about above our heads, often waking to feel their descent to our bunks in search of crumbs and leavings from our food. They would run along the edges of our bodies, using our frames the same way they used the edges of walls to guide themselves.

Each sand bag wall had openings for observation and

firing positions. Rolls of concertina wire lined the perimeter as a defense against sapper (suicide bomber) attacks and attempts by the enemy to overrun the base camp.

Soon after settling in to my new home, first platoon ventured out into the field. It was our turn to patrol the villages and rice paddies that surrounded the south side of Liz. First squad took point and I was second in line behind the point man. The area was declared a free fire zone meaning that anyone running from you or declining to stop when you yelled "dung lai" was assumed to be the enemy and you were expected to open fire. We were told if you didn't detain or shoot them, they would be lying in wait to ambush you up ahead.

We walked down the access road to the southeast base of Liz and turned south walking in line formation into a small village. The first grass roofed and mud walled house was occupied by an old lady and two young children. The older child, a girl perhaps five years old was holding a baby boy who was maybe a year old. The child was perched on her hip, her baby sitting duties fully accepted at such a young age. The elderly mama san used a large round and shallow basket to polish rice, shaking and stirring the basket with obvious experience to separate the hulls from the precious rice grains. She did not miss a beat in her chores as we walked by her house. She did not look up or acknowledge our presence.

The mid-morning sun on this breezeless February day rapidly sent the mercury above one hundred degrees. It was taking its toll, causing all of us to sweat profusely. That drain of precious bodily fluids left a couple of guys in danger of heat prostration, so Sergeant Greene ordered our squad to take a break and pop a couple of salt tablets.

I washed down my salt tablets with a long swig from my canteen of rubber tasting warm water and turned my attention back to the old lady and children. I was curious to see how they would react to me if I tried to be nice. They were still carefully avoiding direct contact or any acknowledgement that strangers were in their tiny village.

I approached calmly, hoping not to frighten the little girl or baby. I reached in the leg pocket of my fatigue pants and felt for the c-ration chocolate bar I was saving for an occasion just like this. It was no Hershey bar but I guessed a child in this poor village would like it anyway. I held the paper wrapped candy in the open palm of my hand, much like I would offer sugar cubes to a horse. I hoped that would demonstrate there was no mischief in my intent.

The little girl acknowledged my movement toward her by looking at me for the first time. Her alert eyes quickly shot from mine to the offering in my outstretched hand, then to the old lady to gauge her reaction. The woman, presumably her grandmother, nodded her tentative approval that encouraged me to move closer to the girl. Still holding her infant sibling, she trotted to me and snatched the candy away before retreating to sit beside the basket of rice.

This gave me the opening I needed to approach the

woman. I wanted to see if I could convince her that we were not there to harm her, her family or her property. I reached into the left leg pocket of my pants and removed a can of fruit cocktail, part of my intended lunch, hoping she would accept the gift I offered. Without hesitation, she stood from her squatting position, laid her basket to the side and walked the few steps between us to gently take the can from my hand.

She sat back down next to the girl who had unwrapped the chocolate and was feeding a broken off piece to the baby. The girl broke off another piece and handed it to her grandmother before taking a bite for herself.

I stood by and watched as they devoured the rest of the small chocolate bar. The melted goo formed a brown coating that covered the old lady's betel nut stained purple teeth as she smiled her appreciation for the treat.

She rolled the green can of fruit cocktail around between her palms looking like she was not quite sure what to do with it. Feeling braver, I took off my helmet and removed the P-38 can opener from the band that held the camouflaged steel pot cover, held it between my thumb and forefinger and approached, signaling that I would use it to open the can for her.

She warmed to my gesture, smiling, and handed over the can. I squatted down next to her trying to copy her posture by sort of sitting on my heels with my thighs resting on my calves. I was surprised that I was somewhat comfortable sitting this way. I opened the can and fished around for the plastic spoon in my pocket. I sunk the spoon in the juicy can of fruit and handed it over. It gave me pleasure to see the expressions of surprised delight on their faces as the woman and little girl took turns tasting the unfamiliar sweet morsels of pears, grapes, cherries and peaches. Once all of the fruit chunks were gone, the little girl carefully tilted the can to allow the baby to drink the juice.

The grandmother picked up her basket and routinely continued to shake the precious rice in a circular motion. I observed that she adeptly tossed the rice into the air every third circle. The polishing process stripped the brown husks from the white grains and the leavings dropped through to the ground below. When only the white rice grains remained, she poured the now finished product into a pail and scooped a new handful of brown rice into the basket.

I gestured that I would like to try the polishing process. She smiled broadly and handed over the basket, demonstrating first how to roll it around proficiently. I caught on pretty quickly and even managed to toss the rice carefully on the third circle like she had been doing. I was pleased to see the dusty husks cover my boots to prove the process was working.

I heard the sergeant instruct us to mount up and regretted that the break was over. It was rewarding to have made these new friends. I realized the relationship had developed without a single word spoken among us. I felt the same sense of purpose that I had experienced with Dam out on Highway One.

"We're here to kill Charlie, not to feed his family," the sergeant instructed me as I passed by him in line behind the point man.

As we followed the path from the village onto a rice paddy dike heading south we spotted a man apparently supervising women who were bent over from the waist working in the rice paddy. He gazed in our direction and briefly froze in startled recognition, then bolted towards a small village to the west. The point man yelled for him to stop but he just ran faster.

Someone yelled for us to shoot him, so I followed the order. I clicked my safety off and fired twice, the first a tracer round that left a red phosphorous line of travel showing me I had missed the target to the right. My second shot found its mark and hit the fleeing man in the torso, his lifeless body dead before he landed, sprawled, among the rice plants.

"I got him, I got him," I heard Franny shout from somewhere behind me as he raced toward the downed man who we presumed to be the enemy. I was glad to hear someone else claim the kill, my first in what would become a long year filled with death.

I would not need to feel guilty now about feeding Charlie's family, I thought.

"He's probably one of the local VC militia who gathered up the villagers and forced them to walk to their deaths when the ARVN were on bridge guard," Sergeant Greene declared.

If true, that would sure put a different slant on how I

felt about taking a life, I thought.

Chapter 4

The platoon sergeant picked me for detail the next day. The army knew how to use busy work to keep you from getting distracted. I was having a little trouble accepting that I had taken the life of another human being and he knew it.

Regardless what you were doing, the infantry seemed to always have a long walk for you attached to your missions or assignments. Sergeant Duke led our six-man detail down the access road and half the one mile distance east out to Highway One. We turned left into an area of tall grasses and underbrush and went about twenty yards to where a fifty foot section of concertina wire was missing. Steel fence posts and rolls of fencing to repair the missing section had been dropped off in advance of our arrival.

Swarms of mosquitoes were so thick you could feel them hit the palms and backs of your hands as you attempted to swat them away from your face. I generously wiped liquid mosquito repellent over my hands and face. Nonetheless, that did not deter them from their incessant buzzing in my ears. I would grow to despise that sound.

My assignment was to carry and install fence posts

every eight feet in preparation for the other guys to roll out and attach the concertina wire to the posts. Over beers I had told a story to Duke and the other guys about cutting and installing a locust post barbed wire fence around land in the Blue Ridge Mountains my dad bought in Watauga County, North Carolina. We used two work horses that belonged to old Mr. Carlton, who sold Dad the land, to drag the locust posts from the woods after we cut them. Locust is a super hard wood that, when stripped of its briar covered bark, makes a durable and long lasting fence post. Duke told me he considered my experience when he picked me for the detail. Gee thanks.

I measured and marked where the first post should go and went to get a post. As I walked back with it on my shoulder I spotted a snake coming toward me from the side. I froze in mid-step as a bright green snake about eight feet long slithered between my legs and continued on its way, not seeming to notice it had crossed my track. I walked over to Duke and described the encounter.

"Bamboo Viper," Duke declared. "It's known as a two-step snake. It's so venomous that if it bites you, you might make it two steps before you're dead."

I was surprised that I was able to just take that in stride. I guess the stuff I had seen in the last few days had numbed the normal death fear I should have felt.

By mid-morning we had installed all of the posts and about half of the fencing so Duke instructed us to take a break for chow. I selected a shaded spot under a small tree, inspected the ground to make sure it was clear of ants or bees nests and sat using the tree as a back rest. I opened a can of peaches using my P-38 can opener, searched through my pack for a plastic spoon and took my first bite, savoring the sweet juice that held the fruit. The tree seemed to move behind me so I felt behind my back. The tree had an odd rolled shape to it, like the candy cane stripe of a barber's pole. On closer inspection I realized there was a huge snake coiled around the tree trunk.

I called Sergeant Duke over and he identified the snake as a Python. "They aren't known for biting but will squeeze you to death if they feel threatened or are hungry," he said. In only a few hours I had encountered man-eating malaria spreading mosquitoes and had close encounters with two deadly snakes. I began to appreciate the prospect of comfort and safety offered by my new home on Liz and was happy to walk back up the hill when our fencing detail was finished.

Chapter 5

Less than a week after I joined the platoon, we went on my first air combat assault. As I packed rations for the three-day assignment I tried to limit the weight of my rucksack by leaving behind anything I considered not absolutely required for daily survival. I left behind extra fatigue shirt and pants and extra socks. On my first extended mission I discovered that hot beer and hot Coke, even though they weighed more, would become preferable to iodine laced water even when mixed with Kool-Aid.

We used iodine pills to purify the local water and prevent infection from disease carrying bacteria. We knew we would risk dysentery if we drank the water without iodine added. We learned never to drink water from a local well or stream without first adding the little orange pill. The locals never seemed to get sick so they must have developed resistance to the worms and things growing in the water.

I packed all the ammunition I could carry not knowing how often we would get new supplies in the field. My greatest fear was running out of ammo. So, I attached two hand grenades to each ammo pouch on my belt. I loaded five twenty-round M-16 clips into each ammo pouch. I stuffed as many refill boxes as would fit into the side pockets of my rucksack. I strapped a tube shaped LAW rocket launcher to the bottom of my rucksack along with my poncho. Once my packing was complete the combined weight of my ammo belt and rucksack was a hefty sixty pounds.

Before dawn, we saddled up and walked down the access road to the bottom of the hill from Liz. The shoulder straps of my rucksack were already taking their toll on my shoulders before we reached the staging area. As the sun peaked over the South China Sea to the east, the horizon filled with Huey troop transport helicopters that were eerily noiseless at first sighting. As they came closer, the thump – thump – thump of their rotor blades became a roar as they began their staggered landings to pick up our waiting eight-man squads. We spaced ourselves four men on each side, ten yards clear of the landing area. We popped green smoke grenades to mark the landing zone for the pilots.

The chopper swooped in raising a cloud of dust and debris that covered us from head to toe in sweaty grit. I struggled to get my footing on the helicopter runner and climbed aboard, straining to maintain my balance under my heavy load. Four soldiers sat on the raised canvas bench seating and the remaining four, including me, sat on the floor. I sat in front of the port side door gunner … precariously close to the door opening.

The takeoff was exhilarating from a combination of excitement and fear. I had no idea where we were going or what we faced. The strength and force of the two dozen or more helicopters flying in attack formation gave me a terrific adrenalin rush. Our Huey bounced side to side and up and down as the other chopper rotors attacked the air around us. My first helicopter experience was like a carnival ride that left my heart racing and my stomach in my throat.

We passed over Highway One and the bridge at the end of the access road to Liz as we headed east towards the sea. Villagers working in the rice gazed up at us as we flew over and their water buffalo ran away, the children tending them in pursuit. To the south I could see the brigade headquarters and the village of Đức Phổ. Quảng Ngãi city, for which the province was named, was off in the distance to the north. The blue-green South China Sea was to our front and its white sand beaches were coming into view.

Cobra attack helicopters, ferocious looking with their gaping painted on teeth, buzzed by us and began their assault on a group of small villages northeast of us, their rockets and machine guns blasting away. Our door gunners opened fire as we began our descent toward the green smoke that marked our intended landing zone. Approaching on full attack mode was the standard clearing procedure for air combat assaults. Green smoke meant our forward attack group was not getting return fire from the ground. Red would have told us the landing zone was hot with confirmed enemy presence.

Our Huey descended and hovered with its runners a few feet above the ground which was spotted with waist high burial mounds. Someone yelled for us to jump. I was afraid I would break a leg. The door gunner behind me, sensing my hesitation, shouted instructions for me to put my feet on the skids and then jump the remaining few feet to the ground. I followed his instructions, hit the ground and bounced around awkwardly. The shifting weight of my pack caused me to tumble. I managed to regain my footing and followed the rest of the squad as we spread out into firing positions to protect the landing zone for the remaining troops to descend.

Once the helicopters had deposited the company safely, they headed back to Bronco.

They reminded me of a migrating flock of birds headed south, the clap – clap – clap from their rotors becoming an echo as they faded from sight. First platoon took point with first squad leading the way. Then we spread out into a sweeping formation stretched side to side to approach the villages.

The coastal sandy soil made forward progress difficult under the weight of my fully loaded back pack. My boots wanted to sink in under the extra weight. The mercury began to boil towards a hundred degrees and it was only mid-morning. My body kept pace with the others although the heat was taking its toll. My vision was getting blurred, the straps were brutally tugging at my shoulders and it was all I could do to concentrate on staying in position.

"You need to sweat." The words from behind pulled me from my stupor. "You got to stay alert 'cause Charlie don't show no sympathy," Sergeant Duke advised. He pulled a Ballantine beer from his pack and handed it to me. "You drink one hot beer. It will make you sweat," he said as he walked on down the line to check up on the rest of the platoon.

That hot beer tasted so good that I guzzled it down in only a couple of chugs. True to Duke's word, I started sweating almost immediately and was surprised how quickly I felt better. I realized how close I was getting to heat prostration so rinsed down a couple of salt tablets with the last sip of beer.

Suddenly, we felt more than heard bullets hissing through the air above our heads and we all hit the ground. Off to our right, second platoon came under sniper attack and a new replacement on his first day in the field was wounded. Fortunately, the dust off took only minutes to swoop in and rescue the injured private. It helped that we were close to their base at Bronco.

When the medevac headed south with our wounded soldier safely on board, we moved into the wooded village fifty meters east. The terrain became predominately sand. We were getting close to the beach.

Thatched roof homes in the village were abandoned with cooking fires smoldering. All of the local residents had moved out in a hurry. The word must have spread quickly that Americans were coming so everyone left or were well hidden.

The simple homes with mud packed walls were well kept. The hard sand yards were newly swept. Carefully placed limestone rocks that had to have been carried from a considerable distance away lined the perimeter of the yard to my front. Since a sniper ambushed us from the village we were extra cautious as we searched. If Charlie was still around there was a good chance he would be intent on setting up a booby trap.

I saw the other guys noisily searching, turning over and scattering baskets of polished white rice, throwing sleeping mats into the dirt yards and knocking over reverently placed altars and breaking the ceramic fixtures that adorned them. Seeing the religious icons callously destroyed bothered me. It did not seem right to desecrate their shrines, Buddha idols and incense sticks.

I cautiously approached the door opening to the house I had chosen to search. I realized I was tip toeing with my rifle on automatic, feeling like there was something about this house to fear. I was careful not to touch anything. A trip wire could be strung across the doorway. A contact detonator would be easy to conceal in the sand.

I peered through the doorway. The living space was a simple rectangle with dirt floor, the center partially covered with bamboo mats. The dirt floor on the left side was elevated a few inches and was covered with four sleeping mats arranged two each, side by side. A narrow table perhaps three feet tall was used as an altar placed with care against the back wall. It was adorned with a finely knitted cloth and on the cloth sat a golden Buddha. The Buddha had what appeared to be little naked people climbing all over it. To Buddha's left was a small offering plate of rice and bamboo leaves. On his right sat a jar filled with incense sticks. One smoking lit stick was in a Coke bottle placed in front of Buddha, its sweet aroma evidence that the people who lived here were not gone long.

I turned my attention to the cooking hearth to the right. Its coals were smoldering and a pot hung above the fire by its handle. I could smell the distinct odor of cooked rice. We had interrupted the family mealtime.

I suddenly heard a moaning noise coming from behind the house. I noticed a narrow opening in the corner beside the hearth and slowly walked over and peeked out. The rear door opened into another room, a grass walled lean to shed attached to the rear of the house. A young woman who appeared to be in her late teens, wearing no pants, was squatting beside a bamboo bed. She was holding on to the side of the bed and moaning, in obvious pain. I took a step toward her, but she held her hand up, palm towards me, signaling me to stay back.

Then I saw the source of her pain. A baby squirted out from her body followed closely by the afterbirth. She efficiently grasped the child with one hand and began the process of clearing the afterbirth from her with the other. She then lovingly cleaned the mucus and blood from around the infant's still closed eyes, nose, mouth and ears. Satisfied that the child was breathing, she raised herself up and, with her baby clutched to her belly, maneuvered herself onto the bamboo slatted bed. Waiting on the bed was a pot holding a knife in water that she used to slice the umbilical cord. Now that the baby, a boy I observed, was free from her she wrapped it in a white cloth and laid it to her side so she could continue to look after herself.

I felt guilty that I had violated this most personal delivery of a new life and backed away. I smiled to her and signaled thumbs up in hopes she would forgive my embarrassed presence. She smiled back at me seeming to understand that I meant her no harm and turned her attention to her newborn infant.

I went back around to the front of the house and decided to take a closer look inside, wanting to feel confident that there was nobody else there and a little concerned that the woman I encountered might have been the wife of a Viet Cong. The father had to be either enemy or ARVN, I reasoned. I knew that, sadly, he could have been both. So, I decided to search the house more thoroughly. I rummaged through the meager belongings of dishes, pots, chop sticks and a few pairs of black silk pajama pants and shirts. But there was nothing threatening in this village farm house so I decided to leave well enough alone.

I cautiously circled back to where I left the new born and mother only minutes earlier. They had disappeared. I saw that there was a raised mound bunker beside the house and knew that was where they went. I decided not to pursue them.

I rejoined my squad as they went through the village searching for signs of the enemy sniper. I felt I had made a secret pact with the mother and child and decided not to report what I had witnessed. I felt that I had been blessed with a near religious experience even though someone had ambushed our soldiers from her village.

It was a long day filled with new experiences…first air combat assault…first wounded soldier and subsequent medevac…and first time humping three clicks carrying a full pack in more than hundred degree heat. Most life changing was witnessing a mother giving birth.

Around mid-afternoon we reached the beach. The company perimeter assignments were made in a half moon shape using the South China Sea as a backdrop. We set about digging our foxholes in the sand then took turns standing guard to allow everyone a chance to bathe in the blue-green water, taking pleasure in the opportunity to wash away the sweat, dirt and sand.

The salt content in the water was so dense that I floated effortlessly on the surface. When I left the water I was entirely covered with salt. Using a towel to wipe away the salt proved futile. The salt stuck to the towel and scratched and scraped when I wiped myself with it. I cleaned myself the best I could and hated having to put my dirty fatigues back on.

I put on my boxer shorts; then stripped back down as soon as I pulled my fatigue pants over them. It was like trying to wear sandpaper. I used extra care to clean sand away from my socks and boots. I put them on and went shirtless for the rest of the afternoon.

Our squad leader, Jeff Green, came by to tell Franny and me that our squad was assigned night ambush. We would leave our rucksacks behind and take only our weapons, ammo belts, canteens of water and claymore mines.

"We'll head out as soon as it gets dark," he said. "We're going back to the intersection of trails we passed on the way to the beach today. Make sure whatever you carry is tied down so you don't make noise, no talking and the smoking lamp is out until we get back to the beach. We'll be moving at a fast walk so be sure and keep up. And Christopher," he said, focusing his attention on me, "you've got rear security."

"What does that mean?" I asked.

"There will be eight of us," he explained. "Rivers will be leading us on point and you'll be last in line making sure nobody comes at us from behind."

At dusk we filed out from the safety of the company perimeter. If there was to be a moon, it was not yet lighting the trail in front of me. I followed the sound of Franny's footsteps. I strained to capture his outline to my front. I could tell when my boots left the edges of the well-worn dirt trail and thought that as long as the trail went straight I would be okay. I realized that I was so intent on staying on the trail and keeping up that Viet Cong soldiers could have been walking right along beside me. With that thought I started glancing to the sides and rear as often as I could without tripping or losing my way. The sound of Franny's boots pounding the trail ahead were my sole link to safety on this insane and terrorizing trek to set up an ambush that would hopefully kill somebody.

It seemed much longer, but in less than half an hour the line in front of me stopped. We had reached the intersection of trails. Rivers led us off to the left just short of crossing the trail to our front. We went to work setting up our trap.

Franny and I had the duty of placing a claymore mine to face down the trail towards the east. That trail ran back towards the beach parallel to the one we were on. Franny held the detonator and spool of wire as I ran the wire twenty yards or so out and set the claymore facing down the trail, arc out, so it created a fifteen foot wide blast zone of destruction. I connected the firing pin to the mine and followed the wire back to join Franny. He had found cover behind a burial mound.

I hunkered down beside Franny. This was my first time in the field at night so I had no idea what to expect. Franny held the mine detonator expectantly as I aimed my rifle in the general direction of the ambush we were setting. I waved my hand in front of my face. I realized I could not see shit.

Our timing worked. We heard animated Vietnamese chatter. People were coming up the trail from the beach heading our way. I did not realize our squad leader was so close to us when he urgently whispered "blow the claymore."

Franny did not hesitate. The explosion lit the night. It silhouetted two people caught by the blast that sent them tumbling. I could hear them moaning after the blast. I could tell they were alive but injured.

Franny and I stayed put, not knowing what to do. Several of the guys ran into the ambush site and began yelling and ferociously firing their rifles at the two wounded people lying on the ground.

"This is for Stewart, you bastards." Someone was angrily shouting from the direction of the claymore explosion followed by bursts of automatic small arms fire. They finished off the two people who had wandered into our ambush. I continued to hear muffled talking in the dark as our soldiers moved to search the two bodies.

I stood up from behind the burial mound. Franny was at my side as we followed the sound of voices to join the others. Somebody produced a flashlight and we formed a circle to get a look at the bloodied remains. Jeff Greene whispered that we had scored a bunch of documents and a lot of money from a couple of Viet Cong tax collectors. He presented the double handful of booty for our inspection.

I was in shock. The warp speed events of the last hour, the terrifying dash to arrive where we now stood coupled with the murderous execution of the ambush, had my brain on overload. It was like someone else was staring at the mutilated bodies through my eyes. I did not believe this scene could be real.

"Time to go," Jeff declared. "If any of their friends are around they're going to know where we are now."

It was still early and moonless. I could hear the excitement in Jeff's speech as he hurriedly called for a head count and instructed us to move out down the trail at a double time pace. We were running back to the company perimeter in the pitch dark. I was still last in the column and was struggling to keep my bearings.

I kept telling myself to just keep putting one foot in front of the other on the dirt pathway. I somehow managed to regain my footing with every stumble. I envisioned Franny's outline from the sounds his boots made and followed the image created in my fear. Franny's movement in front of me as he rapidly shuffled along allowed me to retain the little sanity I could muster from these fearsome events.

Less than thirty minutes after blowing the ambush we arrived back within the welcomed security of the company perimeter. I could hear Jeff excitedly reporting to the company commander as he presented the documents and piasters they had lifted from the bloodied bodies of the tax collectors. It was all I could do to collapse into my fox hole next to Franny eager to close my eyes and try to stop my mind from recycling the amazing events of the day.

The sunrise woke me from an exhausted sleep, the early morning heat staining my already filthy fatigue shirt with sweat. I walked out to the surf and washed my face in the salty water, anxious to clear my head of the terrible images from yesterday's chain of events. Among all that transpired, though, I felt a degree of satisfaction and a secret compassion for the mother I had protected by not telling the others about her.

I returned to the fox hole and began packing my gear

into my rucksack, taking care to clean the sticky sand from my poncho liner. I had slept on top of it without putting the poncho below and it was a mess of sand and sweat. I ate a c-ration can of beans and franks for breakfast and chased it down with warm and putrid tasting iodine laced water. I imagined how wonderful my mother's simple bacon, eggs and toast would taste right about now.

Chapter 6

We invented names for our enemies to convince ourselves of our superiority, names like dinks, slope heads, slant eyes and gooks. We believed because we were taller, better supported and better equipped that we were far superior; but they proved to be a crafty, evasive and determined enemy. They were experienced at war having lived it most of their lives.

While we carried packs full of nutritious canned foods, a Viet Cong soldier could survive for days on a rice ball wrapped in cellophane. They lived under ground in tunnels and bunkers not emerging into daylight for days, weeks or even months at a time. Access to these sanctuaries was well camouflaged, with trap doors hidden in bushes, buried in sand and even under water. Their country was at war long before we got involved and their determination defeated the French years after they repelled occupations by China and Japan. Known as the "Pearl of the Orient" for its pristine beaches, majestic mountains, abundant rice crops and thriving rubber tree plantations, Indochina was a historic and perpetual target for takeover.

My first experience with Viet Cong ferocity came soon after our successful ambush that took out the tax collectors. This combat assault took us east of Quảng

Ngãi city a few clicks (kilometers) north of that ambush site, again along the coast of the South China Sea. We were on line formation moving through an old French plantation with many ruined concrete structures, most likely the scene of a battle between the Viet Minh and French a decade before us.

The area had a bad feel to it, like you knew you were somewhere you did not want to be and perhaps where you didn't belong. The concrete walls that still stood, a corner of a house here and a wall with door opening there, all displayed Vietnamese writings. We did not know what we were reading but had the feeling they were warnings since the words Viet Cong were included in most lines.

Rivers was walking point again. He displayed no fear and seemed obsessed with being the first to make enemy contact. He reminded me of my dad, a fanatic grouse hunter who dragged me along on his tireless day-long hunting trips in the mountains of North Carolina. Rivers' determination to root out our enemy was just like the way my dad tirelessly searched through laurel thickets intent on finding his prey.

Rivers was good at leading our patrols and, like my dad's old pointer Jake seeking grouse, had a nose for finding the VC in unlikely hiding places. Powell, a new replacement, was second in line behind Rivers. I had switched weapons and was carrying an M-79 grenade launcher. It had the butt of a shotgun, but was like a hand held two-foot mortar tube. The ammunition looked like a big bullet. The stock broke down and you loaded the grenade bullet and snapped it shut, just like the 410 gauge shotgun I learned to hunt quail and grouse with as a twelve-year old kid. To fire the grenade round you made a best guess at distance, pointed the weapon skyward and pulled the trigger to launch the projectile like a mortar, arcing high and raining down on the target making a fearsome sounding blast on impact.

I felt relieved when Rivers walked past the last of the French structures and headed south away from the plantation. It seemed we had luck with us this day since nobody hit a booby trap and we had made no enemy contact. I had just reached the last building, about thirty yards behind Rivers and Powell, when bullets zinged past me from the front. Rivers and Powell dove to the ground and Powell yelled "I'm hit, medic…medic."

Rivers was not more than twenty feet from the enemy trench across our front, dug by the Viet Cong to shield the ambush site. AK-47 small arms fire was coming at us over his and Powell's heads, rounds occasionally kicking up dirt around them, to let us know they were intent on killing our trapped soldiers. All of our guys responded, firing in the general direction of the trench, although we could not see the enemy. I walked a few rounds from my grenade launcher from beyond the trench back toward Rivers' position, being careful not to chance a short round that could blow away my own guys. The blast from the grenades along with the barrage of fire from the rest our platoon seemed to work since the automatic firing from the entrenched enemy position stopped, at least briefly.

Powell was still yelling for a medic but nobody chanced running into the ambush to get to him. I did not feel comfortable getting any closer to the trench with just the grenade launcher, so I traded it with one of the other guys for his rifle, quickly showed him how to use it then made a zigzagging run for Powell. Rivers saw me coming so he jumped up and met me just as I reached Powell. We each grabbed an arm and dragged him back the thirty or so yards to the hastily established perimeter.

I could hear other guys behind us yelling they were hit and realized the ambush had taken out more of our troops than just Powell. Somebody shouted that a medevac was on the way so Rivers popped red smoke as I fired strafing rounds to try to clear a landing zone.

The medevac chopper pilots were sent from heaven. They fearlessly zoomed into hot landing situations, taking enemy fire head on, knowingly putting themselves and their crews at risk to extract our dead and wounded soldiers. The Huey marked with red crosses on the door panels came roaring in from above, making a near vertical decent trying not to be an easy target for Charlie. We couldn't tell if there was incoming enemy fire because all of our guys were firing protective cover all around the landing zone, determined to protect the heroic dust-off crew.

I could see the appreciation in Powell's face as Rivers and I lifted him through the open side door of the helicopter. He was conscious. In shock, the wounds to his thigh and buttocks causing him severe pain. Before we could step fully away the pilot raised the tail of the big bird and took off forward, nose down, as it made its anxious ascent away from danger. Not finished, he made a quick decent down again towards more red smoke among the plantation walls further back in our loosely crafted perimeter, intent on picking up more wounded soldiers.

During the days ahead our commanders were determined to root the infestation of Viet Cong out of the villages along the coast. Day after day our missions were repeated, assaulting coastal villages with names like Một Ấp Châu, Gia Ngọc, Phú Vinh hoặc and Tiên Xá. We occasionally got lucky and found an enemy soldier or two and killed or captured them, moved on to the next village only to repeat the process a few days later. Time after time we would draw sniper fire and lose one or more soldiers to a booby trap or Bouncing Betty, a mine that would fly up into the air when stepped on and send deadly shrapnel from the airborne explosion.

We were in the field for our eighth day since Powell was wounded. We were on patrol east of Phú Vinh village. Second squad was on point, first squad was next and I was about tenth in the line formation. Suddenly bullets were flying everywhere kicking up sand all around us. The point man from second squad was wounded and we were all face down in the sand, trying desperately to be invisible. The field radio the RTO in front of me carried was buzzing with requests for air support and Medevac's.

The sand around me kept getting splattered and I

realized a sniper had me in his sights. I raised my head to try to spot him and could almost feel the breeze from the zing…zing…zing of rounds zipping past my head. I squirmed deeper into the sand trying to hide my entire body inside of my helmet. I could not figure out where he was hiding. Everywhere I looked was just sand divided by the path we followed.

Every few seconds bullets kicked up sand around me, one only inches from my head. I decided to stop trying to spot the sniper and play dead, hoping he would think he had hit me. About that time the cobra attack helicopters came zooming in, their thirty caliber machine guns blaring and their rocket propelled grenades exploding. Thankfully, my sniper either decided he hit me or got scared and retreated from the air assault. Now I knew what Rivers must have felt like when he and Powell were pinned down a week earlier.

Once our helicopter support group unleashed their barrage of fire on suspected enemy positions, the VC disappeared into their web of tunnels that seemed to be everywhere. We were able to resume our sweeping operation that was interrupted by the enemy ambush. Search as we might, our efforts proved fruitless. I was hoping to find the guy who was shooting at me dead in a ditch but we would leave this field of battle with no enemy body count, an end that was becoming too common.

It was part of the Viet Cong master plan to hit us and disappear, ambush us and merge into the landscape and booby trap us relentlessly. I could see from the soldiers who arrived in country as a brigade unit a month before me that the tactic was having its desired effect on our morale. Our superiors must have arrived at the same conclusion. A beautiful covey of Huey troop transport helicopters suddenly filled the sky and we were ordered to load up for extraction from the field. We had earned our first stand down, a three-day retreat from the perils of combat.

Chapter 7

The airfield on Bronco, brigade headquarters at Đức Phổ, was buzzing with air traffic. C-130 cargo planes landed and departed every few minutes. They were capable of short field takeoffs and landings and therefore did not require a lot of runway. These airplanes were designed to transport a platoon of soldiers and all of their equipment and supplies. Vehicles like jeeps and armored personnel carriers could be loaded by winch up and down the ramp that folded down in the rear of the airplane. Vital supplies could also be parachuted to remote battle zones only reachable by air drop.

Huey helicopters came and went like worker bees moving troops and supplies. The American military was drawn by its enemies into an unfamiliar jungle and urban warfare. We did not get an opportunity to set up our positions and fight one another line to line. There were no lines. We hopped from one place to another, diving into the jungle on the hope of catching the enemy off guard. More often it seemed we were the ones caught in bad situations favoring the supposed weaker enemy.

Dependence on helicopters evolved due to lack of serviceable roads, difficult to navigate terrain with flooded rice paddies and rivers and streams with no bridges. It was a constant battle to maintain bridges along Highway One and next to impossible to support bridges away from the main highway. Our corps of engineers would build or repair them and the VC or NVA would blow them up.

A rail line formerly ran between north and south. All that remained was the earthen dike that served as the base for the tracks. The tracks were removed and used to build small walking bridges across streams and as foundations for houses and businesses.

In the short time it took us to unload and walk across the tarmac to get clear of the airfield, I saw three airships arrive with red crosses on the doors. The Huey medevac helicopters swooped in to waiting crews from the field hospital who rushed to attend to the wounded or to unload the dead. The two soldiers from the last Huey to arrive were in body bags. The brigade medics delicately unloaded the body bags, unzipped them and checked inside to verify that they were properly identified. We all stopped and stood at attention while these unfortunate troops were carried away, saddened at the loss of guys from one of our units in the field. It was a stark reminder of our own vulnerability and would make returning to the field after our brief vacation that much harder.

We got our quarters assigned, happy to have cots to sleep on. The green canvas tents with raised wood floors weren't exactly the Holiday Inn, but we gave our collective approval as we made claim to our beds.

I dropped my rucksack and ammo belt on a cot closest to the canvas door opening flap, took my rifle and headed to supply, anxious to get some clean fatigues and a shower. I ran into a young Specialist Four named Felix Queen, whom I had gotten to know during my few days spent here before going to the field. Felix was one of the lucky ones to get assigned at headquarters as a clerk typist and did not have to go into the field. Felix joked that it was a dirty job but somebody had to do it. I could feel his underlying guilt knowing the guys he processed through battalion would be sent into harm's way.

Felix was from Asheville, North Carolina, only seventy-five miles from my hometown of Hickory. He told me that, in his opinion, our company commander was the best captain in Vietnam. Coincidentally, he was from Canton, only a short trip up the road from Asheville in the Blue Ridge Mountains. Felix said Captain Joe Rhinehart was in the Army only because he got hurt playing baseball. He said he was a really good catcher for Western Carolina who got picked up for the big leagues by Pittsburgh. His first season he experienced a career ending leg injury so he had two choices, go back to Canton and face working in the pulp mills or go into the army. I remembered the terrible pulp mill odor from driving through Canton as a kid and decided I would probably have opted for the army as well.

Felix offered to take me over to the brigade PX after I got cleaned up. I picked up my clean fatigue shirt and slacks, taking pleasure in being able to get properly fitted in small sizes, and went to the showers. I had to wait in line for a shower head to open up and was happy to see the guy ahead of me had left a good sized chunk of soap behind. The grit and sand from the rotor blades of the helicopters went away pretty easily as the first layer of grime. The grey looking base layer of dirt from being in the field day and night without bathing took a more rigorous scrubbing.

I remembered a kid in elementary school who was mistreated by his family. He lived in a shack and never bathed. One day I took some of my clothes to school at the urging of my parents. We coaxed James into the gym shower, managed to get him out of his filthy and torn clothes and shoes, and thoroughly scrubbed him head to toe. I remember that his sockless toes stuck out the end of his worn out shoes. His skin was a dirty grey color, much the way my skin looked now. He did not know how to bathe and didn't like the experience. But when we got him all cleaned up and into my used clothes, shoes and socks, you could tell he was proud of himself. I smiled at the memory as I scrubbed hard to remove the grime.

I walked over to meet Felix at battalion. He told me he had scored a jeep we could use for the afternoon. As we headed over to the brigade PX, Felix looked me over and told me I needed a good shave. I told him that being light bearded, it was not high on my priority list.

"You have got to try a full face shave by a Korean barber," he said.

I had noticed how clean cut Felix was, pressed fatigues, perfectly cut black short hair and clean shaven. I guessed it was a requirement for keeping the job in the rear.

The Korean barber shop was no more than a shoe shine stand in front of the PX. The "barber" was a slight Korean guy in tailored green slacks and shirt, similar to our fatigues. Felix introduced me and told the guy I needed the works.

He started by lathering up a bar of soap and coating my entire face with it. My barber chair was an ammo box with rope handles on each end. I caught myself holding on to the rope handles when I saw that his barber's razor was a double edged razor blade held by sticking the center of the blade on the pinky finger of his left hand. I sure hoped he was left handed.

He proceeded to shave my entire face, leaving only my eyebrows untouched. He was deft at his strokes, obviously taking great pride in his profession. He wiped my face clean with a sweetly scented towel and smiled upon the completion of his work. It was strangely comforting and cleansing - an unexpected pleasure.

We left our barber and drove up the side of the mountain, affectionately nicknamed Montezuma that overlooked Bronco. It was a second pleasure, getting to see the brigade base from above while looking down on the village of Đức Phổ. To the right at the end of the airfield runway, towards the South China Sea, was the outer perimeter on the east side of the base. I could look north from here and see where we had just departed after our experiences in the field. It was nice to feel safe from this distance, but it made me sad that nothing had really been accomplished while we were out there.

I could see the villages east of Highway One, the ones we had blasted on automatic when we received sniper fire as we waited for the mine clearing team. They looked so innocent from above like this, nestled among the rice paddies. They looked so small and insignificant. Yet, the occupants of one or more intended to deliver death to our small convoy.

I could see Liz to the northwest, its twin peaks silhouetted below the higher mountains beyond. Looking down the southwest side of the mountain, I could see the barren earth that reminded me of the strip mined mountains of West Virginia, where no foliage was left to compliment nature's attempt to reach skyward. The thought of West Virginia took me back to my youthful adventure to visit Janie in the blue 1960 Plymouth Valiant that I purchased from my Aunt Mabel.

I had met Janie from Madison, West Virginia, on a trip to Myrtle Beach with some of my high school classmates. It was on the last day before her family went home from vacation. I was an infatuated sixteen year-old and immediately made up my mind to find a way to see Janie again. So, soon after getting home from the beach, I began saving my money for a trip to drive up to Madison for a visit. I talked my friend Nathan into going along. We drove up through Boone and took the back roads through the Blue Ridge Mountains through the corner of Virginia and into West Virginia. We passed through mining country and when we stopped for gas in Bluefield, the people looked at us like we were nuts for being there.

The visit turned out to be awkward. Janie was only fifteen and her parents prohibited us from spending much time together and only with her friends at the community pool. So Nathan and I decided to go on back home after one night. We routed our trip via the West Virginia Turnpike. We left Madison late in the afternoon and drove through some rugged mountains where they were strip mining, clearing all foliage to strip the coal from the earth. On the turnpike south of Bluefield, I turned on the headlights and the car began to jerk and sputter and the red engine light was flashing on and off. I pulled over to the shoulder and stopped. Nathan observed that we were in the middle of nowhere in the Virginia mountains. The car was still running rough so I turned the lights off. When I did that the engine ran smoothly again.

We were downright perplexed, scared of being in these mountains in the dark, yet unable to turn on the lights for fear of losing the engine. Soon, an eighteen wheeler came into view, so I made the quick decision to fall in behind him and follow his tail lights to the next town, running without my headlights. Out of nowhere it seemed, a Virginia highway patrolman pulled us over, took me to jail and left Nathan on the side of the highway, alone in the rugged mountains to spend the night in the car. I had to wait until morning to call and ask my parents to wire money for the ticket and fine and so I could get a wrecker to go find Nathan and buy a new battery for my car.

"Do you see where the stream runs into the sea?" Felix asked, interrupting my childhood memory as he pointed out the spot along the coast to the northeast. "Just north of there is where you guys ambushed the tax collectors."

I was surprised he knew the story. He explained that he reads all of the morning field reports before they are sent on to brigade.

"Who is Stewart?" I asked. "Some of the guys were yelling his name when they killed the tax collectors."

"I guess that would have been before you came in as a replacement," he answered thoughtfully. "I wasn't there but I can tell you what I heard."

He told me that first platoon was on patrol on Highway 515 and walked into an enemy carrying party. The munitions carrying party, which included several Viet Cong escorts armed with AK-47's, scattered into the countryside. Led by a young first lieutenant, first platoon went after them.

He said that Stewart walked up to a hole in the ground and a VC popped up from the hole and shot him in the knee. Stewart was pinned down lying close to the hole and the enemy would pop up now and then, fire off a few rounds and disappear. He was hollering for help but our guys could not get to him.

The heroic young lieutenant, determined not to let one of his men lay there wounded and dying, ran forward to try to help and was shot and severely wounded. He had a sucking chest wound.

The Viet Cong finally jumped up from the hole to make a run for it and our guys killed him. Only then were they able to evacuate the wounded soldiers. Stewart died from severe loss of blood after getting to the brigade hospital. The lieutenant survived and was transferred out for long term treatment.

Now I understood the anger I heard the night of the tax collector ambush.

Felix guided my view to the location of ambush ally to the northwest. It seemed such a short distance from our tax collector ambush site when looking down from high up on Bronco, however it was at least three clicks to the north.

"That's where you guys got hit and had to evacuate Powell," Felix explained. "I heard you were up for a medal for that."

I was surprised and did not know how to respond to that, so I just let it pass. I did not feel like what I did merited a medal. I just hoped someone would do the same for me.

"I read in your 201 file that you were going to college when you got drafted," Felix said, changing the subject. "Didn't you have a college deferment?"

"I had one," I answered. "I attended for one semester but was having a hard time paying my own way, working two jobs and trying to make passing grades. So, I decided to volunteer for the draft, do my military time and go back to school on the G.I. Bill. It made more sense to me than taking student loans and paying them back the rest of my life."

"Do you regret that decision now that you are in the 'Nam?" he prodded.

"Let me tell you a story that will break your heart," I replied. "I left school in December after the end of the semester. I was scheduled to be inducted into the army as a two year draftee on Easter Monday, so I continued my job driving a delivery truck. When Easter Monday came, I had no orders and did not know where to go to report for duty. The draft board was closed so I had to wait until Tuesday to call. When I called on Tuesday, the draft board lady told me she had no records for me and would have to look into it and get back to me. It was several days before she called to tell me that my files had been misplaced in the veteran's files. She said I would never have been drafted had I not called."

"You've got to be kidding me," Felix laughed. "I bet you'll want to kick your own ass next time you're trying to hide under your helmet while Charlie is shooting at you!"

"I already cussed at myself all the way out and back while I was trying to keep up on that first night ambush, thinking to myself 'you dumb ass'. Anyway," I continued, "I had given up my delivery job and would not be inducted now until August 14, so I had to find another job to get by until then. So, I took a job as a knock up man at a furniture frame factory. My job was to knock together wood frames, matching up the dowel pins into the precut holes and fitting them together with hot glue and a rubber mallet. The chair and sofa arms were marked with pencils and had to be trimmed on a vertical band saw. I had to align the wood pieces up to the rotating saw blade and trim along the lines. If there was a knot in the wood, the blade would grab the wood and shoot it through the other side of the saw. If you were not paying attention or were holding the wood too tight, it would take your hand along for the ride. I was the only knock up man in the plant with all of my fingers. I could not wait to go into the army while my limbs were still intact."

"I heard they are going to promote you to Specialist Four, the same rank as me," Felix offered. "You did not hear that from me, though," he added.

We got back into the jeep and headed down the winding one-lane trail through the big garbage dump on the southwest side of Bronco. Huge piles of wooden ammo crates were strewn among the piles of garbage, a testament to the amazing volume of ordinance the army used against our enemies.

Felix stopped the jeep and we dismounted to look down on the village of Đức Phổ. He pointed out a compound encircled by a concrete wall with an arched entry.

"That's the laundry and orphanage," he explained. "I like to visit and take them stuff. It makes me feel better about being here. I'll take you there tomorrow if you want to go into town."

Chapter 8

The next morning we walked out the main gate into Đức Phổ after the mine clearing crew opened the road. Felix carried a green canvas claymore mine bag filled with baby powder, C-rations, chocolate bars and other goodies for kids in the orphanage. We turned left from the access road onto Highway One, the main street through the village. The street was buzzing with traffic, vehicle and pedestrian. Three-wheeled vehicles that looked like a motorcycle in front and a pickup truck bed in back zoomed about through the crowds, each loaded with more people than they looked like they could handle. Loaded buses trudged along filled to capacity with people riding inside while others hitched rides by standing on the bumpers and leaning precariously from doorways.

Shops lined both sides of the roadway. Young women called to us as we passed offering "number one boom-boom". Felix told me the going rate was five dollars. He warned "you might get more than you bargain for." I told him I thought I would pass although we did see some other guys from the company disappear down alleys with the girls.

A young girl maybe twelve, close to Dam's age I guessed, waved to me from a storefront. She was standing next to her mother so I waved back, wanting to be friendly. She smiled and briskly walked to me and started talking.

"What you want G.I.?" she asked as if responding to me.

"She thinks you invited her to come," Felix pointed out. "When they wave to you moving their hand up and down like that it means come here to them. If you want them to go away, turn your palm down and wave them away and say di-di."

When Felix said the word di-di, she took it that he wanted her to leave us. Her welcoming smile turned to a frown as she backed away.

"Do you know Dam?" I asked quickly, not wanting to hurt her feelings.

"Dam number one girlfriend," she answered. "How you know Dam?"

"I got candles and cigarettes from her on the road," I answered. "She was selling them from her bicycle and had Anh and other friends with her."

"You come my store," she said tugging at my sleeve. She pulled me to her storefront and her mother immediately came forward, showing us the variety of products they wanted to sell us.

Cigarettes, Cokes, chocolate and other products from our sundries packs were neatly displayed on a rectangular table in the center of the open air store. I also noticed Schlitz beer on a shelf behind the table. The black market was thriving in Đức Phổ.

"We're going to the orphanage," I explained as we pulled ourselves away from their aggressive sales efforts. It was hard not to buy something but I was running low on money. "If you see Dam, tell her Jared said hello." I hoped she would remember me.

"You buy tuoc dinky dau?" she asked before we could get clear of her storefront.

"That's Vietnamese for crazy cigarette," Felix explained. "Pot."

"No thanks," I answered as we headed off towards the orphanage.

About the length of a city block from the store we walked through the once stately entrance to the orphanage, two tall columns that could have held gates to a fort. Walls once attached to the columns were now crumbled piles of concrete and stucco that ran along the roadside. The gateway opened into a swept dirt courtyard. Two wide concrete steps worn smooth from years of use climbed to sturdy wood double doors that led to the enclosed part of the compound. Felix knocked on the door and a petite little nun in her black and white habit tugged open the heavy door.

Her instant excitement and recognition at seeing Felix told me he was a frequent and welcomed friend to the orphanage. Her broad smile revealed even white teeth that surprised me on a lady who appeared to be north of fifty. During my short tenure in country, I had become accustomed to seeing only betel nut stained purple teeth on any woman over thirty.

Felix introduced me as "G.I. Jared" which struck me as funny. She extended her arm and a tiny and anemic looking white hand revealed itself from within the black folds of the sleeve of her habit. I was careful to take her hand gently. Everything about her was so delicate. I was in awe of her gentle presence and I felt I was being blessed by her offered touch.

"It nice Felix bring you see us," she offered, her slight voice barely a whisper. "I am Sister Hao."

Sister Hao spoke good English. You could distinguish the past French influence in her enunciation and choice of words. Her drawn face and slender frame defined her beleaguered existence. Her lively brown eyes sharply contrasted the darkly shaded circles below them. I was saddened yet humbled by her presence. I could not imagine the life sacrifices she made for her presence here.

Sister Hao led us further inside. She seemed to float more than walk since her feet were invisible below her flowing frock. Her gracefulness bestowed a religious reverence and I felt comforted being in this place.

My religious experience was interrupted by the sudden appearance of children. The boys and girls surrounded Felix expectantly waiting for him to pass his bag of goodies around. They fought for his attention, tugging at his pant legs and reaching out to be picked up and held. Felix moved among them familiarly, touching their heads and calling those he remembered by name, as he handed out C-ration chocolates, sodas, cans of ham and eggs, beans and franks and other assorted meals. He handed

Sister Hao two plastic Johnson's Baby Powder dispensers which she promptly handed over to a pretty young Vietnamese nun named Lei.

Lei moved off to the next room, the nursery. I followed behind her as she went from bed to bed inspecting the babies to see who needed the precious baby powder. There were more than a dozen infants, many the obvious offspring of black soldiers. The prostitutes would not keep the mixed race babies and would bring them to the orphanage as soon as they had them. It was not so much a prejudicial issue of having a half black child but more because the Viet Cong, also their customers, would ostracize or kill them for having babies obviously sired by black Americans. Children from white fathers were harder to detect as coming from American men since the French occupation had produced a whole populace of Asian and Caucasian mix.

The babies were not covered by diapers. I wondered how they managed to clean up after them. I guess that was something I would sooner not see, I thought. Lei gently applied the powder, not just to their tender little bottoms and also to heads, faces, arms and legs. I saw some really nasty looking rashes and skin ailments that the powder would do little to heal although it did seem to provide temporary relief to some.

"We do not have salves, lotions or medicines to treat the children," Sister Lei pointed out when she saw my look of concern. "Sometimes soldiers bring what they can but it is never enough."

I followed Felix from the nursery into the next large room which was bustling with activity. Five young women were vigorously washing and ironing military uniforms, then neatly folding them and wrapping the bundles in brown paper bound with string. They then carefully labeled the packages with soldiers' names. I noticed the floor of the laundry had once been concrete and was now mostly washed out and rutted unlike the cleaned and polished concrete and terra cotta floors in the rest of the orphanage.

The five girls all had their black silk pants legs rolled up to above the knees and moved about their laundry chores barefooted. I saw that their shapely and muscular young legs were severely marked with round and sore looking scars.

"Are those leech scars on their legs?" I asked Felix.

"Afraid so," he confirmed. "Those girls work here in exchange for meals and a place to sleep. They come from farm families who do not have enough rice to go around. They still go out to the rice paddies and help with planting and harvesting so their families can eat, but they end up back here when supplies run low. It works out," he added. "The orphanage makes enough money from their work in the laundry to help feed the children and provide food, shelter and clothing for the girls."

One of the girls brought Felix a neatly bound packet of cleaned and pressed fatigues with his name neatly written across the top. That explained how Felix always looked so clean and sharply dressed when I saw him. He handed her a few dollars and informed me it was time to be getting back. So we went to find Sister Hao to show her our appreciation for her hospitality and went out the big doors, a trail of smiling and waving children following along behind. As we passed through the columnar entrance back onto the main street I was pleasantly surprised to see Dam standing in the street waving to me and smiling.

"Tôi biết Jared," she shouted. Meaning I know Jared, I remembered.

"My friend, Dam, I was just asking about you," I said, truly pleased to see her. "This is my friend, Felix."

"I know Felix. He number one," she answered.

"Where's your bicycle?" I asked.

"My friend tell me you come Đức Phổ, so I take home to Mama San," she explained.

"Are you ready to teach me some more Vietnamese words?" I was anxious to learn some more from my little teacher.

"I've got to get back to Bronco," Felix interrupted. "You can hang around though. Just be nice to our good friend Dam."

As Felix walked down the road I got to feeling a little nervous about being in Đức Phổ without another American. We were instructed only to go into the village when there were two or more of us. I could see that Dam sensed my discomfort as she patted my arm in a reassuring gesture.

"Okay Jared stay with Dam, no sweat," she smiled.

She delicately grasped my left hand with her much smaller right and led me back through the orphanage columns. I noticed how incredibly cute Dam looked as she led me along by the hand, her curly locks bouncing naturally in rhythm with her stride.

We sat on the second step at the front of the building and Dam started chattering away like she was meeting with a long lost friend. Her version of English was a mishmash of Vietnamese, English with some French thrown in. She said things like "you beaucoup dinky dau" which I figured out from her gestures meant that I was very crazy. I asked how to say "you're very pretty" and she knew right away to answer "em dep qua"; "em" – "young girl", she said pointing to herself, "dep" – "pretty", she described by holding her hands palm out to the sides of her face while smiling and blinking rapidly, and "qua" she defined in French as beaucoup.

We moved on to teaching each other how to count from one to ten. "một, hai, ba, bốn, năm, sáu, bảy, tám, chin, mười," Dam recited. With her patient repetition I was soon counting one to ten rapidly over and over again. Then she reminded me how to count above ten by using multiplication, like two times ten is twenty, hai mười, twenty-one is hai mười một. In one lesson Dam had me understanding how to count to ninety-nine, compliment a pretty girl or tell somebody they were crazy. And I was never very good at foreign languages in school.

I could see that Dam learned faster than me. She had a natural talent for teaching and her retention of English words came easy to her as she taught me words and numbers. Each time I got things right she rewarded me with a big smile and a congratulatory "Jared number one."

My brain had absorbed all of the Vietnamese I could handle for one lesson so I decided to use the opportunity to learn more about Dam. All I really knew about her was the little I learned when I met her out on Highway One.

I asked if she had any brothers and sisters. "No got."

I asked about her father. "No got."

I asked her mother's name. "Tuy," she answered. "Same as me, she added. My name is Mai Thi Tuy Et Dam."

I asked her mother's age. "Hai mươi tám" she answered. I had to count to eight in my newly acquired Vietnamese to figure out her mom was twenty plus eight. That would have made her fifteen when she had Dam. I calculated, Dam would have been born in 1955. I surmised Dam's father was probably French but decided against suggesting that to her. Her features appeared to be part Caucasian. Her answer of "no got" when I asked about her father was likely her way of avoiding a painful subject.

I was so absorbed talking with Dam that I had lost track of time. I checked my watch and saw that it was after noon.

"Where can we buy some lunch," I asked, as I mimicked spooning food into my mouth.

"You wait, I get," Dam declared without hesitation as she trotted off and disappeared into the crowded traffic on the main road through Đức Phổ.

I obediently sat and waited for Dam, enjoying the opportunity to observe the people in the village. Two patrolling ARVN soldiers passed by and eyed me suspiciously but refrained from approaching me. The M-16 I held across my lap probably discouraged them from becoming too aggressive, I assumed.

A deuce and a half troop truck rolled by loaded with American soldiers headed north on Highway One. *Wooly Bully* by Sam The Sham & The Pharaohs was playing on a transistor radio from the back of the truck. The soldiers were singing along loudly as they passed through the village. I gave a big wave and thumbs up as they passed. One of the guys stuck his butt out over the tailgate and mooned me. I flipped him a bird and we waved a friendly so long in mutual understanding. We all hated being here and we needed to keep it light.

As the truck passed by I was surprised to see Lenny Enson and Bart Hitchcock from my platoon appear in its place at an open air shop across from the orphanage. Lenny was holding up a black silk jacket that had a map of Vietnam colorfully knitted across the back. I watched as he negotiated back and forth with the shopkeeper before politely laying the jacket back on the display table and turning away. The shop keeper followed along behind him, obviously trying to sell something to the soldier.

While I was watching Lenny and Bart, Dam walked up pushing her green bike loaded with its mobile store of goods. I was confused when I saw her stop and talk to my friends, knowing that she was supposed to be bringing lunch. But I noticed she was protectively holding what appeared to be food on chop sticks.

I watched as Lenny pointed to the food, apparently inquiring about buying it. Dam turned and pointed to me, and I could tell she was afraid she might offend them. She looked at me and waved and Lenny smiled in recognition and understanding. They all headed across the street towards me, Dam hurriedly aiming her bicycle in my direction, the food awkwardly held above her handle bars.

"I got number one food for you," Dam announced defensively after hurrying to get to me first. The spicy aroma of the beef on a stick with peppers and bamboo shoots smelled so good I could taste the flavor before actually taking a bite.

"Why you got your bike?" I asked, bewildered.

"Mama San say I work now," Dam explained. I guessed her mother had allowed me to waste enough of Dam's time.

"You eat with me first," I suggested, pointing to the food.

"I eat rice with Mama San," she explained. "I go work now."

"Do you think you could go and get us some of those," Lenny asked Dam, pointing to the skewered delicacies.

"Mama San make," I get. "How many you want?"

"Same-same for me and for him as for Jared," Lenny

responded, pointing to Bart.

"No sweat," Dam said as she handed me the three steak sticks, hopped on her bike and started off down the dirt street once again.

I handed a skewer each to Lenny and Bart. We were in the habit of sharing everything and it was natural to just hand it over without needing to ask or offer. The meat was surprisingly tasty and tangy. The hot pepper spices caused us all to unscrew the caps on our canteens with the first bite.

"We didn't mean to steal your food. We could have waited for ours." Lenny was always so polite I sometimes forgot he was a grunt like the rest of us.

I thought of him as a gentleman soldier. At six feet one inch and one hundred and seventy pounds, he was strong and healthy but his aura was totally non-aggressive. He did not fear confrontation and would go to great lengths to avoid in-your-face situations. His fair and unblemished skin gave him a cleaner than most look and his black, plastic framed military issue glasses finished his appearance of studious innocence.

Lenny took his soldiering seriously. He had a job to do and intended to do it to the best of his ability. Like me, he was confused about the political and religious implications of this war and we shared our fears and concerns about the things it was causing us to become.

As our friendship grew we began to keep each other company by doubling up during our turns at guard duty. We normally performed guard duty from atop the bunker since there was a limited field of view of the attack zone from the inside. We spent many miserable nights during rainy periods hunkered under hooded green ponchos attempting to keep as dry as possible, which usually proved to be a futile effort. You were tempted to hunker down under the poncho and use it like a tent but knew you subjected yourself and others to surprise attack for lack of visibility. So, we would sit with the poncho hood tucked under our steel helmets and stare at the moonless darkness, more listening than seeing. We hoped trip flares we attached to the concertina wire would signal enemy encroachment. Charlie often attacked during inclement weather.

Lenny was raised in a village in Alaska called Unalakleet. He described it as being so remote you could only get there by dog sled or snow mobile in winter. His parents were missionaries and they lived a pretty basic existence mirroring that of their charges in severe conditions in a harsh climate.

Yet I found myself jealous of what I saw with Lenny. I could see that his experience in Alaska had shaped his strengths and morals and given him life knowledge that I did not grasp. I knew it was something I wanted yet knew only experience like Lenny had would give it to me.

Many times, sitting on top of our bunker on Liz, we shared our thoughts about what the conflict was all about and attempted to understand our role. On those occasions, we discovered it took a lot of beer to get the conversation to have any meaning. We always arrived at the same conclusion. What in the world are our leaders thinking?

We could not understand why our powerful country was not using its capabilities to support us. We were confused. What was it that our country wanted us to do? We went through training to be good soldiers, convinced that our role was sanctioned by our country. We had no choice but to carry on with that understanding. We could not grasp the concept that our generals would not support us.

"These things are hot," Bart announced, wiping sweat from his brow. I could see perspiration beads in his thick, sandy colored mustache as he smiled to reveal even white teeth.

"Yeah," Lenny agreed. "You think Dam's mother is trying to kill us? Maybe she's VC," he laughed.

I always envied people with healthy teeth and bright white smiles and Bart was one of those fortunate few. My baby teeth turned brown and even as a four-year-old kid, I was so ashamed of them that I never smiled for pictures. It was a long time after my permanent teeth came in before I realized it was okay to smile and reveal my new ones. I even wondered why the tooth fairy would want them when my mother told me to put them under my pillow when they dropped out.

Bart had a million dollar smile. When he smiled his whole face expressed pleasure that made you feel good just to share it with him. He seemed to have an inner happiness about life that made him an odd fit for an infantry soldier. Bart was from Utah and a Mormon.

Except for a girl in high school, I never knew a Mormon. She was gorgeous but because of her mysterious religion, I considered her to be unapproachable. After meeting Bart and looking back, I realized I was mistaken to be guided by ignorance.

"All right, here comes the rest of the food," Bart announced, pointing to Dam. She was riding her bike on the shoulder of the dirt roadway. She waited for a break in the unending line of bikes, scooters and trucks to cross the road in our direction.

"I bring three cold beers," Dam said smiling, knowing that we would want to buy them to douse the fire from the spicy food. She reached into her bicycle basket and removed two sets of carefully wrapped steak sticks and handed them over, then retrieved the beers and distributed them among us. She stood and watched expectantly until I realized I had not offered to pay her for the first food she brought.

"How much you want for the food and beers?" I asked. The other guys took the hint and started digging around in their fatigue pockets for money.

"Meat stick one dollar, beer one dollar." When Dam was in her business mode, you could see that she took it very seriously. I had come to the conclusion that everything Dam sold was one dollar.

Dam efficiently tucked the bills away into the elastic waist of her black silk pants and announced that she had to go work now. I expected it would be a while before I would get to see her again. The three of us waved and called goodbye as she pedaled off to the north in search of more customers, her mũ lá hanging on her back by the strap around her neck, Dale Evans style.

An odd silence remained in the space Dam left, a void vacated by her strong personality. We all felt her absence as we watched the back of her curly head bob up and down while she expertly maneuvered her mobile store through traffic.

"What an amazing little person," Lenny observed. "Too bad they can't all be like her."

We ate the food her mom had prepared. The only sounds we made were the gasping and exhaling the spices elicited with each bite. The cold Ballantine beer was a life saver.

As I observed my two friends enjoying their treats, I noticed that they, like me, never really relaxed. Their eyes roved from person to person and place to place fixedly alert to their surroundings. Except for where we were and the automatic weapons they always held at the ready, these two could have fit right in on any college campus back home. Although denominationally different, both were raised in strict religious circumstances. Their rugged appearance belied the character and morals I knew lay beneath.

"Felix took me to the orphanage this morning," I offered. "It's pretty inspiring if you guys would like to go in and check it out."

They both nodded their approval. It was something different to do to pass the time. Unless you were into prostitutes, drugs or cheaply crafted trinkets, there was not much to do in Đức Phổ.

Sister Hao honored me by remembering my name as she welcomed us through the stately front doors. The older children were gathered for their daily lessons as they sat on the terra cotta floor in a circle. Sister Lei directed as they obediently recited Vietnamese verse in a monotone chorus of young voices.

Bart noticed the young women doing their laundry chores in the adjacent room and wandered off to inspect. Lenny watched the kids with me for a while, then soon trailed off to find Bart.

I squatted next to the gathered children and enjoyed their youthful enthusiasm to learn. Their rhythmic recitations grew louder when they realized a stranger had taken an interest in watching and listening.

Introducing more people to the orphanage became a personal goal when I saw how taken my two friends were by the people and the place. Bart was so entranced with it that we had trouble getting him to leave when Lenny and I decided it was time to get back to Bronco. Once outside the entrance Bart excused himself to go urinate behind a stately banyan tree in the side yard.

"I think Bart's in love," Lenny whispered. "He got talking to a pretty young girl in the laundry and they seemed to really hit it off."

"I can't imagine where that could go," I said, trying to keep my voice down.

"He talked like he was going to come back and might

even want to marry her," Lenny explained, unable to hide how ridiculous he thought that was.

Bart did act like a love struck adolescent during the entire walk back to base. He talked like he was really serious about taking a bride back to Utah with him.

Back on Bronco, smoking grills were lined up outside of the bar we called Red Dog Saloon. *It Tears Me Up* by Percy Sledge blared from the reel-to-reel tape player.

The battalion mess sergeant had arranged to feed us a grilled steak dinner. Our battalion commander commandeered the precious meat for us from the officers club. He wanted his troops to be treated as well as the officers on this well-deserved stand down.

"Man, I can't believe the tunes they've got on this reel-to-reel player," Lenny observed as Sam & Dave singing *Soul Man* resonated from the stereo speakers. As if someone were directing everyone chimed in and sang along. The sing along continued as another Sam & Dave favorite *Hold On, I'm Comin'* followed.

We gorged ourselves on the much appreciated grilled beef and drank a few too many beers. That led to some interesting twists on our field experiences that became believable war stories until we decided it was time to sack out. On the walk to the barracks American Breed serenaded from the reel to reel with *Bend Me, Shape Me* while the last remaining soldiers at the bar chorused along.

Chapter 9

As usual, we had no idea where this combat assault would take us when we gathered at the boarding area. The difference was the location. We were accustomed to meeting the Hueys at the base of Liz in a cloud of red dirt and dust. It was a nice change to stage at the airfield on Bronco where the helicopters were already waiting on the tarmac. We just had to board and wait for the assault group to take off in formation. It made lugging fully loaded sixty-pound rucksacks on board a much less strenuous project.

The pilots were anxiously waiting for the sun to peek its big eye over the South China Sea out east so we could get airborne. We all shared the tension and anticipation that accompanied a battalion sized assault operation. The logistics required when deploying a force of this size, five companies with coordinated artillery and air support, was inspirational. Yet we had lived through repeated exercises like this when our superior force and fire power did little to dislodge a supposedly inferior and outgunned enemy.

Brigade intelligence passed word to our commanders that a Marine corporal was being held captive by the Viet Cong to the west of Quảng Ngãi. According to the report he was being moved from village to village to allow the locals to beat, harass and spit on him. That heart rending news fired us up. In the worst way, we wanted to find and save him.

We took off from Bronco at the first sign of daylight. I was in my usual position sitting on the floor of the Huey next to the open left door. It was an awesome sight to look down and see dozens of helicopters still on the tarmac with their rotors turning as they prepared to join the flight formation behind us.

We headed north from Bronco and followed Highway One until we could see the twin peaks of Liz to our west. Slightly further north at Mộ Đức, our flock of helicopters turned abruptly west and Cobra attack helicopters zoomed by us flying low to get positioned to attack. In less than ten minutes we could hear explosions to our front as the assault began. The mass of cannon and machine gun fire preceded us to prepare the landing zone for our descent.

I was relieved to see green smoke when our pilot skillfully eased us down in the middle of an acre of grassy pasture. Even with my sixty-pound pack, it was an effortless dismount to be able to use the runner to step to ground level.

We established a hasty perimeter to allow the rest of the company to land and unload, then assumed a line formation and briskly headed west toward our target, a small mountain marked on the map as Hill 328, its height above sea level. The other companies landed to the north, south and west of the mountain intending to surround the enemy and cut off his escape routes.

I was on point leading the rest of first squad as we followed the open footpath that led us through Minh Long village at the base of the mountain. I walked at a faster than normal pace. I was concerned that the adrenalin rush from our desire to rescue one of our soldiers would make us careless. I did not want to lead us into an ambush. I knew we needed to hurry.

Artillery rounds fired from the battery on Liz whizzed over our heads and began pounding the hill five hundred meters to our front. The 105mm rounds flew directly over us, all sounding dangerously close.

I heard intense whistling that sounded like a jet about to land behind me when a deafening explosion sent me tumbling off of the dirt path to the ground. A short round had fallen from the sky ten meters to my right. My ears ached from the concussion, but I was conscious enough to quickly inspect myself to see where I was hit, certain that a blast so close would have sent shrapnel flying in my direction.

Once convinced that I was unhurt, I turned my attention to the guys who were following close behind me. Other than the obvious shell shock, we had somehow escaped the blast without a casualty. The low angle and trajectory of the artillery round had evidently sent all of the shrapnel to our front.

It took me a few minutes to gather my wits. I felt dazed and confused from the surprising short round blast but I was relieved to be alive. I was anxious to get my head cleared enough to continue on, knowing we had a ticking clock marking the window of opportunity to get to the corporal.

"I think you need me to take over point for a while," Franny said, appearing from somewhere back in the line. "If you're up for it you can walk behind me."

"I am feeling some shell shock, Franny," I admitted. "I'm sorry to bail on you, but I've got your back," I promised.

"Come on, let's do this," he shouted back to the rest of the platoon. He knew we were all feeling desperate to execute the rescue. Franny always took walking point as an honor to be in charge. He ducked his head low as if sniffing out the right direction then headed out the trail we were on before.

Ahead, where the terrain began its ascent upward, the foliage thickened to forest and heavy undergrowth. I could see smoke and dust from the shelling and helicopter gunship attacks that sprinkled the mountainside.

We covered the few hundred meter distance to the base of the hill in less than half an hour and Franny cautiously led our climb up the narrow hillside path. I heard a clicking noise and thought Franny had stepped on a mine. Instead it was the detonator from a chi-com hand grenade in the dense tree line a few meters ahead. Luckily, the shrapnel and explosion that followed was absorbed by the forest growth. Charlie was close to our front.

We were even more convinced, now, that the enemy had our fellow American on the hill above us. Knowledge that an American prisoner might be in the midst of the

Viet Cong force we were approaching made us super cautious about opening fire on whoever was tossing grenades at us.

Within twenty meters or so I heard the now familiar click of another chi-com grenade being thrown followed by a thud as it landed a couple of yards behind Franny and directly on the path in front of me. In a blur I caught sight of Franny running at me. He tackled me low and took me to the ground knocking the air out of me in the process. We landed hard on the dirt path, both of us pulling our helmets down over our faces to shield us from the expected blast. But the explosion never came.

"I think it's a dud," Franny shouted from under his helmet as we crawled back down the hill to get a safe distance away from it.

It was the first time I had seen one of them up close. It resembled one of my soup cans mounted on a Christmas bell handle. When thrown by the handle, the jerking motion sets off the timer on the firing mechanism and it detonates a few seconds later. Like AK-47 rifles, the grenades were supplied to our enemies by China, called chi-com for Chinese communist.

We marked the hand grenade's location with rocks so the rest of our troop would avoid it and a little at a time Franny led us as we inched our way up the hill. We were stalled by the sound of more grenades exploding on the hill ahead of us. The forest and foliage protected us by causing the projectiles to land short each time. It appeared that we were being delayed by a limited number of enemy soldiers to give them time to retreat. Sadly, it was working and we knew that each delay meant our chances of rescuing the prisoner got slimmer. Our hope was that the Viet Cong would retreat into an ambush by our sister companies who were hopefully blocking their avenues of escape.

When we finally reached the top of the hill, we found evidence of a recently deserted camp with fires still smoldering and uneaten rice in pots. However, there was no sign of the enemy and no reports of our soldiers who surrounded the mountain making contact. They just disappeared. There had to be a tunnel or cave somewhere.

We spread out and searched, but we had to move very slowly since we fully expected to encounter booby traps left by Charlie. We knew that every minute we spent trying to find where they went reduced our chances of rescuing our captured ally.

We were in the middle of a well-used Viet Cong base camp. There were several lean-to shelters surrounded by rows of rough cut wood seating, suitable for training and instruction of large groups of soldiers. Caches of rice in woven baskets were abandoned giving evidence that the camp was deserted in a hurry. There were no mines or booby traps like Charlie would normally leave behind for us, further proof that we had caught them by surprise.

Our company commander ordered us to establish a perimeter and secure the area while we waited and hoped for news that one of our sister companies would make contact with the retreating VC. As the day wore on without any news we acknowledged the dreaded truth that our rescue mission had failed. We knew there had to be a cave or tunnel. Our efforts to find one were proving futile. At our request, the brigade commander sent Chu Hoi soldiers from Bronco by helicopter to help find and enter the tunnels.

Chu Hoi's were enemies who surrendered and became scouts and interpreters for the Americans. They were familiar with methods the VC used to conceal tunnel entrances. Soon after their arrival, they discovered the entrance to a sophisticated and well-constructed tunnel. The entrance was concealed by a moss covered trap door at the base of a rubber tree. The main tunnel was dug into the mountain and had a ladder that led more than fifty feet straight down then branched off in all directions. Regardless of hours spent searching, no enemies were found. Neither was there any sign of where they took our Marine corporal.

A steady stream of helicopters brought in equipment and engineers to destroy the base camp and blow up the tunnel system. Recon platoon took over our responsibility for securing the perimeter around the captured enemy base camp and we headed west on patrol down the mountainside. The ground vibrated beneath our feet when we started our descent as the explosives started blowing up the tunnel complex within the mountain.

I was relieved not to be walking point. The close call with the artillery round and chi-com hand grenades had left me feeling pretty jumpy. But I was comfortable to be walking second in line behind Franny. He paid close attention to detail and did not take unnecessary chances.

This side of Hill 328 wore the scars of previous battles. The foliage and undergrowth, once a dense green jungle, was now a dead zone of barren trees, stumps, leafless vines and root systems. The entire mountainside looked like a fierce firestorm had blown through leaving a discolored dredge of burnt orange behind.

Crop dusting equipment was attached to our airplanes to rain orange death on Charlie's hiding places. From the bleak appearance of the land, I suspected that the chemical defoliant could do as much harm to our enemy as our search and destroy missions it was intended to facilitate. The destruction we saw was evidence that we were not the first to attempt to uproot the Viet Cong from this base camp.

I had heard stories about the defoliation campaign. We saw entire mountains during combat assault flights that were turned barren. We patrolled dense jungle and swamp areas where we often wished defoliant would have been used, jungle so thick we had to cut trails with machetes.

The charred hillside gave way to a pastoral lea in the river valley below. The contrasting landscape was a testament to the extremes between war and peace that we walked and flew in and out of every day. While it was a relief to know Charlie had no good concealment, no hedgerows to cover his ambushes or booby traps, I had a bad feeling just walking through the area. Even the air smelled musty and tainted. If the chemicals could destroy the flora to this extent, I wondered how it might be affecting us being exposed to it. And what effect would the toxic spray have on villagers who passed through or lived near areas where it was used. I hoped that we would not have to dig in and sleep on the poisoned ground.

On direction from our battalion commander, we waited until we were several hundred yards into the plush green river valley before we set up our night perimeter. We put extra effort into digging our fox holes deep since we had proof that we were in Charlie's domain. Fortunately, digging in was easier than usual thanks to the fertile grassy soil in the valley.

As I looked around, I could see that we were a dejected crew. It was heart rendering to have been just minutes from saving the Marine. We could all envision what he must have experienced while we were so close. He was probably dragged and beaten to get him through the tunnel system and away from us.

As the descending sun began to blanket the valley in shadows, I folded my spade and strapped it back under the base of my ruck sack. I realized I had not eaten since we left Bronco so I poked around in my pack to find my favorite LRRP ration packet of spaghetti and meat sauce. I poured the contents into my metal canteen holder and added water to the freeze dried mixture. I used my Zippo lighter to fire up a blue heat tab and in a few minutes I was spooning away at my Italian dinner.

"Duke came by while you were cooking," Franny said

as he popped the top on a warm beer and sat down beside me. "He said we are leaving one man in each position and taking one man out for night raids tonight."

"What's a night raid?" I asked

"He didn't elaborate," Franny answered, shrugging. "He did say we are supposed to draw straws between us to see who goes and who stays. Whoever is going is supposed to meet up at the CQ for instructions as soon as we draw straws."

I drew the short straw. I was not sure whether or not to be disappointed. The thought of manning a fox hole alone twenty meters away from the next perimeter post was not so appealing either.

I walked the thirty or forty meters to the center of the perimeter for the meeting. Twelve of us would be going out led by Sergeant Jeff Greene. Our assignment would take us around the base of Hill 328 and back to the village of Minh Long. The idea was to sneak into the village and try to catch a prisoner by raiding the houses one by one. The mission was to try and get more information about the force that occupied the mountain base camp. There was still a flicker of hope among us to learn more about the marine corporal.

I saddled up packing light, carrying only my rifle, ammo belt with canteen and one claymore mine in its canvas bag with a shoulder strap. There was no need for sleeping gear since we would be on the move and would stop only when we returned to the perimeter after raiding and searching the village. We were to carry no food or cans of soda or beer in our pockets. It was important we had nothing on us that would cause us to make noise and give our presence away.

When dusk gave way to darkness, we left the perimeter and headed southeast around the base of the mountain. The terrain was a grassy valley with a well-worn foot path running through its center. We were on the west end of the same trail we used to assault Hill 328 earlier.

Jeff elected to walk point and I fell in behind him to walk second. Jeff had earned my respect and admiration when I joined his squad as a replacement back in January. Although my first experience in the field with him when we executed the ambush after my first combat assault still gave me nightmares, I had grown to understand the angered retribution against the two tax collectors that I witnessed that night.

Jeff was a Midwestern farm boy who told stories about his experiences flying crop dusters and operating big farm equipment, tractors with enclosed cockpits and stereo systems. He told me a story once about how he had misjudged a power line while dusting a field. He flew into it and the prop wound around the wires which suspended his airplane fifty feet in the air. He had to be rescued by the fire department.

I asked Jeff why he didn't become a helicopter pilot since he was already a pilot before he entered the army. He responded that being a pilot taught him how to read the sky.

"You always gauge the direction and strength of the

wind and look for cumulous cloud build up and movement," he explained. "The one thing you never want to do is go towards towering clouds that form a thunderhead. They can crush a small aircraft. Every time we board the Huey's for a combat assault and see red smoke when we approach the landing zone, it feels to me like we're flying into the storm. I admire our Huey pilots, but I figure you can only fly into the storm and live to talk about it just so many times before your luck runs out."

Jeff was about my height and had the build, I thought, of a golfer or tennis player. He seemed athletic to me, yet he didn't appear to be a team sport sort of guy. In some ways he struck me as a loner. That probably stemmed from his apparent desire for privacy when asked about anything other than his farming and flying responsibilities. I guessed that he came from a wealthy family. I wondered why he could not have found a way around serving in this war.

He was a good looking and solidly built guy with a slightly pointy nose who appeared to have been well brought up. Vietnam was giving him a lot of skin issues. The repeated walks through tepid rice paddy and swamp water left him with skin lesions and rashes better known as jungle rot. His skin would just about get healed up when we would be off on another mission in wet conditions.

Jeff came to Vietnam with the brigade from Schofield Barracks, Hawaii in November. He never allowed himself to get sucked into conversations about the politics of the war. He took his responsibilities seriously, while not gung ho. He just wanted to be a good soldier and for that reason was a good leader. He wasn't fearless but was sincere in his determination to seek out and confront our enemies. We all knew we could trust Jeff to be there for us when we needed him. I hoped tonight would not be a test of that need.

Aided by the early evening moonlight, Jeff briskly led us the thousand meters to the village. We spread out in three four-man teams intent on catching the villagers by surprise. I took the flashlight and volunteered to enter the first hooch while the other guys surrounded the front and back. I took my rifle off safety and stooped down to clear the short doorway and flipped on the flashlight. To my surprise, a guy with a white sidewall haircut, a distinguishing mark of a North Vietnamese soldier, leaped from a hammock slung between the walls of the grass and mud house and dove through the wall of the hooch. I instinctively fired several rounds in his direction from the hip. I was pretty sure I saw a pistol in his right hand.

I looked around to see that an old mama san and two young children were huddled in a corner of the hooch. Although obviously frightened, they did not seem to me to be upset over my shooting at the man in their home. I suspected he was there by force, not by invitation.

I was disappointed to learn that I had killed him. We were supposed to try to capture an enemy soldier for interrogation. My reaction to his sudden leap from the hammock and attempted escape through the wall could have cost us another shot at information about our captured comrade. Our chance of capturing any other enemy soldiers who might have been hiding among the villagers would now surely be lost.

Since our position was given away we would need to beat feet back to the safety of our company perimeter in a hurry. Our twelve-man patrol would be vulnerable wandering around at night in enemy infested territory.

Jeff led us back onto the path we used to enter the village, passing word down the line for us to keep up because he planned to move at a double time pace. The moonlight was a welcome aid to our movements but its brightness would also make our silhouettes an easy target to ambush.

We had covered about half of the thousand meter distance back when Jeff signaled that he detected movement to our front. We dropped down on both sides of the trail trying hard to maintain silence. My heavy breathing from the rapid pace we were setting that was almost a trot concerned me that I might give us away. As I stooped down off the side of the trail I realized that I could hear the others gasping for breath as well.

Zack Rivers quietly eased up through our column and tapped me on the shoulder as he passed. I could hear him whispering to Jeff, and then he disappeared forward as he went to scout the trail ahead for a possible enemy trap. He had a real instinct for snooping Charlie out. In less than five minutes we heard a burst on automatic and then silence once again. I hoped Zack was the shooter. I was relieved to see his hunkered down image return to Jeff and heard them whispering.

Jeff signaled to me that we were moving again and our column followed obediently along, this time with Zack in the point position. When we signaled our arrival back to our guys on guard of the perimeter I realized we had been gone only one and a half hours.

We went directly to the CQ to describe the results of our mission. I reported my reasons for killing the NVA soldier and ruining our chances of taking him prisoner. The company commander simply responded that he would report one enemy killed in action.

Zack reported one possible KIA. He said he spotted the outline of a sniper thanks to the bright moonlight and fired a burst at him on automatic but could not confirm the kill.

Zack Rivers was the most fearless soldier I knew. If he was ever afraid he did not show it. He was the one guy among us who would voluntarily go one-on-one with an enemy soldier any chance he got. It almost seemed entertaining to him.

He never showed any emotion although I sensed constant underlying anger. I walked up on him in a village once and caught him punishing the village residents for no particular reason. He had acquired part of a pool cue stick somewhere, the kind that come in two pieces and screw apart, and was walking around rapping villagers on their heads with it.

Another time I entered a village courtyard to find Zack

directing the entire village populace as he had them doing push-ups. On both occasions he just stopped and walked away as soon as he knew I was watching. Zack would not talk about these things. When I asked why he did them, he just shrugged and turned away.

I saw Zack as a time bomb waiting for an excuse to explode. His anger and lack of fear struck me as some sort of personality issue that had the potential to be dangerous. While the rest of us would experience shock and fatigue after deaths, injuries or severe and prolonged fire fights, Zack would show no emotion or strain. He would just go along unaffected by the traumatic events around him.

I joined Franny at our shared fox hole. He was anxious to hear details about the night raid. He had heard the shots fired by Zack. He needed assurance that we were not imminently facing an enemy attack. The guys manning the perimeter were on high alert.

"I screwed up," I explained. "When I entered the hooch and turned on the flashlight, this wild eyed guy jumped out of a hammock right in front of me. I'm pretty sure he was holding a pistol but he did not open fire or point it at me. It all happened so fast and he just took a big leap and literally jumped through the grass wall. I guess there must have been a flap or some sort of escape hatch since he went through so easily."

"Our other guys were guarding the back and I probably should have given them a chance to capture him," I continued. "I was worried he would confront them with the pistol. I guess I was too startled to think it through. I fired a burst through the hooch wall on automatic and killed him. I blew our chance of interrogating him about our Marine."

"Better him than you," Franny declared. "Don't second guess yourself. He could have killed one of our guys just as easily. How would you have felt then?"

I knew he was right. But I kept seeing the image of the young man's startled face blinded by the flashlight. I had never been in a face-to-face situation like that before.

I volunteered to take first watch. I was too wired to relax anyway. I sat with my back against the dirt wall of our shared fox hole and stared into the darkness. Like Franny, I was extra watchful after all the enemy activity we had encountered around this mountain. Fortunately, the night passed without further activity. I was relieved to welcome the sun as it teased me with a sliver of bright orange over the top of Hill 328 during my final turn on guard.

We saddled up and headed down the trail towards Minh Long to begin our long hump to return to Liz. The mission to assault the mountain and try to save a prisoner was declared ended. Second squad was assigned point today. It made sense to give first squad a break after yesterday.

A few hundred meters down the trail, Zack left our column and carefully walked towards the base of the mountain, his rifle at the ready. We passed word forward to stop and wait for him. I knew he was checking to see if there was any sign of the enemy he had encountered.

He had not walked fully out of site when I saw him kneel down. When he stood up he was proudly holding an enemy AK-47 with a big grin splitting his face. The body of the soldier he killed was still in a sitting position, leaning against a tree and stiff from the effects of rigor mortis.

Chapter 10

It was a full day's hump to make Liz before nightfall. We were anxious to get back to the comfort and safety of our bunkers on the hilltop. We walked up the west side of the hill with the setting sun at our backs just in time for hot chow. It made us appreciate our mess hall guys when we learned they had a hot meal waiting for us.

Bravo Company alternated manning Liz as their base camp when we were not there. When we departed Bronco for the assault on Hill 328, Company B was also included in the effort to save the captured marine. They returned to Liz earlier in the day, so we found ourselves in a crowded chow line. With two companies on the hill, we would have twice the number of troops in each bunker. That was a good thing since it cut our guard duty requirements in half.

Although I badly wanted a shower, I opted for the hot meal first. I really wanted to clean up after a long day of sweating under a full pack but needed food more. I quickly filled my steel mess tray with instant potatoes and covered them with the beef and gravy mixture that was the main course. I selected a cold Budweiser from the ice barrel and went to find a seat at one of the picnic style tables. The mess tent was already crowded with a lot of faces that I didn't recognize from our sister company, so I just took the first empty space I spotted.

I was surprised to sit down beside a Vietnamese guy. I thought at first he must be a chu hoi, then realized he was just a young boy. Someone had given him a fatigue shirt and pants to wear that were much too large for his small frame. The shirt sleeves were rolled up so the normal length to the elbows landed at his wrists. The pants, held up by a cut off claymore mine bag strap, were rolled up around his ankles. The nametag on the shirt was Briscoe.

"Hello Sergeant Briscoe," I teased, hoping to learn more about him. "I'm Jared."

"I not sergeant," he answered with a frown. "I Quang."

"Sorry. Nice to meet you, Quang," I corrected. "But you look like a Sergeant Briscoe to me," I added, touching my finger to the nametag on his fatigue shirt.

This elicited a big smile when he realized I was teasing him. He looked around as if checking to see if anyone objected to our talking. Nobody seemed to be paying any attention to us.

"Why are you here?" I asked, and used hand signals to try to support my question.

"Sergeant bring," he answered, pointing to the nametag. "I hurt, sergeant take me doctor. Mama san, all family, dead. VC kill."

At that he turned and raised his shirt to show me a newly tended wound in his lower back. The reddening scar, a two-inch long evidence of his terrible experience, was proof that his story was true.

My soft heart turned to mush. I knew that the other guys thought of me as too concerned about the Viets. I hoped they would understand my taking an interest in Quang.

"How old are you?" I asked. He looked puzzled so I clarified by adding, "I'm hai mươi, how many are you."

He smiled broadly in recognition of my question and limited understanding of his language. "I Le Van Quang. I mười hai," he announced proudly. He looked younger than twelve years old.

"There's a movie up at artillery tonight," somebody announced. "Eight o'clock for anyone interested."

I could tell Quang did not understand the announcement, but I was intrigued at the prospect of introducing him to something he might never have seen before, and that made the idea of a movie intriguing to me.

"I see you have a new friend." I looked behind us thinking someone was speaking to me when I realized one of the cooks was familiarly addressing Quang. The specialist turned his attention to me.

"He came in with some of the guys from Bravo a week or so back," the cook explained. "I heard his family was killed by an enemy RPG that hit his hooch down in Quảng Ngãi. He didn't seem hurt badly enough for a dust off so they brought him to Liz to be treated by the medics. They sent him down to Bronco the next day to get the shrapnel wound stitched up and then the medics there sent him back here a few days later because they didn't know what else to do with him. He's been hanging around ever since."

"Where is your family, Quang?" I asked. "We need to find a way to get him back to them," I said to the cook.

"No got family, all dead," Quang declared as tears welled up in his sad eyes.

"Somebody from Military Assistance Command came and checked his identification papers and is supposed to be trying to find relatives who will take him," the cook added. "That's the last we heard," he continued. "Maybe you can do something with him," he added before going back to his post on the chow line.

I studied the little boy before me whom I now knew to be twelve years old. He somehow seemed even more vulnerable than before. He appeared to shrivel down into the oversized clothing, lost in unfamiliar surroundings without loved ones or possessions.

The fatigues he wore were clean enough, I guessed, although I was probably not the best judge. I was used to wearing the same clothes day after day until they could stand by themselves. The pleasure of getting fresh clothing was one of the main rewards of returning each time to Liz.

I took Quang's hands in mine and inspected them. They were soiled a familiar grey from going extended periods without washing.

"Come with me," I instructed Quang. "We're going to clean you up. Then I take you to a movie." I was not sure how much he understood, but he came along without further prodding.

I shouldered my pack and led Quang down the winding path to our bunker. Franny was sitting on top smoking a cigarette pinched in his familiar style between the thumb and forefinger of his right hand. The damp green towel draped around his neck told me he had already showered.

"Who's the dink?" Franny asked pointing to Quang.

"He's my new friend, Quang," I answered. "He might be staying with us for a little while until we can find his family. And, this is Franny, Quang," I introduced as I ducked into the bunker doorway and dropped my pack on a wooden bunk. I fetched two sets of clean fatigues, soap and towel from my green wooden locker box and went back outside. I wore size small fatigues and knew they would still be too big but would hopefully fit Quang better than what he wore.

Franny was wordlessly studying Quang from atop the bunker. I could see that I might have a challenge getting him accepted, so I quickly added that the cooks were looking after him. That seemed to make it okay that Quang was here. Franny turned his attention back to cleaning his rifle and alternately dragging his cigarette and sipping his beer.

"Did you eat?" I asked Franny. I knew he had a habit of drinking and smoking instead of taking advantage of hot meals when they were available.

"I'm going up when the rest of the guys get done," Franny explained. "You know I don't like the crowds when they're putting on the feed bag."

It was a zoo when a hot meal was laid out and the guys

had been on C-rations. I felt the same way Franny did. I had never liked the regimentation the Army created in its offering of meals. Get in line, hold out your steel dinner tray and have the guys manning the chow line slop out spoon loads of food.

"If you've got the bunker covered for a few minutes, we need to go shower," I plead.

"No problem. The other guys will be here any minute," Franny assured.

"Do you think I could get by with taking Quang up to artillery for a movie?" I asked. "I'll pick up whatever guard duty nobody else wants afterwards," I promised.

"I got you covered," he smiled. I knew I could always depend on Franny.

Chapter 11

The Good, The Bad, And The Ugly was bigger than life on the screen the artillery guys created from a sheet. To a bunch of guys who were fighting every day against an elusive enemy, the prospect of being able to face down and quick draw an opponent Clint Eastwood style had a certain appeal.

My extra set of size small fatigue shirt and pants, while still large on Quang, fit him much better. We only had to roll the sleeves and cuff the pants a couple of turns. He looked less sad all cleaned up and in fresh clothing. I made a mental note to find some boots small enough for his bare feet.

I couldn't tell if Quang was excited or scared when the movie started. The piercing sounds of gunfire, the fantastic music that built each scene to crescendo along with the larger than life gunfighters had him mesmerized. Quang was holding on to my leg with a death grip. His face was electric with excitement.

Giving a kid the opportunity to see a major motion picture like this for the first time was a terrific and gratifying experience for him that I wished could be afforded to every Vietnamese child. I often imagined what it would be like to share modern technology with poor village boys and girls when they came begging for chop-chop and souvenirs. I envisioned opening doors to a brightly lighted grocery store and letting them peer in for the first time.

I was overwhelmed by the circumstance as I reveled in Quang's new adventure. It was an epic movie that I found myself seeing only in my peripheral vision. My entertainment for the night was watching Quang. His resilience from recent loss impressed me. The joy he displayed from this new experience, the excitement pure as can only come from a child, was more touching than anything I had ever known.

Following the movie, the crowd that had gathered dispersed quickly. Each soldier begrudgingly headed back to the reality of their duties for the night. I steered Quang toward the mess tent to get a cold soda for him and a beer for me before I took him to face the rest of the squad down the hill at our bunker. I stuck four extra beers in my fatigue shirt and pants pockets for whomever might be awake when we got back.

I was still worried that somebody might object to him and cause a confrontation. The truth was, he could go back to wherever he was sleeping before we arrived and still be okay. I think I wanted to be close to him as much as he needed someone. It felt good to feel needed and share happiness in a place that did not know much of it.

I popped the top on my beer and helped Quang with his soda after his pop top broke. I used my knife to punch through the perforated outline where the opener should have worked. I held my can out to his and said 'toast to a fun night.' I had to demonstrate the bumping of cans followed by a sip. He seemed to understand there was some significance to the ritual.

"Him shoot," Quang declared as he demonstrated his quick draw, his right hand formed to an imaginary six gun. "Bad man, same-same Viet Cong. Quang and Jared shoot, maybe VC no more."

It took me a minute to figure out that the movie had stimulated a desire in Quang to seek revenge for the killing of his family. In his mind, he had assumed the role of the "good." The "bad" and "ugly" represented the people who killed his family. I desperately wished I could be that bigger than life gunfighter who could seek out and destroy evil, especially the hateful people who murdered Quang's undeserving relatives.

We left the mess tent and started down the dark narrow path. Lights were not allowed on our mountain fortress except on top of the hill. Liz was far safer for us than being out in the field. We knew we were vulnerable to attack every night, even on our fortified base.

It was after ten-thirty when we got to the bunker. Lenny was perched on top with his rifle across his lap.

"How was the movie?" he asked. Lenny's voice and manner were always upbeat, calm and reassuring. In those few words he let me know that Franny had filled him in about Quang and he had no problem with him being here. "Come on up, it's a nice, quiet night."

"The show was terrific," I answered as we climbed up

the sandbag steps to the roof. "The best part was watching Quang see a movie for the first time. He flat got into Clint Eastwood." I handed Lenny one of the cold beers from my shirt pocket.

"So, you liked it okay?" he asked, turning his attention to Quang. "I'm Lenny."

"Number one," Quang enthusiastically replied followed by his quick draw demonstration. He walked over to the edge of the bunker and peered down into the darkness.

"There was one segment that got him pretty emotional," I whispered. "I was really more intent on his reactions to the movie than paying close attention to the screen. When they showed a segment with a huge civil war battle and soldiers from both sides being massacred, tears were rolling down his cheeks. I acted like I didn't notice. I didn't want to embarrass him. It made me wonder how much ugliness this kid has seen in his twelve years. Vietnam has been at war his whole life."

"I heard his family was killed," Lenny said. "I wonder which side his father was on."

"Hey Quang, where is your papa san?" I asked. I remembered that he had only said that his mama san and family were killed.

"Papa san dead long time," Quang declared. "Him ARVN. VC kill."

"Come on Quang, I'm going to take you down below," I instructed. "It's not a good idea for you to be standing up here in the open making a target for Charlie. Do you think anybody will mind if he sleeps in the bunker with us?" I asked Lenny, not wanting to just assume it would be okay with the others.

"Franny brought it up and we kicked it around some while you were gone," Lenny explained. "I don't know about long term, but nobody seemed to mind him being here tonight."

I kept an extra poncho liner in my locker for when the other got wet. I dug it out and directed Quang to the foot end of my bunk and demonstrated for him how to use it to cover up completely to keep the mosquitos off. The wooden bunk was long enough for us to sleep feet-to-feet. He followed my instructions without protest and was asleep before I could sneak out to relieve Lenny on guard.

Chapter 12

"This wound is getting infected," the medic scolded. "If he was going to shower he should have had that wound cleaned and new bandages applied.

"I'm sorry. It was dark when we showered and he didn't complain about it hurting," I explained. "I didn't think about checking on it."

"We're going to have to get him to brigade to have it looked after." The medic was indignant. He wrote out a sick call authorization normally intended for our soldiers and suggested I get permission to take him to Bronco today. "One of our guys is making a supply run so you can probably catch a ride in his jeep if you can get back here in a hurry."

Sergeant Duke was his usual easy going self when I found him sitting on a bunker having his mid-morning beer. I introduced him to Quang and showed him the sick call authorization.

"Go take him to Bronco," Duke waved. "Make sure they patch him up good." Then he pulled me aside and whispered, "You need to take him to the orphanage 'cause MACV said they can't find any relatives who will take him."

Even Duke heard that I had taken Quang under my

wing. I did not mind the responsibility and looked forward to the opportunity to go into Đức Phổ. I liked the people at the orphanage and hoped Quang would be accepted there.

We walked back to the bunker so I could get my ammo belt and steel helmet. I kept an extra steel pot and helmet liner in the bunker for emergencies, those times when you dive for cover and your head gear goes tumbling away. I adjusted the liner band to its smallest size, inserted it into the steel helmet and handed it to Quang.

"You have to wear this when we go out on the road," I explained.

He smiled enthusiastically as he plopped the heavy hat on his little head. He had to work at keeping his head from wobbling side to side from the weight but he finally learned to keep his neck straight and use his hands to balance the load when he turned to the side or leaned one way or another.

We had one more stop to make before heading up the hill to catch our ride. I hoped supply would have a pair of boots small enough for Quang and I needed another set of fatigues to replace the ones Quang now wore.

"Sorry, clean fatigues haven't come in yet," the supply clerk informed me when I asked about my size small shirt and pants. "And the best I can do on the boots is a size seven. He'll need some socks to go with the boots," he added, pleasantly.

A proper fit would have probably been size five. Quang anxiously sat on the ground and pulled the socks up to his knees and slipped into the oversized jungle boots. He awkwardly stood without lacing up his shiny new footwear. I sat on the ground in front of him and laced the boots as tightly as they would go. Even though his feet had extra room to move around, tying the laces around the canvas part of the boots around his ankles made them comfortable enough so he could walk. Running would probably be a challenge.

"I soldier now," he beamed with pride.

He did resemble a Kit Carson, the nickname given to boys taken in by soldiers who often served as interpreters and scouts to their American benefactors. I remembered the black and white television series *The Adventures of Kit Carson* from back in the early fifties when I was seven or eight years old. I never quite understood the Kit Carson tag used for these Vietnamese kids though.

Quang sat up front with the medic and I took the less comfortable bench seat in the back. It put me up higher so I could be on guard for the ride down Highway One. I held my rifle at the ready as we descended down the access road and out to the dirt highway.

Traffic was the usual snarl as our driver nudged in among the throng of scooters, bicycles and pedestrians. He had to weave side to side to avoid the numerous ruts and holes in the dirt surface. Bomb craters our jeep could fit into were blown away from the edges of the road, evidence that Charlie had been busy during the spring Tet offensive. I hoped the explosions were set off by our mine sweeping crews and not caused by vehicles or pedestrians detonating them.

Quang was having fun. His new right boot was perched high on the open door frame visible to people we passed. I saw that he had his helmet tilted over his right eye with attitude. He had also given close attention to rolling his shirt sleeves tightly above the wrists so his uniform appeared to fit.

Except for a lot of stopping and starting and bouncing around, the trip to Bronco was uneventful. We turned left at the north end of Đức Phổ and cleared through the front gate before noon. Our driver headed straight to the brigade medical bunker. He reminded me to be back by early afternoon if I wanted to ride back to Liz with him.

The medical staff tended to be gruff with us soldiers but the doctor was gentle in his treatment of the boy. I could see that Quang was determined to be brave as the doctor removed his stitches and redressed his wound. He did really great until the doctor produced a syringe and pulled down Quang's fatigue pants to administer a tetanus shot. I thought at first Quang was going to break and run from his terrified expression. That needle did look awfully long.

The doctor declared that the wound was sufficiently healed that he would not need to see the patient again unless further problems or infection arose. So we headed over to the latrine to wash away the road grime we accumulated during our dusty ride from Liz. We passed by Vietnamese peasants dressed in black pajama pants rolled up to the knees who were standing by their burning barrels of human waste, the gray kerosene smoke billowing skyward and spreading the stench across the compound.

"Number ten stink," Quang declared as he pinched his nostrils trying to fend off the smell.

"Yeah, are you ready to go eat some lunch?" I teased.

"You crazy G.I.," Quang laughed.

We hurried to clean up and get away from the latrine area. I had a plan. I had promised myself that I would bring some gifts to the orphanage next time I visited and that would give me the excuse I needed to introduce Quang to the sisters.

So, we went to pay a visit to the battalion supply sergeant. I talked him out of some mosquito repellant, foot powder, a couple of bars of soap and a case of C-rations. He packed it all into a green canvas back pack, the kind that were replaced by the ruck sacks we now used. The old style did not have a metal frame so you could not comfortably handle as much weight. I shouldered the pack and Quang followed as I led him out of the gate to Highway One.

I was pleasantly surprised to spot Dam and her green bicycle store perched outside the gate. She was carefully scrutinizing each soldier who walked by before pouncing on them with her sales pitch to buy candles, sodas and cigarettes. I caught her glance and noticed her immediate recognition as she saw me walking with Quang.

"Tôi biết Jared!" she shouted, trotting her bike towards us as fast as her sandal clad feet would carry her.

"Mai Thi Tuy Et Dam!" I called back, proud that I was able to remember her entire name. "Come and meet my new friend Le Van Quang," I invited, wanting Quang to feel important at the use of his full name. I could see that he was surprised I knew someone in the village.

"Why you come Đức Phổ?" Dam asked.

"We're going to visit the orphanage," I answered. "First we were hoping to get some of your mama san's beef sticks for lunch."

"No sweat," she replied. "How many you want?"

"Three for me, ba for Quang and ba for Dam if you will eat with us." She grinned at my use of the Vietnamese for three, showing me she was proud I remembered her teaching. "And maybe three cold Cokes too," I added.

"You go orphanage, I bring," she instructed as she mounted her bike and expertly maneuvered among traffic on the main street into the village.

Quang seemed bewildered at all that was going on around him. Much had happened since we met the day before. It was asking a lot for him to trust me to be so involved in his life so fast. I guessed the real test of that trust would come with his introduction to Sister Hao.

The crumbled gated entrance was unchanged from when I saw it last with Lenny and Bart. We sat down on the wide staircase below the tall wooden front doors to wait for Dam to bring our food. I was not sure if Dam would go inside the Catholic orphanage based on her Buddhist beliefs and I did not want any awkward moments to deter from my mission. We would be content to eat our food and visit outside for now, I decided. Besides, I wanted to give the two children a chance to get to know each other.

I guessed Sister Hao did not know we were coming to see her. It was crucial for her to be willing to take on a twelve-year old orphan. I did not remember seeing kids his age during my earlier visit and wondered if there was an age limit.

We could hear children inside reciting their school lessons. The stucco walls reverberated the chorus of voices into a rhythmic high pitched humming, the happy sounds in contrast to the drone of truck, bus and motorcycle engines on the street to our front.

I set the back pack full of gifts on the step in front of Quang.

"When we go in to visit, you should look through the pack and decide what you want to keep," I suggested. "You can give the rest to the sisters and children."

Quang smiled broadly and possessively pulled the pack between his knees. He started to open the top flap but I stopped him.

"You wait. Maybe see what they need before you decide."

"Mama san have number one chicken sticks, no got beef," Dam apologized as she pushed her bicycle into the courtyard and joined us. She carefully leaned her bike against the banyan tree, removed the Cokes from the basket and gave ours to us and kept one for herself as I had asked. I was glad to see that she was accepting my offer to buy her lunch.

Dam distributed the chicken sticks and sat beside Quang. The chicken was flavorful and skewered with onions and peppers. We consumed the delicious food while slurping away at the canned Cokes to ease the burn from the spices.

Dam turned her attention to Quang. She was rapidly speaking Vietnamese. I could tell she was asking him questions and I was able to pick up just enough in his responses to understand that he was relating the loss of his family in Quảng Ngãi. He raised his shirt to explain how he was wounded. I heard bác sĩ, the word for doctor, so I surmised that he was explaining why we came to Bronco.

I enjoyed watching them gobble at their chicken treats as they chattered away between bites. They seemed to be getting along fine. Dam occasionally glanced at me and paused at things Quang would say, then dive right back into intense conversation.

Finally, when she seemed to have learned all she needed to know, Dam stood and came to sit on the step to my right away from Quang. Without prompting from me, she began to relate what she had learned, serving as my self-appointed interpreter.

She related Quang's story about the VC killing his family in Quảng Ngãi. She pointed to her lower back as she explained his wound and his trip to the doctor. She said he told her he had only known me for one day but we had become number one friends.

"Yeah, the soldiers took him to Liz to see the medic and he was there when we returned to base," I added, providing a few more details to his story.

Dam went on to explain that Quang knew he was being sent to stay at the orphanage but did not like the idea. She pointed out that he was Buddhist and the orphanage was Catholic. She said he told her he wanted to stay with the soldiers on Liz, especially me.

"I go work now," Dam declared as she stood to face me. I guess she decided she had finished performing her duties as interpreter and wanted to be paid for the lunch so she could go make some money.

I thanked her for her help and paid her in U.S. dollars. She said goodbye to Quang and said some things rapidly in Vietnamese, then mounted her bike and rode off down the edge of the street.

"Dam number one you think?" I asked Quang.

"She okay. She say she come see me in orphanage," he added as tears welled in his sad eyes.

I was relieved to learn that Quang knew the plan to place him in the orphanage. I was struggling to figure out how to break that news to him. I guessed the guy from Military Assistance Command – Vietnam (MACV) must have mentioned the possibility to him.

"Let's go meet Sister Hao," I suggested as I knocked on the heavy door.

Sister Hao opened the door without hesitation as if she was waiting expectantly on the other side. She acknowledged me with a gentle nod then turned her attention to the boy at my side. I was not sure she remembered me.

"Is this Quang?" she stated more than asked. "We take good care of him," she assured as she directed him into the building and closed the door behind her. Someone from Bronco must have given her notice that Quang was coming today. Whoever it was must have also exerted some influence since there was no question about his being accepted.

I was a little bewildered at being left standing on the steps. The more I thought about it, I decided Sister Hao knew what she was doing by making the handoff brief. I needed to get back to Bronco, anyway, so I could catch my ride back to Liz.

Chapter 13

The midday traffic on Highway One was light so the ride back took less than an hour. We turned off on the access road to Liz and saw that a column of soldiers was descending from the hill in full gear. Drawing closer I saw that it was my platoon and Lenny walked point.

When we got close enough Lenny informed me that they were going on an emergency combat assault. A Chinook helicopter was shot down on the beach and they were being sent out to protect it. Duke recognized me from further back in the column and waved the Jeep driver over.

"Take him up to get his gear and bring him right back," Duke instructed the Specialist. Turning his attention to me he added "and you need to plan to be a few days. We don't know much except that a "hook" is down and needing our help."

The driver revved the Jeep engine and raced up the hill beside the column of troops. I hurried down the path to my bunker and gathered up my ruck sack, poncho and poncho liner then added four hand grenades and extra magazines of ammo. I tossed in my stash of LRRP rations, made sure my canteen was filled to capacity and yelled up the hill to the driver to go grab me six or eight beers from the mess hall to add to my pack.

As we sped down the winding lane from the top of Liz I could see the formation of helicopters coming towards us from Bronco. The driver skidded to a stop next to Lenny and Franny and they reached into the back and grabbed my gear just in time for him to maneuver the vehicle clear of the landing Huey's. It was a familiar and automatic maneuver as we lined up and boarded the moment the skids touched down.

My brief reprieve from combat duty was over before it started. It was hard to believe that just yesterday we had the forced march back to Liz. Since then I had gotten to know my new friend Quang only to make the trip into Bronco to dump him off. And here I was looking down on the rice paddies and coastal villages as we flew once again into harm's way.

I saw the white sandy coastline ahead. It appeared to me that we were headed to the same section of beach we knew as ambush alley where Powell was wounded.

I silently hoped that I would not be sent out on ambush, at least not on our first night on the beach. It made sense that ambush patrols would be sent out to extend security beyond mortar range from the downed helicopter. I just wanted to be guarding a perimeter tonight instead of humping around in the dark.

I could see Cobra attack helicopters circling like buzzards around prey as the Chinook came in to view, perched on the sand. They were strafing the terrain trying to protect the downed bird as we came in to establish a perimeter around it. It looked to me like the pilot had not crash landed but rather managed to land normally, except that the wheels were sunk to the axles in the soft sand.

I could sense the urgency of the situation. An opportunity to rescue a downed helicopter and its crew had my adrenaline flowing as much as during our efforts to save the captured Marine corporal. I hoped we would get it right this time.

Our covey of Huey's swooped in to drop us off simultaneously on three landing zones that were marked by red smoke to the north, west and south of the hook. I heard bullets whizzing by and popping into the steel above my head. Fortunately, nobody was hit and the helicopter's performance did not seem to be affected as our pilot hovered our runners above the sand.

I jumped from my perch in the left doorway using the runner to break my fall and managed to land in a stooped position, not pretty but still upright. I ran beside the others to make a circle out about twenty yards surrounding the downed helicopter on all sides except east towards the South China Sea. Charlie could not shoot mortars at us from the water.

We all began frantically digging in the sand with our utility shovels. I spaced myself an equal distance between Fanny and Lenny on the north side adjacent to the lowered rear ramp. The helicopter crew had evidently escaped under fire and had to leave the ramp tilted open.

I used my shovel folded like a spade and dug like a dog, wildly throwing sand to quickly create a trench in the sand. I could lay in it if we came under fire before I had it ready to use as a firing position. I then extended the handle to shovel straight down about three feet so I would be able to sit upright with only my steel pot exposed above ground. Before I could get my hiding place completed I heard the hollow sounding thump of a mortar round being launched. I dove into my shallow trench tightly gripping my helmet while attempting to burrow deeper into the sand.

The mortar round sounded like a low caliber when it exploded to the west and well short of our perimeter. I guessed the Viet Cong were using a hand held mortar tube, one held between the legs that used the ground as a base instead of a fixed platform. That would explain the problem they were having with distance and accuracy.

Duke and the platoon radio operator were busy requesting artillery support using the AO map to guess Charlie's position. The first several rounds were just location markers since we were so close to the target area. As soon as Duke and the artillery battery were comfortable they had the range zeroed in, I heard Duke give the order to fire for effect. I quickly unrolled my poncho and spread it out to cover the sand in my trench, then dove on top of it. I had managed to shake most of the sand from my fatigues from before and hoped not to have to grovel in it again.

The artillery explosions that ran along a parallel line to the sea shook the ground in an awesome display of power. They made the VC mortar rounds seem like pop guns. I was relieved to learn we would be using artillery through the night instead of sending out patrols. While the artillery battery did their job we were able to properly finish our circle of fox holes. They needed to be deep enough so it would take a direct hit for Charlie's mortar attacks to harm us. I hoped they would not get lucky and hit the downed Chinook.

The artillery strafing continued for more than an hour. When the thunderous onslaught abruptly ended it was replaced with an eerie and expectant calm, like when you know lighting is going to strike, but you don't know when or where.

Feeling confident that our show of firepower had backed the Viet Cong down for now, Duke stood in the center of the perimeter and explained our situation and plan. He said a Huey came in with the initial Cobra assault squadron and was able to land and rescue the crew. Nobody was injured or lost. The VC just got lucky shooting small arms at the helicopter and hit hydraulics that caused the chopper to go down. The plan now was for us to guard against attack until a repair crew could attempt to get the craft airborne in the morning.

Duke's speech was interrupted by the ding-ding of small arms fire hitting the fuselage of the Chinook. Duke yelled for everybody to get down as he dove for cover. Fortunately, it seemed Charlie was more interested in destroying the helicopter than taking aim at us.

As dusk settled over our exposed fortification that was precariously intended to protect the mammoth machine,

Charlie's efforts intensified. Luckily his aim remained imperfect. Mortar rounds exploded in twos and threes followed closely by our artillery as Duke tried to direct fire to where the thumping originated. The return fire repeatedly sent Charlie into hiding giving us the chance to relax until the artillery support ceased. Then the thumping of a round dropped into a mortar tube would start again as the enemy tried relentlessly to destroy his target.

The light show of mortar blasts and artillery explosions continued until early morning. I sat in my fox hole peering over the edge, straining to catch sight of the enemy assault that we expected to follow each mortar attack. The ground attack never came and the mortar rounds finally stopped exploding. I guessed they must have used up all of their ammo before they could complete their mission. The sun managed to spray its welcome rays of light over us as it rose above the sea to find our troop and our charge still intact.

By mid-morning, repairs were done and the flight crew was back on board. The whining of the front and rear rotor blades slowly brought the massive bird to life. A whirlwind sandstorm was sucked into the air by the huge blades thoroughly coating my clothes, hands and face. It didn't matter. We accomplished our mission and nobody was lost. It felt terrific to win one.

"You guys want a ride," the crew chief yelled from the open hatchway, confident the helicopter was now fully functional.

We gathered our gear and trotted up the ramp relieved

not to be having to take the long walk back to Liz.

Chapter 14

We took turns carrying buckets of water from the rubber water blimps to use in our makeshift shower. It was a welcome relief when my turn under the bucket came. The sand molded together with my sweat required two five-gallon bucket loads to wash away.

I picked up my gear and headed toward our bunker with only my boots on and my towel wrapped around my waist. Then I remembered I had given my only set of spare fatigues to Quang so I stopped off by supply and scored a fresh set of size smalls and put them on along with some brand new socks. I noticed for the first time that the manufacturing stamp in white on the green socks read "Burlington Mills, Greensboro, North Carolina." It gave me a brief pang of homesickness to see a product from so close to home.

My rifle was coated with sand so I asked the supply clerk for a new cleaning kit and oil. I started down the hill and was shocked to see Quang sitting atop my bunker. He was wearing his helmet and trying desperately to look like a real soldier.

"What are you doing here?" I was tired and irritated that my efforts to get him settled were wasted.

Quang shrank into himself, his little shoulders hunched

in fear of retribution. Tears welled in his downcast eyes and his lips formed a pout.

"I no like orphanage, I no like sister, I no like…" his little hands formed a cross, his way of saying Catholic. "I run away, come stay with you."

I was bewildered and did not know what to do. My orders were clear. Take him to the orphanage where his own people could look after him.

"You stay here," I said sternly. "I've got to go find out what to do with you." I needed to let somebody know he was back.

I wondered how he managed to get from Đức Phổ to Liz, and so quickly? I had to give him credit. He surely was a resourceful little guy. But what had I done or said for him to think he should look to me for dependence? Surely other soldiers were nice to him and helped him, like the guys from Bravo Company who brought him here in the first place.

More importantly, what would my superiors think when they learned that he was here with me again, I worried. No matter what I did, it would look like I went against my orders and brought him back from the orphanage. Somebody at Bronco had gone to extra effort to make sure he was accepted by the sisters. I imagined that Sister Hao would lose face, too, at the loss of her new charge.

Duke was nonchalant about it. He said just to let him stay as long as he didn't cause any trouble. Nobody except me seemed to see it as an important issue. In the grand scheme of things, the disposition of one more Vietnamese citizen had to be low on the American military priority list.

I wondered about the position I was putting myself in if I went back and told Quang it was okay for him to stay with us on Liz. I knew that meant more specifically staying with me, under my care and custody. I had the feeling I was creating a monster.

How were the other guys going to feel about having a Vietnamese boy around all of the time, especially knowing a lot of soldiers disliked any contact with the locals? I had enough problems with resentments over my "gook lover" image as it was.

What the hell, I decided. Just take it day at a time and let it play out. It would be hard for this little boy to be hurt any more than he already had been, so what could it harm to try and let him feel some happiness.

By the time I got back to Quang at the bunker, it had started to rain. I found him inside sitting on my bunk, the back pack full of food and things for the orphanage secured tightly between his knees. I had warmed to the idea as I hurried down the hill in the rain and found myself excitedly informing him that it was okay for him to stay.

His response to the news was like it was no big deal, like he knew he was supposed to be here and did not expect anything different. He saw the cleaning kit I held and offered to clean my rifle. Quang was anxious to assume his role as my "Kit Carson."

Chapter 15

The next day it continued to rain. It rained so hard and long that we didn't see the sun for days. We wore our ponchos with the hoods over our heads under our helmets. It helped to protect our fatigue shirts from being totally soaked, but everything else was wet.

The monsoon rain flooded the rice paddies surrounding Liz. The water got so deep it covered many of the dikes and even flooded the access road to Liz. After a week of constant rain it got to be impossible for helicopters to bring in supplies. Air combat assaults were suspended. It was even difficult to get trucks and jeeps up the hill to Liz since the roadways turned to mud.

We joked about needing to build an ark so we could float off of Liz. We sat around listing all of the animals we would need to gather up in pairs; two water buffalo, a chicken and a rooster, two wild boars, two tigers, a pair of geese from under the bridge out on Highway One, two crates, two bamboo vipers, two Burmese pythons, two fish for our nuoc mam, two rats from our bunker and the list droned on.

It was finally necessary for deuce and a half trucks to make the trek through the flooded waters to Bronco to get supplies and transfer soldiers back and forth. The mine clearing team had been waiting out the rain to clear the access road. They were finally able to saddle up and wade down the road to try to make sure Charlie did not set booby traps in place.

It was difficult to tell where the road edges stopped in the sea of flooded rice paddies that overtook the elevated roadway. A young mine clearing specialist carrying the heavy electronic sweeping gear ventured too close to the roadway edge, slipped off the bank and down into the rice paddy. He drowned before anyone could pull him too safety. He could not free himself from the gear strapped to his back and chest. That would be a difficult bereavement letter for his commanding officer to write to his family.

We were trapped on Liz for days. That was not a bad thing since there were no air combat assaults or patrols beyond the high ground around the twin peaks of Liz. So, we were not out humping in the boonies or getting ambushed and booby trapped by Charlie.

During the weeks stuck on Liz my relationship with Quang nurtured into a special friendship. He followed me around like a puppy, always looking for an opportunity to fill a need. He learned to break down my rifle, clean it and reassemble it faster than I could do it. He scrubbed and polished my boots, something none of us ever did. I was used to my scruffy looking boots and liked the tough combat soldier image they portrayed. But I saw how he beamed with pride when he presented my shiny boots for inspection and decided to put up with the crap I got from the guys over my rear echelon boots.

By the end of June the monsoons ended. I had gotten used to Quang sitting on top of the bunker with me during my stints at guard duty. Charlie had not attacked us in weeks thanks to the high water around Liz so I did not feel like his safety was an issue. We were sitting on the sand bags under our ponchos when the rain stopped. The sky suddenly opened and we welcomed back the stars and the moon and even the Southern Cross in the vastness overhead.

The sun and heat that replaced the rain were a welcomed relief. The flood waters began to subside and we could see the rice paddy dikes peaking up from the sea of water. The access road from Liz was finally draining so it would be possible to safely navigate between the shoulders that dropped off abruptly into rice paddy water.

When the terrain was flooded the enemy believed he could affect our access to supplies by eliminating the bridges on Highway One, the only navigable north to south roadway. So, we were assigned bridge guard duty on the same bridge where I saw the bodies of the slaughtered villagers killed by ARVN soldiers guarding the bridge.

We geared up with supplies and ammunition for our three day assignment the same as we would have packed for a full field operation. We knew that once we reached the bridge after the one mile walk out from Liz we would be staying put so we packed heavy, electing not to leave behind luxury item extras like clean fatigues, towels, beer, c-rations and hand grenades.

As we started down the hill on the winding road leaving Liz, I started to question my decision to pack heavy as my boots sunk into the red mud. The mud sucked at my boots as they sank to above my ankles. Yet when we reached the bottom of the hill and started out the access road the ground was surprisingly firm, especially considering that it had been under water for weeks.

I had not walked down this road since my early days in country when Duke brought us out here to repair the concertina wire fence. I caught myself instinctively checking the fence for breaks as we walked. I saw that the section we repaired was still intact and felt a sense of pride that our workmanship survived. Little that we did seemed to have any lasting effect. At least the fence was still standing.

I remembered the snakes I ran into while working on that detail. I had come in contact with many dangerous snakes and other tropical vermin since then. Those early encounters served to make me aware of the dangers in the jungle. I handled them better now after months being around Duke and learning from his calm acceptance that the animals belonged and I was just a visitor.

"Leave them alone and they'll leave you alone," he would declare. "They're not going to come looking for you and won't bother you unless you bother them," he would say. I tried to keep that same perspective in mind about the Vietnamese people.

While that was true of the people I got to know in Đức

Phở, I learned that most people outside of the village were not our friends and would come looking for us, determined to bother us as much as possible. They wanted to kill us if they could.

"Remember when we came down here to fix that hole in the wire?" Lenny was evidently sharing my nostalgia.

"I was just thinking about that," I confirmed.

"Did you ever hear why that section of fence was missing?" Lenny continued. "Following the Viet Cong attack on the bridge, our recon platoon was patrolling the terrain alongside the access road since the mine sweepers were finding too many booby traps," Lenny went on before I had a chance to respond. "A young PFC was walking point. He was an experienced card player who had a reputation for taking all the money and had an especially successful night of gambling up at the mess hall tent the night before. It was not safe to leave all of his winnings in the bunker up on Liz, so he carried the money along with him on the patrol. On the path beside the concertina wire we replaced he stepped on a mine. It blew a big hole in the fence. The story was that all of that money, a combination of American currency and MPC came floating down from the sky and the other guys in the platoon chased around picking it up before they realized it belonged to the ill-fated gambler. He was reported missing in action because no remains were ever found."

That must have been another tough letter for somebody to write home, I thought.

The mosquitoes were still here. They were bigger and

more aggressive than ever. The flooded paddies were the ideal breeding grounds. Normally the bugs were not so bothersome in the midday heat. They were out now and ferocious. I dreaded nightfall knowing that we were going to be next to the mosquito infested water by the bridge. I had two bottles of repellant in my helmet band and wondered if that would get me through the next three days. I had been coating it on my face, neck and hands since we left Liz and the buzzing in my ears didn't slow down at all.

Up ahead, traffic on Highway One was back to normal packed with buses, motor bikes, bicycles and foot traffic. Our column turned right onto the highway and joined the flow that carried us to the bridge a short distance to the south.

The soldiers from B Company waved and shouted their pleasure at seeing us, happy they were getting relieved from the boring, yet hazardous duty. They gave us a tour of the meager accommodations under the bridge that would be our sleeping quarters, bare red dirt with no place to hang hammocks. We would have to lay our ponchos out on the ground and cover up with the poncho liners to try to keep the mosquitos at bay. Not so different from being out in jungle or coastal areas we patrolled, except that we would at least have a roof over our heads.

The guys we relieved pointed out where they had placed their trip flares and claymore mines. They reported having no enemy contact during the five days they were on duty except that the geese around the bridge sounded off occasionally, an alarm we were advised to take seriously. I had a vision of the Viet Cong herding the villagers towards the ARVN soldiers guarding the bridge and knew I would not want to be faced with that dilemma.

A deuce-and-a-half supply truck came by and the B Company guys waved him down. Luckily for them, he was headed for Liz. They tossed their gear in the back and were on board before we could ask any more questions about our duty assignment. So, we stowed our rucksacks under the bridge, kept our ammo belts on, and went to take positions on both sides of the road alongside the meandering traffic.

I had not eaten since breakfast before sunrise up at the mess hall tent. I decided to reward myself with a meal of LRRP ration spaghetti and meat sauce, so I lit a blue heat tab, filled my canteen cup half full with water and poured the contents of the cellophane bag into the water. In just a few minutes I was able to devour my spaghetti and lick my plastic spoon clean before rinsing it and my canteen holder thoroughly to avoid attracting ants. I was situating my canteen and holder back onto my ammo belt when a jeep pulled over to the side of the bridge next to me.

"I need somebody to help me with a medical emergency," the specialist four announced.

"What kind of emergency?" I asked.

"We have a problem just a short distance north of here in Mộ Đức, and I need somebody to help me take a villager up to Liz for examination," he declared. "I'll bring you back when we're finished," he promised.

I agreed to go with him and got in the jeep. I told the guys I would return shortly. This looked like a nice break from usual duty to me.

"I'm Jim," the medic said, offering his hand.

"Jared," I answered. "What's the crisis?"

"You'll see," he said, sarcastically.

Riding in the jeep was an unexpected distraction from our assigned job. Jim the medic drove north just shy of Mộ Đức village and stopped beside a grass walled shop on the right side of the road. Two soldiers walked out of the shop just as we arrived.

"Have you guys had sex here?" Jim asked.

No answer was needed. You could tell they knew that they had just done something they would wish they hadn't.

"Wait here and we'll take you up for treatment," the medic directed. "Unless you used condoms, you've probably just been exposed to gonorrhea."

We went into the hooch and an attractive woman appeared from a back room.

"My name Mai," she introduced. "What you want?"

Jim simply took her by the arm and declared that we were going to take her up to the bác sĩ for an examination. She started screaming and fighting his grip on her arm so he yelled for me to help. We managed to restrain her and get her to the jeep. Jim gunned the motor to head us off toward the access road. Somehow, I got saddled with the job of trying to keep her from jumping out of the jeep as we raced off toward Liz.

We stopped and picked up the two soldiers who had started walking back and who Jim, to my relief, assigned the duty of holding onto a screaming and uncooperative Mai. It was an almost amusing ride the rest of the way up the hill to Liz, the woman yelling and the men sweating through their now known serious transgressions.

I enjoyed the ride as the jeep slipped side to side in the muddy tracks in the winding hillside roadway up to the top of Liz. When Jim pulled to a stop, no encouragement was needed for the two soldiers to roughly unload Mai and lead her into the medical bunker. Their fear of the disease she carried had turned to anger for exposing them to it.

The chief medic ordered Mai onto an examination table. It took Jim the medic, the two soldiers and me to hold her down while the chief removed her black silk pajama pants so he could examine her. I was holding her right leg and gagged when the odor of infection from her exposed genitalia hit me.

"Did both of you men have intercourse with this woman?" the chief asked the soldiers.

They both nodded guiltily.

"Did that smell not alarm you or were you too into the opportunity to notice?" he continued.

The soldiers simply shrugged, their heads bowed in embarrassment.

The chief gave all three patients penicillin shots in their hips and scheduled them for a series of follow up visits. He told Jim to take Mai back to where he found her with instructions to bring her back for her follow up treatments.

Turning to Mai, his voice became stern as he instructed her "no boom-boom, you number ten sick down there. If you boom-boom, is very bad, you die." He jokingly added "you boom-boom VC okay, but no boom-boom GI."

I asked Jim if I could take a few minutes to get some cold beers for the guys back on the bridge. I went over to the mess hall, found an empty C-ration box and retrieved the beers from the washtub of ice and got an extra for Jim. I also fished a Coke from the tub and gave it to Mai who was now calmly perched on the Jeep's rear bench seat.

She gratefully accepted the drink and acted as if the nasty ordeal we just experienced had never happened. Jim dropped her off at her roadside hooch and instructed her one last time with an authoritative tone, "NO BOOM-BOOM!"

She just smiled and went through the doorway. I had a feeling that she had no intention of obeying the no-sex instructions. I just hoped all of her customers would be Viet Cong.

I told the guys back on the bridge the story of my adventure with the woman and the now infected soldiers as we drank the cool beers. I would not have to worry about any of us making a trip to see Mai in Mộ Đức any time soon. After seeing and smelling the nasty effects of gonorrhea, I doubted I would ever find Vietnamese prostitutes tempting.

Guarding the bridge following monsoon rains was easy

duty. It was nearly impossible for Charlie to attack unless he came at us from the roadway thanks to the flooded rice paddies. The man on guard had to sit above the bridge next to the roadway, so we decided the risk of someone falling asleep while on guard was pretty slim. So, we agreed to take one and a half hour shifts starting at dusk with only one man on guard at a time.

We awoke to a hot and humid sunrise after a fitful night fighting off incessant mosquito attacks. My poncho liner had slipped off of my face and my eyes were nearly swollen shut from the bites. I seldom slept through a night in this country but had not stirred since my turn at guard was over at midnight. The varmints must have feasted on me all night.

I opened a can of beans and franks for breakfast and reminded everyone to take their malaria pill. In the early morning haze I could see the mine clearing team making their way towards us as they trudged along the road from Liz. At a distance the lead man with the metal detector resembled a circus elephant with its trunk gently swaying from side to side.

Guarding the bridge was really about the night duty, making sure Charlie did not have a chance to plant mines or explosives to blow it up. Nonetheless, I felt nervous when the mine clearing was completed and the throng of waiting traffic started to cross the bridge. The people passing by paid us little attention.

I was surprised to see Jim, the medic, following close behind the mine sweepers in his jeep. When the mine team walked across the bridge Jim pulled to a stop and waved me over. The doctor had interviewed the two soldiers that we found with Mai. He was now concerned that she had been with many more troops. He wanted to question her to find out as much as he could about who might have been exposed.

I told the guys I would be back soon and climbed into the jeep. Jim steered the vehicle in a tight circle and headed north towards Mộ Đức. Mai's little store was only a mile or so away, but I realized about half way there that the mine clearing team had not yet cleared that section of road. We would have noticed from the bridge if a team had come from the direction of Quảng Ngãi. The team that crossed our bridge going south came from Liz.

At my suggestion, Jim spun the jeep around and stopped. I got out and walked south to see if I could identify our tire tread marks on the red dirt roadway. If we had not detonated a mine so far it would make sense we would not if we could stay on the same tracks. I could clearly see our path since nobody else had traveled the road yet, so I mounted the hood and told Jim to go slow and stay exactly where I guided him. He cautiously crept along following my left and right hand signals.

We made it to the safety of the already cleared Liz access road turnoff when a loud blast sent a billowing cloud skyward north of us.

"I hope that was the mine clearers from Quảng Ngãi," I yelled to Jim.

"That could have been us," he answered, his voice

trembling.

We sat in the jeep and waited expectantly. Since he was a medic, Jim half expected to get a call on his field radio to respond to injured personnel from the explosion. It was a relief when no call came and the mine clearers crept into view on Highway One a few hundred meters to our north.

We finally managed to pull in next to Mai's shop around mid-morning. Traffic from the north was at full flow behind the mine crew but we had the northbound lane to ourselves. The traffic from the direction of Đức Phổ had not yet caught up with us.

Mai was perched at the front of her grass and mud hooch which sat only ten feet from the road edge. Dust from the clay roadway coated the grass roof above her giving it a red glow from the easterly morning sun. She held a mu la, pyramid shaped leaf hat, upside down in her lap. Uncut bamboo leaves extended from the edges. She was in the process of weaving a new hat.

"Hello G.I.," she greeted us, smiling. Unlike before, we seemed to have gained her trust.

I kneeled down beside her, doing my best to mimic the way she was sitting on her feet, buttocks on heels. I was sincerely interested to learn how they made the hats.

"You sit, I show," she motioned to Jim, waving her hand up and down to him.

Jim copied my sitting position the best he could and Mai stood, holding the mu la up to the sunlight giving us a view from the underside.

"Mu la tell story," she explained. "Boy meet girl, man farm rice, boy ride water buffalo," she described, pointing to each scene that we could see were intricately woven with layers of bamboo leaves. She held a little curved knife that she used to trim out the images, truly an artist at home in her craft.

"Beautiful!" I was impressed and happy to see Mai had another means of support.

"You buy, five dollar," she offered. I was sold and fished around in my fatigue pants to find a five dollar MPC note. I thought it would be a cool souvenir to send to my mother.

Mai went into her store to get me a finished hat. She held it up to the sun so I could see that it was of equal quality to the one she was making.

"I need you to come with me again," Jim instructed, anxious to see what kind of fight he was going to get. Surprisingly, Mai simply put her weaving project away inside her house and willingly followed us to the jeep.

I dismounted the jeep at the entrance to the access road so Jim would not have to fight turning around in the now heavy foot and vehicle traffic. He said it made him nervous maneuvering around among the crazy moped riders, especially stopping and turning around while they carelessly zoomed by.

I could see somebody furiously waving to me from the bridge as I walked towards it. Dam and her troop had ridden their bicycles all the way from Đức Phổ to sell their wares along the highway. She had recognized me from the distance and beamed her beautiful welcoming smile in my direction.

When I drew close I could see that she was angry with me, the corners of her normally smiling mouth turned downward.

"Number ten boom-boom," she announced. "Mai bad sick, make G.I. sick." It was a shock to learn Dam would know about such things at her young age.

"No, we just take Mai to see bác sĩ at Liz, maybe make her better." I was anxious to explain. "And we told her only make boom-boom with VC," I added, wanting to humorously point out the absurdity of Dam's concern for me.

That seemed to satisfy her as her white teeth beamed approval. It was a pleasure to have some more time to spend with my friend. Dam and her friends sat around the bridge with us for hours, singing Vietnamese songs and playing hand games that resembled Jacob's ladder, which my sister played with a string when we were kids.

As the lowering sun signaled the arrival of late afternoon, Dam and her friends said their goodbyes and pedaled their mobile stores off towards the south. Their pace was quickened by their empty baskets. We now owned their candles, cigarettes and Cokes and they most of our MPC.

Chapter 16

"This operation looks like a big deal," Gerry declared, handing over his rucksack from inside the resupply chopper so he could help unload the cases of c-rations, Cokes and other supplies.

"Looks like your timing could have been better," I agreed as I carefully placed his pack on dry ground and turned back to assist with the unloading process. "It's the biggest combat assault I've seen since I've been in country. We just flew in this morning and it has been red smoke all day. We've been hearing fire fights around us all afternoon but we haven't had any direct contact yet." I wanted to fill Gerry in. He needed to get back in combat mode after returning from R&R.

He had been a late comer to our platoon as squad leader for third squad. He was a graduate of NCO School. We affectionately referred to them as ninety-day wonders.

Gerry was a handsome, six-foot blond with an admirable, bushy and sandy blond mustache. He wore a peace sign on the lapel of his fatigue shirt and was the anti of gung ho. He frequently quoted verse from *The Prophet* by Kahlil Gibran. He had a smooth resonate voice and he captivated me with his discourse when he quoted the verses "On Love" and "On Children". He had the entire chapters of both memorized. It was easy to visualize a prophet addressing a crowd of followers as Gerry spoke.

I was so taken with my introduction to *The Prophet* that, back in June when I went to Hong Kong on R&R, I went in search of a copy to give to Gerry. I searched all over Kowloon for a book store until a Korean suit maker suggested I try Hong Kong Island. So, I took the ferry across Hong Kong Harbor and walked up and down streets until I came across a store that had books on display in a street side display window.

I studied the books in the window display and noticed they all had red binders with gold print. I guess I should have realized that was odd before I casually entered the store. Two Chinese guys immediately approached me from the back of the store addressing me accusingly, asking what I wanted in their store. I noticed they both had white side wall haircuts, a sign they could have been military or politicos. Rumors were common about American soldiers disappearing when they wandered across the Chinese border from Hong Kong.

At that unwelcomed reception, I looked more thoroughly around the store and realized ALL of the books in the store had crimson red bindings with gold print. I had entered a communist Chinese book store. Suffice to say, I returned to Vietnam without a copy of *The Prophet* for Gerry.

That recollection brought back pleasant memories of my seven-day vacation in Hong Kong, though. American soldiers were treated like celebrities for our free spending habits. Venders of every type wanted our American currency. It was there that I learned our dollar mark originated from a "U" placed over an "S" because the merchants all referred to money in terms of US dollars versus Hong Kong dollars.

I pleasantly remembered my surprise when I checked into my room at the Grand Hotel in Kowloon to find my telephone ringing. I knew nobody in this vast city, and nobody except the Army, was aware of my whereabouts. When I answered it, on the other end of the phone was a sexy and pleasant girl's voice that instructed me to go look out my fifth floor window to the street below.

There, standing next to a pay telephone with the receiver to her ear, was a cute and smiling Chinese girl in a bright yellow and very short dress. "You like I can stay with you, only fifteen dollar, twenty-four hour," she announced.

I asked her how she got my number and she responded that she saw my room light turn on and counted windows and floors. She would call the hotel operator and ask for a specific room number. She really had her system down, I fondly recalled.

I did not take her up on her offer because I had a plan. Before I blew all of my money, I wanted to buy some tailor made clothes to send home. I checked out a few of the Korean tailors in Kowloon. I did not like the aggressive approach they used, grabbing me by the arm and literally guiding me into their shops. So, I inquired for a referral to a good tailor from the hotel and was directed to Hong Kong Island.

The tailor I found was called the Yung Ziang Trading Company. The little shop was located on the second floor above a Chinese spa and bath house. To my surprise, the two hundred dollars I had saved for clothing bought me three sharkskin, silk and wool suits, two top coats and a very heavy mohair sweater. The tailor promised they would be silk lined with my name stenciled on the inside pocket, including the sweater.

They only managed to finish one suit and the two top coats before I left to return to Vietnam so I paid extra to have the other two suits and the sweater shipped home. I took the rest with me to ship from Vietnam for free through the APO system. On my first night back in country in Da Nang, all of my tailor-made clothes and souvenirs were stolen from beneath my bunk while I was sleeping.

My R&R memories, brought to mind by Gerry's return, were suddenly interrupted. "I brought you something," Gerry announced. He handed me a book packaged in brown paper wrapping. He had been more successful than I on R&R while he was in Hawaii. He found a copy of *The Prophet* for me!

I grabbed Gerry around the neck and hugged him. He looked around embarrassed and pushed me away. Soldiers weren't supposed to do that.

I walked with Gerry over to his squad position in the company perimeter and helped him dig in. When we were satisfied the fox hole was deep enough to provide adequate protection, we sat on the edge and opened warm beers.

"How was your R&R?" I asked.

"Unreal and over too fast," he answered. "My fiancé was waiting at the hotel when I arrived. Man, she looked so beautiful. I was surprised to see her with short hair though. She was in a car wreck and had a head injury so they had to shave her head. It was still pretty the way it grew back, just a different look for her. She had what they called a bouncing brain. It is a type of concussion that makes it dangerous for her to get bumped around and she shouldn't get too upset or emotional. They said it could put her into a coma or even kill her. I sure hope nothing happens to me because I'm not sure what it would do to her."

"We've just got to make sure nothing happens to you. That's all." I did not know how else to respond. I could see the desperation he felt.

Dusk was fast approaching. I shook hands with Gerry, told him I was glad he was back and returned to my own squad position. I checked to make sure our guys were all situated and the guard schedule worked out before settling into my fox hole for the night. I could not stop thinking about Gerry's story and his concern for his fiancé.

We had become good friends as soon as he joined the platoon back in the spring. He was assigned as an infantry squad leader directly out of training. I could not imagine coming into this country and being expected to know how to lead without some sort of field experience. He knew he lacked the hard learned lessons of a Vietnam combat infantryman and was smart enough to follow Lenny's lead running the squad.

He wanted to be called Gerry instead of Gerard, his given name. He thought Gerard sounded too formal. At twenty-one, he was a year older than me. He had left his job working for a newspaper in New York when he entered the Army.

His compassion for people was pretty well defined for me one night sitting on top of a bunker on Liz. In between quoting lines from *The Prophet*, he talked about a homeless guy in front of the newspaper office who was there every day when he went to work. He said the guy always had something pleasant to say to him, so he would fish around in his pocket and give him all of the change he had. He said that guy was always quoting excerpts from *The Prophet* and that's what got him interested in Kahlil Gibran.

Gerry and I had both been lucky during our brief tenures as squad leaders. Neither of us had lost anyone from our units although we had been in some pretty intense situations. I was careful not to voice that fact for fear it would jinx us. We had survived plenty of booby traps and snipers and had killed or captured our share of enemy combatants.

The night was unusually dark but thankfully quiet. There was only a crack of light showing around the edge of the new moon and it did little to illuminate the dry rice paddies and hedge rows that surrounded us.

I was always concerned one of our guys might go to sleep during his watch, but not so much on this night. There was too much enemy activity going on in this desolate looking place. We expected more of the same, and who knew whether it would come tonight or tomorrow. I spent the entire night expectantly straining my eyes to see through the shroud of blackness, feeling certain something bad was going to happen. I guessed the rest of the company was feeling the same way.

Sunrise found us sleep deprived although all in one piece. Neither our company nor the other units in the battalion made enemy contact during the night and that was a terrific relief. It made me wonder what Charlie might have planned for us today.

I started the early morning off with breakfast of c-ration ham and eggs, not one of my favorites. But Lenny had traded me out of my last LRRP ration spaghetti and meat sauce by throwing in a beer in the barter. I finished with a can of peaches, sucking the sweet juice from the tin once the fruit was gone.

I buried the cans and remains from my breakfast. We knew never to leave behind anything Charlie could use against us. Our cans were often used, stuffed with explosives, nails and glass, to create damaging booby traps. While these "mini" mines seldom resulted in death, they could cause serious injuries to hands, feet and legs. Like bungee pits, they were designed to incapacitate our soldiers and reduce our numbers.

An hour after sunup, I had my sixty-pound rucksack

packed up and shouldered, ready to take the lead, as first squad usually did, on our day's patrols. I took my usual position behind the point man.

I observed as we walked in a column that there were no villages and no signs of life. Coconut and palm trees lined areas of raised ground where it was apparent villages once existed. We walked across elevated dirt foundations where houses once stood. It was hard to imagine why Charlie would care whether we were here since there didn't seem to be anything for him to protect or defend.

Confirming our fears of an active day, we started hearing explosions and small arms fire in the direction of elements of our cadre to the north. Our field radios came alive with reports of enemy attacks. "Look out for snipers behind you," a desperate voice announced.

Based on hearing that, we switched from walking in single file to a side-to-side line of assault, which would cover a fifty-yard swath of terrain with one platoon.

"Burn the hooches!" screamed another excited declaration over our radios. Small arms fire echoed behind the shouted warnings as the radio mikes were squelched.

We walked on dry, cracked and crusted unfarmed soil. I imagined the area awash in knee-deep irrigated rice fields with villagers bent at the waist planting or harvesting the fertile landscape. The fields would normally be flooded this time of year, especially so soon after the end of the monsoon rains. For now, stubs of untended rice plants crunched under our boots.

The total lack of villages, homes, people or animals where they had obviously once flourished gave me the eerie feeling that this was a battleground where much life had been lost. I wondered if the evident history of devastation drove Charlie's hatred and determination, making him intent on driving out the American plague that had taken so much away.

Duke caught up to our squad, walking beside me now, on the left side of the platoon. Second squad was to our right, then Gerry's third squad with forth squad to the far right flank.

Up ahead there was a raised area where a village once stood. As we entered on the left edge, Duke approached the only hooch in sight and torched it using his Zippo lighter. The grass and mud house did not burn easily. Instead it smoked and smoldered as the flames slowly took hold.

Beside the burning hooch, there was a mound that covered the bunker where the villagers would seek refuge from war. I removed a grenade from my ammo pouch and yelled for anyone who might be inside to come out. It was a half-hearted warning since I believed that anyone here would be an enemy combatant. I pulled the pin and tossed the grenade into the opening and yelled "fire in the hole." Nothing happened. My hand grenade was a dud. So, I removed another, pulled the pin and lobbed it in, this time without issuing a warning. The explosion sent a cloud of smoke through the opening, but it was an attack into an empty hole.

We moved forward through a well-worn courtyard where residents had thoroughly trampled the soil at some time in the past. The dirt was hard packed reminding me of the mama sans I had seen sweeping the dirt around their meager homes as I traveled through dozens of villages during my time in Vietnam.

We walked across it into an open dry rice paddy. We were about halfway through the thirty yard expanse when machine gun fire exploded in front of me. The dirt kicked up around my feet and in the soil to my front and sides, but somehow I was not hit. Duke dove to the ground next to me. We held our helmets protectively to shield our heads.

From the wood line to our front, Charlie had us in the crosshairs. I propped up on my elbows and fired my M-16 on automatic. I had no idea where the enemy fire was coming from. Duke rolled over next to me.

"Give me grenades," he instructed as he reached over and took my last two hand grenades from my ammo belt. He pulled the pins on both grenades, then jumped up and ran hard toward where he thought the enemy firing position was located, and threw the grenades. The loud blasts stopped the bullets from coming at us and hopefully killed the bastards.

Duke ran back to me and shouted instructions for me to get our guys back. He then took off running down the middle of the dry rice paddy yelling "I got to go get my boys."

I had not seen Duke move like this before. His heroics

were like watching a movie. He was aware what was happening on the entire battle line and somehow knew our guys were injured to the right of us. He ran down the center of the wide open paddy firing his rifle in the direction of the wood line, now to his left.

I got to my feet and, following Duke's orders, yelled for everyone to pull back and take cover. We retreated to the cluster of tropical trees that had once been the village perimeter.

I heard someone shout that Duke was hit. So, I took aim and wildly fired my rifle on automatic at the far side of the dry rice field. Everyone around me did the same creating a deafening barrage of covering fire. The entrenched enemy still popped off rounds toward our soldiers who were pinned down in the open. We continued exchanging fire for a half hour or so until I could see something more needed to be done to help our guys still out in the open down the line to my right.

I moved further back into the center of the abandoned village to find the company commander. He was hiding together with his company quarters group among the mounds that once protected the villagers. I did not understand where our helicopter gunships were when we needed them. Now I saw that the captain was too busy cowering to give us the help we needed.

I remembered Felix Queen talking about what a wonderful leader Joe Rhinehart was and I had witnessed how he would always be up in the front leading his troops into action instead of sending them. I sure wished he was with us today instead of the coward Captain O'Grady who I now saw looking after his own ass with no regard for his men. It was a disappointing day when Captain Rhinehart left us in the field for his promotion into the brigade headquarters at Bronco.

I approached the captain and told him we had people pinned down in the dry paddy, and I told him he needed to get us air support. His response was "you need to go get them out of there." Nonetheless, I was relieved to hear his radio operator call for air support as I walked away.

Without a plan, and without thinking clearly what I was about to do, I started off around the back side of a new-looking grass hooch that stood at the right edge of the elevated village perimeter. Perhaps the hooch would give me some cover as I tried to get to our soldiers who were pinned down, I thought. Suddenly, I saw Franny run up behind me.

I heard the captain yell, "Franny, you don't have to do that."

Franny shouted back, "they are my friends. I've got to help them."

Franny and I eased around to the front hugging the hooch walls for cover. An oval shaped bomb crater was in the center of the paddy twenty yards to our front. I could see the tops of helmets inside that told me our soldiers were trapped there. Others were scattered face down in the dry paddy, not moving. We started towards them and were stopped by automatic rifle fire that sent bullets zinging by us from across the open field.

We dove to our bellies behind a row of rocks that lined the courtyard of the hooch. As we hit the ground face down, a bullet kicked up the dirt between our heads. We turned and gazed up simultaneously to see the barrel of a sniper's rifle as he pulled it back into the folds of the grass roof. We aimed our M-16's and both attempted to shoot him. Both of our rifles failed to fire. They had overheated from too much shooting on automatic.

We jumped up and ran back towards the hooch, hoping to get clear of the sniper's line of sight. We were too slow. The sniper fired twice. Both rounds hit Franny in the belly. He started to fall but reached an arm around my shoulder still in full stride. We stumbled together towards some of the CQ guys who were watching the events unfold from the right of us.

"He's in the roof!" I desperately shouted to them.

We had covered the entire twenty-yard distance to the mound where they hid before somebody managed to come up with an M-79 grenade launcher. He breached the weapon, loaded the bullet shaped grenade into the chamber and snapped it closed. He then took aim and fired towards the hooch. It seemed to me that everything moved in slow motion.

Franny collapsed dragging me to the ground with him.

"Get those sons of bitches," he groaned. The panic in his eyes belied his final attempt at bravery.

The medic appeared from somewhere and dove to the ground next to us. He gently pried Franny's hands loose from me and went to work treating his wounds.

I hated leaving Franny but I knew our mission to help the others was not finished. The hooch was fully engulfed in flames now, the gray smoke billowing skyward. I trotted to the edge of the paddy and saw Chester Wong get to his feet from his face down position and move to the body lying next to him. I ran to his side as he rolled the lifeless soldier over on his back. Gerry's glazed eyes stared skyward. He was shot in the back of the head by the sniper, likely dead before he hit the ground.

A Medevac chopper flew low overhead, circled and landed between the wood line and the bomb crater. Those trapped in the crater started to emerge, the uninjured helping the wounded. I saw that Duke's right arm was dangling loosely as Lenny assisted him. The sniper's bullet had shattered his shoulder blade as he raced to the aid of "his boys."

Lenny and Sanders then found Ed Woods and carried him to the chopper while Wong and I loaded Gerry's lifeless body through the open doorway. Lenny and Sanders headed back to the crater to retrieve Mo Vogler who had taken five rounds but was still alive and conscious. Still under fire from the wood line, Sanders was hit in the back and lay wounded in the open paddy.

Under heavy enemy fire, the Medevac chopper took off towards open terrain to the south. Lenny saw that they were leaving behind more wounded and knew they needed to be called back. Duke's radio operator had been hit and his radio destroyed. So, Lenny stripped off his gear and did a zig-zag run back to find the captain's RTO to get the helicopter to return.

The Medevac swooped in again and we quickly loaded the two remaining wounded soldiers. Those of us left in the paddy retreated back to join the captain and his small remaining troop behind the village bunkers. Only minutes after all of our soldiers were clear of the dry rice paddy, the air strike we requested roared past overhead making a recon run to make sure they had the target area zeroed. They were so close and loud that everyone dove to the ground expecting bombs to explode. The two jets flared skyward in a wide arc then dove back in our direction. Massive explosions shook the earth as the bombs brought fire and destruction to the wooded area that had concealed our enemies.

Our first and second platoons had taken a terrible beating that left four dead and twenty-two wounded. I watched the remaining frame from the smoldering hooch collapse and wondered if we actually killed the sniper or if he escaped into a tunnel or bunker. I knew I would be haunted by not knowing for sure if Franny's killer survived. Why did he have to target Franny instead of me? We could not have been more than six inches apart. I felt terrible guilt that I had led Franny to his death.

What about poor Gerry and the plight facing his fiancé? Of all the terrible stories I had heard and witnessed because of this war, that one had to be the crown jewel. I knew I would cherish my copy of *The Prophet* forever.

Chapter 17

We had a reprieve from combat assaults for a couple of weeks that gave us time to rebuild our battered company with replacements. We were a dejected crew. We were thankful for the opportunity to shake off the beating we took.

We questioned ourselves a great deal about the events of August 25. Why did we walk into that open rice paddy without air support after hearing all of the reports coming across the radios? Why didn't someone see the sniper in the roof of the hooch, who, we later discovered, was the shooter of most of our dead and wounded? More importantly, why did we not burn the hooch as ordered? Why did it take so long to get air support?

Each of the questions could only be answered with excuses since there were no good reasons for any of it. We were sent into the open by a company commander not fit to command. We did not realize the sniper was there because he was firing with us. Lenny informed me that Gerry did attempt to torch the corner of the hooch when he passed by, but he did not wait long enough to verify it caught on. Nobody could reason why the request for air support was not called in earlier. Once again it fell back on our cowardly captain.

By the end of the first week of September, it was time to get back to the business of war. We boarded the Huey's at the base of Liz and headed north, the rotor blades louder than usual as they thwack…thwack…thwacked, fighting westerly winds that wanted to push us off course to the east. The pilot was forced to fly a skewed course with his nose pointed northwest to maintain a northerly heading.

The mission was taking us to the Sơn Hà area in the mountains west of Quảng Ngãi. The Hà Thành Montagnard Special Forces camp was under enemy siege and we were going in to bail them out. The entire battalion was mobilized including an artillery battery. Firebase Dragon to the north of Liz was the designated staging area. The five light infantry companies that made up third battalion were scheduled to meet there to form a major combat assault group.

We were flying low over rice paddies, perhaps fifteen hundred feet, to cover the fifteen-mile distance north from Liz to Dragon. Below I could see a hedge row at the edge of the rice paddy that bordered dense jungle growth of elephant grass to the west. These weren't the kind of towering and manicured boxwood hedge rows you would see surrounding Palm Beach mansions. These were rows of unkempt scrub brush left over from decades earlier when the rice fields were carved out of overgrown terrain.

Not all of our operations took us air mobile. Following the VC ambush that wounded Powell and others, we were assigned daily patrols across rice paddies and in villages throughout our primary area of operations between Đức Phổ and Quảng Ngãi, mostly concentrating on the eastern side of Highway One where the enemy occupation was strongest. We soon learned that there were no safe places. No matter how calm an area appeared, trouble seemed to always lie in our path.

Before our brigade moved into the area from Hawaii, a marine regiment had occupied Quảng Ngãi Province. The marines were pretty brutal in their tactics and left behind alienated village leaders and families whose rice was destroyed, whose villages were bombed out or burned and whose family members were killed or captured. When the marines moved out, the area they vacated became a hot bed of enemy determination fueled by hatred and anger towards Americans.

Day after day we covered the same terrain on search and destroy missions. We were supposed to seek out and kill or capture the enemy by invading the local villages, rummaging through their belongings, scattering their caches of rice, trampling rice paddies and burning their homes any time we felt they gave us justification.

Over and over snipers would pop up from their well-concealed hiding places, spider holes or tunnels, along the hedgerows or from within the villages. They would fire bursts from their Chinese supplied AK-47 rifles and disappear. Most of these sniper attacks left one or more of our soldiers dead or wounded. Because the well planned attacks were over as quickly as they started, we seldom saw the enemy no matter how thoroughly we searched.

The harassment took its toll and filled our soldiers with anger and hatred of Vietnamese people over seeing our friends wounded and maimed. We did not get many opportunities to exact revenge by killing or capturing the perpetrators.

I got pretty good at walking point and with experience learned I actually did not mind the assignments. I had good instincts and paid close attention, never allowing myself to relax or drop my guard. I got a fast education from the many sniper attacks and from the booby traps that were exploded along hedge rows, on paddy dike paths and in villages. It seemed common sense to me never to walk in a straight line or pass through hedgerows on beaten paths, but rather to walk through rice paddy water and cut new paths, never taking the easiest route. The enemy set traps based on where they thought we were headed and would execute their plans only minutes ahead of us.

Walking point was an onerous responsibility. You were given an assigned destination. You were responsible for making route decisions. The guys following your lead, whether a squad, platoon or entire company of soldiers, were depending on you. Those decisions could either save lives by avoiding enemy contact or cost devastation and death because you made the wrong choices.

It became hard to distinguish one area of terrain from the next. The rice paddies all looked the same. The villages, on raised ground they surrounded, were indistinguishable one from the next with their mud walled and thatched roof houses and brushed dirt yards. The insides of the houses were pretty much identical. On one side was a hearth for cooking fires with a rice pot dangling over the fire. Bamboo sleeping mats lined the walls.

An altar containing a small statue of Buddha would be centered in the house. He would be surrounded by rice cakes, incense sticks and other symbolic offerings from the home dwellers. These hungry and often starving people never failed to share their meager food supplies to honor their religious icons. To the side of the house would be a mound of dirt with small door opening, a bunker for protection from overnight air strikes and artillery fire.

During the day the villagers worked in the rice, leaving only old people and children to mind the homes. Children were trained to sound the alarm when Americans were sighted. They ran from the villages shouting to us to "souvenir baby san chop-chop", the word souvenir learned from days of the French colonialism.

When the villagers were at home and heard we were coming, they gathered at one house, huddled together defensively, squatting calves against thighs. There were no chairs in the houses and this squatting position was their way of sitting around the house relaxing. They were careful not to make eye contact with us, afraid any effort to communicate might be interpreted as hostile. I wondered how we could ever win over a people who were turned so totally against us, whose language we did not speak and who we treated with so little respect.

We learned to appreciate our helicopter rides even though they often took us into hostile situations. It beat humping long distances with loaded rucksacks. We got accustomed to searching for signs of the enemy as we flew and would point out suspects to the door gunners who would unleash barrages from their M-60 machine guns.

I dangled my left leg out the door as I scanned the terrain for signs of the enemy, the door gunner doing the same behind me. The whizzing sound of bullets interrupted my search and banged harshly into the upper side of the helicopter fuselage above our heads. I instinctively sought protection from within by rolling to my right and jerking my left leg inside to safety. Fortunately nobody was hit but the helicopter started performing strangely, swaying from side to side. The pilot shouted for us to hang on as we abruptly turned nose down in a dive attitude, the ground coming up at us fast.

I could see the co-pilot talking through his mouthpiece to the door gunners as the pilot scrambled to maintain control. The door gunner behind me leaned into our compartment and shouted for us to be prepared to jump on command before we hit ground. We were going in fast and to jump at this speed would be suicide so we all just held on tight. The pilot and co-pilot tugged hard on the controls and managed to bring the nose up just enough as our skids bumped the ground hard. The Huey somehow managed to absorb the impact without crashing. Instead, the runners bounced off the dry rice paddy and we managed to maintain flight only a few meters above ground.

The door gunner relayed the pilot's message to us that he was going to try to make it to LZ Dragon rather than risk putting down and becoming a sitting duck for Charlie. Flying low without the ability to maneuver would make us an easy target.

Behind us we could hear explosions, the thump – thump – thump of rockets launched from Cobra attack helicopters as they pounded the area where our sniper might have been hiding. The two Cobras assigned to provide protection to our assault group zoomed in above us then dipped low to strafe the potential enemy positions along our crippled path. The red clay firebase, devoid of foliage, was easy to identify when it came into view ahead. Our pilot, our new best friend, managed to set the damaged chopper down gently, delivering us safely from our terrifying ride.

Had I been on a commercial airline, it probably would have been some time before I was ready to board another flight. But the army did not put it to a vote. They had us boarded on another Huey in minutes and back in formation with our combat assault group. We left Dragon and began a steady ascent northward, climbing in sync with the rest of the helicopter formation to ten thousand feet before turning west into the mountains around Sơn Hà. From this altitude, we experienced a panoramic view of the majestic mountains of thirty-five hundred feet or more. They abruptly dipped into winding river valleys at sea level. I had not flown this high in a helicopter before and my legs were safely tucked under me well inside of the open door. I noticed even the door gunner behind me leaned safely back into his seat.

After Duke was wounded, there was no senior NCO to take his place. I was promoted to act as platoon sergeant. I was still getting accustomed to being responsible for keeping up with our whereabouts on the area of operations map. As we flew, I kept track of our location and found Sơn Hà at an elevation of 3,573 feet. The Trà Bồng river valley, at sea level, was less than two miles away.

We began a circling descent around the tallest mountain peak. The top of the mountain had been cleared of trees and growth. It appeared to have been used as a base camp before, although vacant now. A solo bunker rested atop the highest peak to the south. A steep footpath connected it to the wide flat surface of the mountaintop. The Trà Bồng river valley was to the north with the fortified Hà Thanh Special Forces Camp occupying the southern segment of the valley.

Our Cobra attack helicopters began strafing the mountain with rocket propelled grenades and machine gun fire to prepare for our landing. The helicopters transporting our company began our final descent to make a combat assault landing while the other companies branched off to their assigned destinations. Even though green smoke grenades marked our intended landing areas, all of the door gunners on the dozen or more helicopters opened fire on automatic creating a deafening roar, their bullets kicking up dust all over the mountain.

Since we were not under attack, the pilot landed with his runners on the ground, making it easier for us to unload with our fully loaded rucksacks and ammo belts. We took up positions on either side of the landing area and awaited our orders, watching the other platoons move into their positions on the quickly formed perimeter.

A steady convoy of Chinook helicopters brought in support personnel, supplies, mobile command and communications center buildings, ammunition, rations, water blimps and a mortar platoon. An artillery battery with 105 and 155 millimeter cannons came next. The big guns were capable of targeting fire missions to all of the mountainous areas surrounding the Special Forces camp in the valley.

The Viet Cong and NVA occupied the mountains looking down on the camp. They had been bombarding the Montagnards for weeks with mortar and rocket propelled grenade attacks. Our special forces, charged with supervising the native mercenaries, badly needed relief from the siege.

Before Duke was wounded, he had assumed the roles of both platoon sergeant and platoon leader. We were without a first or second lieutenant who would normally fill the leadership role. So, as acting platoon sergeant in Duke's place, I held senior rank. So, for now at least, the company commander communicated his orders directly to me.

He walked over and informed me that he needed a squad to man an observation post in the bunker on top of the hill to the south, about three hundred yards outside of the company perimeter. I had a good view of the dugout sand bag bunker with a lean to style roof when we flew over on our approach. I felt a pang of pity for whoever might be stuck up there all alone. It did not occur to me that it could be a squad I would have to assign.

This would be my first test at being responsible for making the difficult decision about which of our people to send into harm's way. So, I elected to accompany third squad, now led by Lenny, to man the hilltop post.

The third squad guys overheard the orders and, although grumbling about the lousy assignment, set about gathering as many trip flares, claymore mines, hand grenades and all of the extra M-16 ammo we could add to our already fully loaded packs. It was late morning by the time we were ready to set out on our climb up the thirty degree incline to the remote and unprotected hilltop. Even during daylight and from within the safety of the heavily armed company perimeter, the bunker atop the mountain was a frightening and lonesome looking destination.

We began our ascent feeling vulnerable to the vast and mountainous jungle that surrounded the sand bag fort awaiting our small troop. The climb, under our heavy loads, left us soaked with sweat and exhausted by the time we reached the summit. We dropped our rucksacks on the crudely formed sand bag beds in the bunker and decided on an hourly guard rotation. One of us would be standing guard atop the bunker at all times while the rest prepared our defenses around the perimeter.

We put out flares on trip wires on all sides, leaving only the footpath down the mountain open in case we needed to make a hasty retreat. Every twenty yards or so we placed hand grenades on trip wires with pins pulled almost all the way out. If someone bumped against the wire, it would pull the pin out the rest of the way. Last, we surrounded the bunker with claymore mines positioned so they faced out every thirty feet or so. Their detonators lined the top row of sand bags, easily accessible from within the bunker.

It was late afternoon when we finished securing our outpost and it was time to think about food. I tore open a cellophane LRRP ration packet and poured the contents into my canteen holder, arranged some rocks to elevate the improvised cooking pot, added water and put a blue heat tab under the pot. In five minutes I had a hot meal of beef and rice.

We agreed to a watch schedule starting at dusk with two hour shifts that would take us through to morning. The viewing windows inside the bunker gave a panorama of two thirds of our surroundings from northwest to the south and around to northeast, leaving the north side out of view. All eight of us sat on the roof nervously awaiting dark, our weapons at the ready. We felt vulnerable and expectant, our guts telling us Charlie would be coming for us this night.

As the sun settled beyond the mountains to the west,

the sky to the southeast exploded in a rumbling light show from a B-52 bombing raid. We were awed by the ferocity. Even though the dozens of bombs were exploding beyond the next mountain range we could feel the ground vibrate beneath us. You did not hear or see the airplanes in a high altitude B-52 attack. Five- hundred pound bombs just fell from the sky and shook the earth.

When the bombing raid ended we moved inside of the bunker and took up our night positions. I sort of reclined in a sitting position next to the door opening, my back resting against the sand bag wall. I did not really want to sleep but had confidence we could depend on all of our guys to stay alert. I slipped into a light sleep while Russell took first watch.

I was awakened by the back blast from a claymore explosion and saw Baker, who had relieved Russell on guard, feeling for another claymore detonator. A trip flare was burning down the hill on our east side and Baker had blown the mine closest to the flare. A claymore suddenly exploded twenty yards to our front on the south side of the hill.

"I didn't blow that one!" Baker shouted. "Charlie must have cut the detonator wire."

A trip flare and one of our booby trap hand grenades simultaneously went off to our west, telling us we were surrounded on at least three sides by the enemy. Baker saw movement to the east, close in, and detonated another claymore.

This had all of the markings of a sapper attack. The

enemy would send suicide squads to penetrate our perimeters, either wearing vests loaded with bombs or carrying satchels filled with explosives mixed with nails, glass and anything else that would kill or maim from the blast.

I made a quick decision to call in mortar support. I hooded my map with a poncho and shined my flashlight long enough to get coordinates. It would be a risky request for support since the mortar rounds would have to fly close to our position to be effective, including going directly over our heads. I believed that was our only hope for protection of our southern exposure. Short rounds were a serious risk, yet I decided one worth taking.

I got on the radio and ordered a mortar platoon fire mission. I read the map coordinates that would put the first round directly over our heads to land fifty meters to our front. The mortar platoon sergeant personally responded that he thought it was too risky. A short round could take us all out. I responded "fire at will", which meant "don't wait for me to clarify but send the mortar rounds now."

The welcome explosions to our front told us the mortar platoon was dead on target. I radioed amended map coordinates to bring in mortar rounds to the east and west. We could hear our hand grenade booby traps exploding from the impact of the mortar blasts. Trip flares illuminated the mountain top. We were relieved to see shadowy silhouettes fleeing, defeated by our counter attack.

Daylight brought relief to our beleaguered crew. Our preparations, combined with the precision efforts of the mortar platoon, had kept us alive.

We spread out and inspected the hillsides that surrounded our bunker. We found blood soaked ground where our claymores and hand grenades had exploded. There were no bodies or weapons. We knew we had killed or wounded some of the attackers. They had removed the evidence during their retreat.

Sleep deprived from a difficult night, I was relieved to see a squad of soldiers climbing the footpath toward our position to take over the outpost. We gave them a guided tour of our remaining hand grenade booby traps, trips flares and claymore mines before beginning our descent down the mountain. The young sergeant in charge of our relief force informed me that the CO wanted me to report in as soon as I reached the company area.

I went straight to the CO's tent as ordered. The company commander and the mortar platoon sergeant were waiting for me. The sergeant seemed pretty distraught.

"What were you thinking?" the sergeant began. "We could have wiped out your squad with one short round. You should know that 81mm mortars are not accurate enough to pull stunts like you pulled last night." The red haired Irishman was so agitated that his face was bright red.

"I want to thank you, sergeant, for saving our lives," I responded as calmly and sincerely as I could. "They were coming for us on all sides and I don't think we could have held them off without your support. We owe you big time," I added.

The sergeant left the tent shaking his head.

"Congratulations," the CO began, as soon as the mortar sergeant was gone. He stood up and shook my hand. "You brought all of our boys back and that's what matters. Do you have an enemy body count?"

"No sir," I answered. "They cleaned up after themselves but we did find blood trails in three locations, so it is reasonable to assume we got at least three of them."

"Roger that," he responded. "I'll report three enemy KIA. And, first platoon will be leading our combat assault into Hà Thanh today. Get your guys ready."

As usual, the captain would be sending units of his company into the valley to confront the enemy while remaining in a protected area. Even the disastrous events of August 25th had not changed his ways.

Chapter 18

The helicopter ride down into the valley to the north of Sơn Hà was a winding ride east towards Quảng Ngãi before circling back to follow the Trà Bồng River westward. We landed in a mountain valley to the north of Hà Thanh Special Forces Camp, the tall grasses blowing in waves that reminded me of riding horses on the Cone Estate near Blowing Rock.

It was a beautiful memory of a trail ride where we followed a path across a mountaintop in the Blue Ridge Mountains. We were on one of the many trails designated for horses only and the wind was blowing the alfalfa field so it looked like gentle waves on a lake. My horse, mistaking the hayfield for water, abruptly lay down and started rolling, saddle and all. I wished so badly that I could go back to those simpler times.

We moved out towards the woods to the west as soon as everyone was on the ground. The terrain was hilly, not steep. We walked from one wooded hill to the next, dipping down a few meters and back up again. We heard intermittent enemy fire to our north signaling that units of our force were making contact. We heard the familiar thunk…thunk…thunk from a fifty caliber machine gun. The heavy rounds sizzled as they buzzed over our heads.

The RTO reported that some of our soldiers were under attack on the wrong end of a captured American Sherman tank. The radio buzzed that one of our helicopters was shot down by the fifty caliber gun. We were fortunate to be in a sway between hills, out of reach of the heavy caliber rounds.

We emerged from the forest northeast of the Special Forces camp. The fortress was a series of bunkers connected by a web of subterranean trenches. A lone bald mountain stood in the center of the valley to the west of the camp.

Our assignment was to hook up with second platoon and establish a defensive perimeter on top of the grass covered mountain. A young lieutenant and his RTO had joined their platoon as a forward observer, responsible for spotting enemy positions and coordinating artillery support. The idea was to establish an observation post with panoramic visibility for the artillery spotter. We were there to surround and protect him.

We followed a steep and winding trail to reach the top of the hundred-foot tall mountain. When we reached the summit, I felt déjà vu over the similarity to our assignment of the previous night. We were exposed on all sides to higher mountains that surrounded the valley. While the location would provide excellent visibility to the lieutenant, it would also give our enemies a clear view of our position.

No orders were needed. Every man could see the precarious position we were placed in. We spread out around the crest of the mountaintop and began the harried task of digging, anxious to limit our visibility to the surrounding mountains as much as possible. The dirt was thankfully soft, so we were able to dig deeply with little effort.

By early afternoon our initial burrowing efforts were enough to provide protection from attack. We still had plenty of daylight left to dig deeper and wider and decided it would be a good time to break for lunch. I had received some cans of Campbell's soup in a care package from home, so I rewarded myself with a can of vegetable beef. I opened the can with my P-38 can opener and heated the soup in the can with a heat tab.

The thumping sound of rocket propelled grenades being launched from the mountains surrounding us interrupted our lunch plans and sent us diving into our fox holes for cover. I had not noticed until now that the lieutenant had chosen the highest and most visible spot on the mountain to erect a tent, about fifteen feet above my fox hole. He and his RTO sought shelter in the tent when everyone was yelling to take cover. They took a direct hit from the first RPG that found its mark and exploded, killing them both instantly.

More rounds came at us from the surrounding hills. Each launch of an RPG made a thumping sound that gave us an idea where they were coming from, so we were able to estimate fire mission coordinates. I ordered an artillery fire mission with the request to fire at will. Since we could not pinpoint Charlie's locations, it made no sense to try to zero in with smoke rounds. The artillery shells sizzled and hissed over our heads as they bombarded the mountains around us. We could see and hear explosions but had no way of knowing if we were successful.

We were sitting ducks on top of the bald hill. The ferocity and power of our artillery attack should have quieted the enemy assault. Each time our attack calmed, we would hear a thump launching another RPG in our direction.

My RTO had ordered a medevac as soon as he realized the two men in the tent were down. It swooped up the more protected eastern side of the mountain and abruptly landed on the hilltop. The guys from second platoon raced to retrieve the bodies of the two dead soldiers and load them aboard the helicopter so it could quickly disappear back down the way it came.

"We've been ordered to abandon our positions and move down to the camp," my RTO reported, relief and excitement in his voice. Our commanders thankfully recognized the senseless peril of leaving us exposed on the hilltop.

Chapter 19

Montagnard is a French term meaning "people from the mountains." The South Vietnamese referred to them as "moi" or savages. The Montagnard natives were pushed from the fertile lowlands into the mountains as the migrants, mostly from China, took control and became the people known today as Vietnamese. The dark skinned mountain people resembled tribes of our American Indians. Their plight with loss of land and rights mirrored our Indians. They did not like the Vietnamese but were amiable to a relationship with the French.

Montagnard soldiers were mercenaries. The French recruited their assistance against the Viet Minh and North Vietnamese back in the 1950's to provide a buffer between the borders of Laos and Cambodia and the central highlands of South Vietnam. They were brutal soldiers who were feared by their enemies.

The French made a tactical error and placed Vietnamese officers in charge of Montagnard Special Forces camps and the Montagnards rebelled, abandoning their camps. That error in judgment opened up enemy supply lines, leaving the French forces vulnerable to enemy build up and attack from the North Vietnamese.

Our commanders learned from the French mistakes and

sent only American Special Forces soldiers to establish relationships with and lead Montagnard villagers. The camps they formed became formidable defenses against invasion from the North Vietnamese and Viet Cong. We heard stories about the Montagnards sneaking into enemy encampments under the cover of darkness, cutting the throats of perimeter guards, then moving through the enemy perimeter and methodically killing sleeping soldiers.

The Hà Thanh camp was populated not just by the Montagnard mercenary soldiers but also by their families. The Special Forces camp was their village. They went about their lives routinely despite the ongoing enemy attacks and battles.

Our descent down the mountain led us onto the main trail through the village. A briskly flowing mountain stream ran alongside the trail. Dark skinned men and women were sitting in the stream bathing, the women vigorously scrubbing the backs of their men with rocks smoothed by the stream's ageless flow.

A woman smiled and waved as we passed by, her betel nut teeth dark red to the gums. Her body being exposed to our line of foreign men did not embarrass her, nor did I feel awkward in the presence of her nudity. It was too natural to be taken any other way.

Further into the village, there were subterranean bunkers along the edge of the trail. The roofs at ground level were heavily fortified with sand bags. The doorway to enter a bunker was just a hole at the edge and I observed that you would have to crawl to get inside.

I discovered how fast I could navigate a bunker entrance as mortar rounds slammed the valley from enemy positions on the hills east of the camp. It was like a bunch of college kids trying to see how many guys could fit into a phone booth as we scrambled to get the sand bag roof above our heads. I slid into the bunker feet first and landed in mud that covered my boots to the ankles. The guy behind me came in head first and landed belly down in the fetid smelling mush. We were lucky this time. Nobody was injured from the attack.

Grass huts on stilts were haphazardly scattered around the valley. They provided housing for the villagers and their families. One of the mortar rounds from our last attack exploded into the hut directly across from our bunker. The grass roof fell inward causing the entire structure to collapse from the blast. Fortunately the dwellers were down stream bathing. It was sad to see them sift through their destroyed, meager belongings when they returned. The woman who had waved to us was holding a cooking pot that she pulled from the debris, likely her most valued possession.

The Special Forces sergeant in charge of the camp came by to inform us that he would take the Montagnard force on patrol to try to root out the enemy mortar and RPG squads. He wanted us to man the bunker perimeter in the valley for the night, and call in artillery support if he requested it, or if we needed it. He said the mortar and RPG attacks eased off at night. Charlie couldn't see our positions after dark from the hills and mountains around us. The sergeant wanted his mercenary force to try to take the enemy by surprise since they had been shelling us all day.

"Don't get frisky with the village women," he warned. "Montagnard men will offer you their women if they like you, but they will come find you and slit your throat if you try to take what is not offered."

I wondered at the warning, knowing that the local women we had seen lacked any sexual attraction that I could imagine. The only ones we had come in contact with had drooping breasts and betel nut teeth. Maybe the Special Forces sergeant had been in country too long.

I ventured out of the bunker and grabbed my rucksack, which I had dropped when I jumped for cover. I opened my last can of Campbell's soup since I wasted one on top of the hill. This one was chicken noodle. I had not eaten since daybreak and the soup qualified for five-star all the way. This simple pleasure could compare to a night of fine dining on a satisfaction scale. Of course a twenty-year-old like me would consider hamburger steak and green beans cooked with bacon fine dining. Still hungry, I finished with a can of C-ration pears.

The sun was slowly settling behind the mountains to our west as a column of scruffy looking, dark skinned soldiers walked by us from another part of the camp further up the river valley to the east. The men were taller than the ARVN soldiers we were used to seeing. They looked lean and mean aside from the colorful necklaces and bracelets that adorned their long slim necks and thin wrists. They were well armed with M-16 rifles and belts of machine gun bullets draped across their shoulders. Aside from their American supplied armament, they had machetes strapped to their sides and some carried hand crafted bows and arrows they would use to unleash silent attacks on unsuspecting enemies. They were a fearsome looking troop whom I would not want to meet up with at night.

These were mercenary fighters who we paid to choose our side of the conflict. Without their loyalty, our access to the enemy supply lines from the western borders of Laos and Cambodia would be untended. The Ho Chi Minh Trail that already bled a constant flow of ammunition, troops and supplies directly into our precariously held provinces, would become an overwhelming flood from the north. That explained the continuing enemy attacks on the compound and the determined effort from the North Vietnamese to dislodge the Montagnards from their favor with the Americans and South Vietnamese.

Having the opportunity to observe these proud fighters, the people whose ancestors truly belonged here, humbled me and added a sense of pride and purpose for our being in their country.

The rumble of B-52 bomber strikes hammering the mountains throughout the night eliminated any possibility of sleep. The attacks kept Charlie in hiding and that prevented him from his usual mortar and RPG assaults on the camp we guarded.

The mercenary patrol returned with the sun. They looked just as calm and self-assured as they appeared when they paraded past us the evening before. I overheard the Special Forces sergeant call in the results of his night raids; five enemy dead and two mortars captured. I was also relieved to hear him report to the battalion commander that he didn't think he would need our support any longer, thanks to the perceived success of the massive bombing missions.

Chapter 20

It felt good to be getting back to Liz after the difficult Hà Thanh mission. Quang greeted me as soon as I walked up the hill from the helicopter landing zone down below. I was happy to see he was still here and being accepted. I was immediately concerned to learn that Liz had been under enemy mortar attacks while we were away.

The cooks looked after him as they promised and made sure he was in their bunker at critical times. I could tell he was still a frightened and bewildered little boy who looked to strangers for safety and food.

I started to question my efforts to keep him on Liz with us. I was not sure whether we were protecting him or exposing him to more danger than if he were in a village somewhere. But, it felt good to walk down to the bunker with him and feel his boots against mine as we slept foot-to-foot on the wooden bunk.

It looked like it was going to be another fitful night trying to sleep, constantly interrupted by commotion on top of Liz. The mortar platoon launched airborne illumination flares every half hour or so from their 81 millimeter mortar tubes. Launching the flares made the same thumping sound as mortar rounds being fired. Instead of hearing an explosion, the flare would make a popping sound when it illuminated and its parachute would open to dangle the light from the night sky.

It was an imperfect light as the parachute swayed from side to side, eerily causing shadows to move about among the concertina wire on the hill below. The flares would not be shining unless someone had called in a mission to the mortar platoon, which meant they believed the Viet Cong were making an attempt to assault our perimeter.

Depending on weather conditions, the flares would provide light for only a few minutes before they burned out or descended to earth. The darkness that followed would be intense, like the effect you get when you look at a light bulb then turn it off, leaving you with night blindness until the next flare popped on. I almost preferred not using the flares. I felt more vulnerable with my vision affected after them. When you're staring into the darkness for hours, the flares provided a welcomed relief.

"Gooks in the wire!" someone yelled from several bunkers away, followed by automatic M-60 machine gun fire down the mountain to the west, every fifth bullet leaving a red light trail marking its phosphorescent path. I could hear the radio chatter as the company commander sent out a red alert for all platoons to be at the ready.

We had heard about fire bases north of us being overrun amid rumors that Americans were taken prisoner. We lived in fear that the enemy would mount an assault on Liz and guessed that such an assault would come from the mountains and the Cambodian border to the west.

Intermittent small arms fire continued through the night from Liz's western exposure. Now and then the squad in the bunker on top of the hill, our northern outpost, would fire off a few rounds, we guessed to make Charlie feel threatened in case he wanted to attempt an attack. It reminded me of our night under attack on the mountain above Hà Thanh. I knew how lonely those guys would be feeling on this dark and active night.

My RTO brought me the field radio. The company commander wanted me to do a perimeter check. I set out, rifle at the ready, and ran to the bunker on the rim of the hill to the east. I called out to second squad to let them know I was coming and found everyone to be wide-eyed, alert and at the ready. On a night like tonight, it did not take a lot of commanding to keep everybody on their toes.

Just as I started out of the second squad doorway to make a run to the next bunker, mortar rounds exploded uphill from us between the mess hall and command and control bunkers. I dove for cover, glad to be in the company of second squad, all of us watchful to see if enemy soldiers were coming up the hill. The mortar platoon fired illumination flares in close succession now, each new flare sent aloft before the last had a chance to burn out.

Our mortar guys were methodically pumping 81mm rounds down the mountainside. They walked the fire from side to side along the western side of Liz, where someone spotted the enemy and sounded the alarm. The machine gunners in the west side bunkers strafed the valley outside the concertina wire, keeping up a barrage of covering fire, intent on keeping Charlie from breaching our perimeter.

Brigade responded to the company commander's request for air support by calling in "Puff The Magic Dragon," a C-130 fixed wing airplane equipped with major armament. We were awed by the amazing light show of fire power as Puff let loose its payload on the valley below. I had heard about this super weapon from the sky, but had not seen it in action. It supposedly landed a bullet every square inch and covered an area the size of a football field in about a minute.

Puff completed its fire mission, blanketing the valley around Liz in minutes, and departed to the north heading back to its base at Chu Lai. A delightful silence that would last through the rest of the night brought peace to our once threatened camp.

I rejoined my squad, and Quang, in our bunker. I slept an uninterrupted sleep for the first time since before we left Liz for Hà Thanh, secure in the knowledge that if Charlie was still out there, he was probably dead meat.

I awoke before sunup with an overwhelming feeling of dread. For reasons I could not conjure, I knew today was going to be a bad day. Worse yet, I was convinced something was going to happen to me. I pictured myself tripping a booby trap, walking into an ambush or being hit by a sniper.

As I might have suspected, after all of the activity during the night, patrols were being dispatched in all directions to seek out the enemy in the valley surrounding

Liz. Regardless of my disconcerting expectations, I was oddly calm facing the possibility that something dreadful would happen if I led a patrol today.

We started out through a gap in the concertina wire on the west side of Liz. Our patrol would take us south and west of Liz through an unpopulated jungle area thick with elephant grass and heavy undergrowth. We followed a narrow footpath for a few hundred meters until it opened onto a wide expanse of dry rice paddies, evenly bordered by dikes that served as pathways, well worn by foot traffic. I decided to separate myself from the rest of the platoon and walk right flank, meaning I would walk twenty or so meters to the right side of the rest of the column. That way, I reasoned, if something was going to happen to me, it would not jeopardize the soldiers around me.

This area was considered to be a free fire zone. Nobody was supposed to be in this vicinity for any reason especially after last night's activities. It was believed to be Viet Cong occupied and controlled.

By early afternoon I was starting to feel foolish about my death and destruction premonition. I had told Lenny about it and the word spread through the platoon about why I was walking flank, a maneuver not generally allowed by commanders of their sergeants. At the same time, I knew other guys had experienced these feelings of fateful expectation that on occasion proved out. This was one of those times you did not want to be right.

The midday heat was taking its toll on the platoon. We

took extra time for our lunch break since we had no specific mission or destination to reach by a certain time, except that we were expected back on Liz by dusk. The guys were sort of lethargic after the extended lunch reprieve. The enemy seemed to hit us most often when we were not paying good enough attention, so I was extra watchful as the platoon entered a dry and unfarmed rice paddy. I walked along higher ground that ran beside a hedge row parallel to the paddy. Experience proved to us that hedge rows were not our friends. Too often the enemy set their ambushes using the hedges for cover and concealment.

I thought I saw movement around a haystack about one hundred meters ahead. The hay was piled ten feet high. It sat on a rise beyond a dike that was at the end of the paddy we occupied. I flipped off the safety on my M-16 and sighted down the barrel now feeling sure I had seen somebody moving around.

In a blur of motion, two people appeared from behind the hay and ran to the right down the path on top of the dike. They had spotted us and were fleeing, presumably not friendly villagers. The runner furthest to the right was much faster, so I took aim in his direction wanting to cut off their escape. I squeezed off two rounds intending for them to get scared and surrender. I misjudged my lead and the second bullet dropped the black pajama clad second runner like a duck in a shooting gallery.

My shooting prompted the platoon to unleash a barrage of automatic weapons fire in the general direction I was firing. The second runner escaped into overgrowth of elephant grass to the right and was out of sight before I could zero in on his fleeing silhouette.

The runner I dropped lay squirming in the dust on the paddy dike path. Our point man reached him first and I heard him yell for the medic as he cautiously approached. Concerned that we might be ambushed, I continued to concentrate on spotting the one that got away until satisfied that he was no longer around.

Probably ten minutes passed before I caught up to the point man and medic who were kneeling down tending to the enemy soldier. I was devastated to find them caring for a boy not more than ten or twelve whose leg was severed above the knee. The boy was smiling and eating C-ration fruit cocktail with a white plastic spoon.

I was consumed with guilt upon the realization that I had crippled and possibly killed a child. It was even worse that he seemed happy to be in our care as he lay spooning the last drops of juice from the can, smiling and talking in a constant buzz of Vietnamese language none of us understood.

"He's in shock," the medic announced, his effort to explain the apparent good humored chatter. "I've got a medevac en route."

I was fixated by the view of this young boy happily eating while his severed leg lay beside him. The stump that remained was now bandaged to cover the raw ugliness of the wound. The severed leg still had the knee attached and it was bent as it would be in a casual sitting position.

"I'm sending the leg with him," the medic offered, seeing the pain in my expression. "Maybe they can do something with it."

The walk back to Liz after the medevac departed was somber. None of us wanted to witness this brutality on a kid. I guessed my premonition was real after all. Something terrible did happen to me. Although I was not physically wounded, I knew I would suffer guilt from this event for the rest of my life. It would be hard to face Quang when we arrived back on Liz.

As soon as we were inside the wire after the long walk back to Liz, I went to see the company commander. I had been thinking about it for some time, and decided today was the right time for me to submit an application to adopt Quang and take him home to America when my time was up.

Chapter 21

The company commander seemed more stressed than usual when he directed the platoon and squad leaders to his command bunker after dinner. He ordered us to report to the base of Liz at our usual landing zone to depart Liz on a combat assault the next morning at 0500. We would meet up for a search and destroy mission with other companies of the battalion east of Quảng Ngãi. He told us the area was known to be enemy infested. We would be hooking up with a platoon of armored personnel carriers who would lead our sweep into a place called Pinkville.

The name Pinkville was familiar to me. I had heard rumors about units of another battalion in our brigade getting cut to pieces back in the spring at the height of TET. They had walked into a mine field and lost most of a platoon before they could figure how to get out.

I unbuttoned the right leg pocket of my fatigue pants and retrieved my area-of-operations (AO) map. I had learned to keep it handy in that pocket wrapped in a waterproof, self-sealing plastic bag. I spread it out on the ground and studied the map trying to find a village called Pinkville. There didn't seem to be an area by that name on my map.

Lenny was sitting next to me so I asked him about it.

He took on sort of a blank look as he gazed at my map, then stood up and went over to ask the company commander for help. I watched as he waved his hand over an area on the edge of the map, so I went over to listen in. He explained that there was no place named Pinkville. He pointed to a cluster of villages with the same names repeated again and again, Mỹ Lai and Mỹ Khê. They were followed by a numeric designation in parentheses like Mỹ Lai (1). There were six areas named Mỹ Lai and four named Mỹ Khê. The villages covered an area that started at the edge of the Sông Kinh River that ran beside the South China Sea and continued inland about three clicks. Along the river next to Mỹ Lai (1) was an area shaded in a rose color that extended a thousand meters south to north and five hundred meters east to west.

"That pink on our military maps designates an area of dense population," the CO explained. "This particular one is known to be a Viet Cong stronghold and has a reputation as a booby trap haven. It got nicknamed Pinkville by troops who got in trouble there."

The mood among the guys on Liz was somber. We had observed the body language of our commanders long enough to recognize when a mission smelled bad, and this one had a definite stink to it. Everyone moved with a sense of urgency, wanting to be as prepared as possible for a hazardous mission to an area that was new to us.

I was one of the seasoned soldiers now, having survived repeated enemy encounters. I was strong and could handle my fully loaded ruck sack with ease whether humping up a mountainside or wading through waist high rice paddy water. I had learned what necessities to carry, so I always had room for more ammunition, hand grenades and rocket launchers.

We did not know how long this mission would last. Although the monsoon season had officially ended at the end of September, we were still getting periods of rain so I packed my poncho and liner. The poncho could be used as a pup tent when tied together with another one from a comrade. We could dig a two man fox hole and erect the tent over the top.

The poncho liner was made of a polyester fabric, light weight with material that mosquitos could not bite through. It was the size of a single bed blanket and that is how I used it. When not on guard duty, I would tuck the poncho liner in carefully so my entire body was covered and I would pull it up over my face to hide from the malaria spreading insects. Even with the poncho liner, it was necessary to spread pungent smelling liquid mosquito repellent over exposed areas like face and hands.

Back in the spring we went out on a full-pack mission. I carried my plastic bottle of mosquito repellant in the waist side pocket of my fatigue shirt. As we walked along, the shirt slipped around so the pockets were in front and back with the button-up opening turned to my side. When we stopped for a break, I unloaded my ruck sack and adjusted my shirt. I unbuttoned my fatigue pants to take a leak and noticed a gooey wetness in my crotch.

The second I exposed my peetong to the air, it felt like someone had doused me with gasoline and set me on fire. On closer inspection, I saw that my right shirt pocket was soaked. The lid on the mosquito repellant bottle had come unscrewed from the motion while walking, and the liquid poured onto my personals, soaking my pants in the process.

I removed my boots and stripped off my pants. The added exposure to the air intensified the burn. I took a canteen of water from my ammunition belt and doused myself with it to no avail.

I called to the platoon medic for help. He simply handed me another canteen of water and told me to keep pouring. I went through four or five canteens before the burn began to ease enough for me to get dressed. I was in pain, but could not continue to delay our mission.

Three days after the mission ended and we returned to Liz, I was able to shower with soap for the first time since the incident. As I soaped up, I saw that all of my brightly reddened skin was peeling from my penis, testicles and the insides of my thighs.

Weeks later my crotch was still red and healing, so with that reminder I discovered a new place to carry my bug juice. I had noticed other guys secured the bottles in the bands that held the camouflage helmet covers on their helmets. I found that trick worked well. I was able to secure a bottle on each side of the helmet.

Our supplies for the upcoming mission were stacked up by the mess tent on top of the hill on Liz. I walked up and sorted through the cases of C-rations, sundries packs and cases of soda and beer. I found a case of LRRP rations and picked out packages of beef and rice and spaghetti with meat sauce. They were my favorites so I took enough for nine meals, three per day for three days. I turned to the C-rations and selected a few cans of cheese and crackers, peaches, pears and fruit cocktail. I went to the sundries packs and scored a few packs of Marlboro cigarettes, a couple of chocolate bars and a new toothbrush. Some of the guys routinely shared their tooth brushes. I wouldn't even do that with the girls I dated.

I had started smoking again when the mosquitoes got real bad at the beginning of the rainy season. The smoke helped drive them away. The more important use for cigarettes, though, was to help remove leeches. The slimy little buggers would insert their tiny heads into pores of your skin while they were no larger than a piece of thread.

We rolled up the bottoms of our pant legs using elastic bands wrapped around the tops of our boots. It helped but did not keep the leeches out. The leeches were so small they could crawl through the eyelets in our boots to get to our skin. Once they attached themselves to you, they would bloat up with your blood until they were the size of your thumb. If you scraped them off while their heads were still in you, the head would break off, get infected and leave a permanent scar. Touching them with a lit cigarette would cause them to pull their heads out so you could flip them off.

Mosquito repellant was equally effective to remove

leeches without scarring. You could douse a little on them and they would immediately remove their heads. After my episode learning how toxic the liquid was to my skin, I preferred to limit its use to my hands and face.

Last, I negotiated with the other guys to trade my ration of Cokes for their beers. I had developed a taste for warm beer as compared to iodine laced water, cool aid or hot Coke. By carrying the light weight LRRP rations, I learned I could tote as much as a case of beer in my pack. When Duke was with us, we often shared our stashes of beer. He had developed a much higher capacity for alcohol during his army career than I could ever match, or so I hoped.

Next I went over to the black, rubber fresh water blimp, rinsed out and refilled my canteen. The iodine laced water got stale real fast in 110 degree heat.

I picked up a new cleaning kit for my rifle. I verified that I still had four hand grenades and ten twenty-round clips of M-16 ammo, plus the one already locked and loaded in my weapon. I picked up one red and one green smoke grenade and a LAW rocket launcher that I strapped under the bottom of my ruck sack below the rolled up poncho and liner. Since my horrible experience finding myself unarmed when Franny needed me, I was determined to overburden myself with armament.

Now that my ruck sack and ammo belt were fully loaded with necessities, I found room in a side pocket for a few more boxes of M-16 rounds and a clean pair of socks. I went into the bunker and found the five boxes of

M-16 tracer rounds that I kept tucked away. I had learned to load red tipped phosphorous tracer rounds every third round. I could then gauge windage and elevation using the point and fire method instead of trying to use the aiming sight on the breach of my rifle. The tracer round left a red trail that would tell me how to adjust my aim to hit my target. I removed the tracers when we were on Liz or back at brigade headquarters on Bronco. The way I was using them wasn't really approved.

Quang joined me as I took the boxes of tracer rounds and my ammo pouch and climbed up on top of our bunker. I opened a warm beer and gave Quang a can of Coke. I removed my survival knife from its sheath and showed Quang how to work it back to front over my whet stone. I took pride in keeping the blade clean and sharp since I used it for everything from cutting up my meals to chopping firewood.

On occasion Duke had borrowed it to kill and cut up a chicken to cook a stew for the platoon to share. He would disappear into a village and return a short time later with a chicken, some bamboo strands from which he would extract bamboo shoots for flavoring, and wild grown hot peppers. Those peppers made Duke's stew so hot you broke into a sweat as soon as you ate it. Honing that knife was my favorite distraction from everything Vietnam. My mom gave me the knife as a going away gift when I shipped out, so it was special to me.

I took the ten M-16 clips from my ammo pouches and removed the one from my rifle and ejected all two hundred rounds. I then got Quang to help as we reloaded all ten metal jackets, adding a tracer every third round. I liked the confidence it gave me to know I could zero in on the enemy and had proven to myself that I could be effective bringing down my targets using the tracer rounds. I had been warned, though, that the enemy would find it easier to see where I was shooting from when I used this ammo.

I spotted Lenny coming down the hill with his towel around his neck. He waved hello and climbed up on the bunker part way.

"You should go up to the latrine and catch a warm shower," he said. "The mess sergeant has his crew heating up water for showers for us."

I went below and grabbed my towel and a small bar of soap I had been saving and headed up the hill. The mess squad was heating five gallon buckets of water over a fire made from broken up ammo boxes for firewood. A fifty-gallon barrel was suspended from what looked like a hangman's gallows with a ladder running up the side.

I stripped off my fatigues and stepped under the craftily designed shower while one of the guys from the mess hall crew climbed up the ladder and poured the heated water into the barrel. Holes were punched in the bottom of the barrel so the water trickled through, shower style. It was a rustic accommodation, yet luxurious compared to the baths we took in rivers and streams in the boonies.

I heard someone announce there would be a movie up by artillery at dark. They were showing *Bat Man.* I hurried back to the bunker and asked Quang if he would like to see another movie with me. I guessed this would be more of a movie for kids than the one I took him to see the first time.

It was pretty cheesy but Quang loved it. After the day I had, it was a welcome distraction. I was happy to spend some uninterrupted, pure enjoyment time with Quang. His favorite character was the "Penguin." He quickly learned to mimic the squawking noises he made. I was feeling excited about my decision to adopt Quang, if they would let me.

Chapter 22

My last watch ended at four o'clock, so I went to the mess for breakfast. Since it was still dark out, we ate in silence with the green canvas that served as shades covering the sides of the mess tent. After visiting the latrine, we saddled up and walked down the winding dirt road to the base of Liz. We assumed our usual positions around the landing zone, lined up and ready to board the Huey helicopters when they descended upon us from the south.

I was comfortable in my knowledge of what to do on combat assaults, but I could not get happy with the windstorm of dust and debris the flapping helicopter blades whipped around us. It coated my face, hands, clothing and rifle with red dust. The dirt always managed to get under my shirt so the straps of my ruck sack irritated my skin until I could unload and shake everything out, which was often halfway through the day.

I was in my usual spot on takeoff next to the left side open door with my boot resting on the runner. The door gunner seated behind me on his perch nodded hello and snapped a new belt of M-60 ammo into the breach of his machine gun. I checked to make sure the first round in my clip had a red tip and locked and loaded it into the chamber of my M-16.

We took off into the wind heading west then abruptly banked to the northeast. The nose low takeoff attitude felt like a carnival ride. Once we achieved climbing speed, the column of Huey's ascended steadily to cruise at about three thousand feet, I guessed. In less than five minutes we were passing directly over Quảng Ngãi city. I could see firebase Dragon off to the west and the rice paddies and hedge rows back towards Liz, where the sniper had landed a lucky round in our fuselage and nearly crashed us on our mission to Hà Thanh.

I could see the majestic mountain ranges that bordered Laos off to the west, only fifty miles beyond LZ Dragon. I was starting to question the purpose of our committing such a massive effort into a fight over so little real estate. This narrow neck of Vietnam land stretched only about eighty miles from the South China Sea to Laos. Flying at this altitude I could see half of the entire width of the country. It was hard to comprehend why we had a half a million soldiers fighting down there in the villages, rice paddies, jungles and rubber tree plantations with about fifty of us dying every day. I knew there was a good chance some of our guys on today's mission would be going home in body bags, or without arms or legs.

The white sandy beaches along the South China Sea were very close now off to the right side of the helicopter. I could see that we were descending into an area only a few clicks north of ambush alley. The memory of how ferocious those VC soldiers were that day filled me with a feeling of dread over what Charlie might have in store for us down there.

The pilot assumed a nose down attitude and we began a rapid descent as the door gunner behind me opened fire, strafing the villages and hedge rows as we passed over. Cobra attack helicopters buzzed by us firing their rockets and thirty caliber machine guns to prepare our landing zone. Red smoke followed the westerly breeze and covered the ground with an eerily pink film, an appropriate prelude to our landing in a place called Pinkville, I thought. I knew the red smoke meant we were going into a hot LZ. Somebody up ahead of us was receiving enemy fire.

As we approached the red smoke that marked our landing zone, I spotted five armored personnel carriers below us. They were lined up side to side facing into a wooded area outside of a cluster of several villages to the north. Machine gunners sat atop each of the APC's firing on full automatic into the dense forest.

Our helicopter landed fifty meters south of the line of our armored support. My RTO brought me the radio as soon as our helicopter took off so I could listen in on the instructions we were getting from the company commander.

"Line your squads up behind the APC's and make sure your troops walk only in their tracks," he ordered. "We suspect this area is heavily mined."

The APC's made tracks like those left by bulldozers. I watched as our squads carefully fell in line behind the armored protection, every man cautiously stepping only within the rutted paths the tracks created.

Less than a hundred meters into the mission we heard a loud explosion. The lead track hit a mine. Its running gear was destroyed leaving the APC helplessly disabled. We could see that some of the crew members were wounded as the squad that had been following along moved forward to help get them out of harm's way. I could hear calls for a medic and the radio was alive with calls for a medevac.

We anxiously awaited orders as all forward movement stopped. The remaining four track commanders were asking for permission to pull back and regroup to try to figure out what to do with the disabled equipment.

When the order came to pull back we reversed our direction and carefully followed the tracks out the way we came in. We studied the map and saw that west and north of the villages marked on the map in pink were areas of dense underbrush. We cleared the wood line and turned west towards Quảng Ngãi, electing to forge our way through the thick foliage where it was unlikely Charlie would have planted mines. As soon as we got underway, the order came down to stop and set up a perimeter to help protect the disabled APC until they could decide whether it could be salvaged or would have to be destroyed.

I was relieved to hear news that the Pinkville operation would be abandoned. Somebody made the decision to destroy the severely damaged APC and we were on our way south by midday.

As we entered the next village to the south of Mỹ Lai, I

spotted a young woman suspiciously raking sand around. We moved in and stopped her, then required her to rake the sand back from the spot she was covering. She was screaming the whole time and crying "em bé, em bé" which I recognized was Vietnamese for baby. When she refused to continue raking, I kneeled down and carefully wiped more sand away. I uncovered a wooden door seated in the sand. It had a hole in the center so I stuck my finger in and yanked. An explosion sent me reeling backwards when the wooden trap door slammed into my chest. The impact knocked the breath out of me and the blast left my ears ringing. Once the shock wore off I inspected myself closely and found that I was otherwise uninjured.

I was fortunate. The people in the hole were blown away by the hand grenade they had wired to the trap door.

Lenny and his squad searched the cave-like hole in the ground and found two dead VC. Upon further inspection, they also found a dead baby underneath them. The young woman's infant child was in the hole with the two Viet Cong soldiers. I believed that they had taken her baby into the hole against her will and required her to help them. Why else would she agree for her infant to be taken from her to help these men?

Nonetheless, I was required to restrain her and bring her in for questioning. So, we tied her hands behind her and led her, weeping, toward the beach where we would establish our night perimeter.

It was hard not to notice her beauty. She appeared to

be part French, her eyes were rounder than normal and her hair was a tint browner than typical of the black silky locks of Vietnamese women. Her sadness at the loss of her infant child rocked me. I was heartbroken to see the progression of events surrounding her unfold.

We were just a few hundred meters from the South China Sea, so the walk to our intended night bivouac was thankfully brief. I led the prisoner to a tree and signaled for her to sit with her back against it. She promptly defecated and wiped her feces all over her silk pants and blouse. I presumed that she had seen propaganda advising her to do that to make her appear ugly to her captors.

Before I could decide what to do with her, now that she was a mess, the company commander ordered me to take my squad out and set up an ambush. As we saddled up and moved out, I looked back to see that guys from the CQ had taken the young woman out into the surf of the South China Sea and were bathing her, naked. I could see that she was trying to cover her breasts with her arms.

"Hey lady," I heard someone yell. "If you're going to drown those puppies, can I get the one with the brown nose?"

A chorus of laughter followed, and that seemed to make the project of bathing her less menacing. But, I still felt nervous about leaving her in such a vulnerable state.

When we returned early the next morning from an uneventful ambush effort, I went to check on the prisoner. She was on her knees and bound next to the company commander's tent. She was crying and in obvious pain.

She was pleading with me. I could not understand her words. It seemed unreasonable for her to be bound like she was so I cut her restraints. She immediately grasped her breasts and began squeezing them to relieve the built up milk from them. It appeared to me that she had been raped, but I could not prove it and nobody seemed to know anything, or would not admit it if they did. I reasoned that if there was a story to be told about how she was treated in my absence, it would come to light when she was interrogated back at brigade.

When the resupply chopper came in, the guys from the CQ bound her hands again and loaded her onto the Huey. I watched as the helicopter took off low and headed east toward the sea. It began a steep climb once out over the safety of the water. The pilot banked sharply to the right to go south to Bronco. To my dismay, I saw the lovely young prisoner dive from the open side door, her long hair streaming behind her, as she floated downward and disappeared into the water.

I felt dirty. I was responsible for the horrible events she endured at the hands of our soldiers, for the loss of her child and for her ultimate death. I should have handled things differently. I should have refused the ambush assignment until I had my prisoner dealt with in a reasonable manner. To have done so would have meant I was insubordinate and refusing orders while on a combat assignment.

I wanted to bring somebody to justice for her treatment. What could I prove? I had not personally seen anything and could not find anyone else willing to make a statement. Now that she was dead and there was no body, nothing could be done. I knew that these evil actions of others would rest heavy on my conscience for the rest of my life.

Chapter 23

The rice paddies remained flooded after the end of monsoon season. They were surrounded by dams that were formed by dikes. The dikes served as pedestrian trails winding among the submerged rice fields and in and out of elevated plots of land that formed farm villages. These trails provided the sole access to villages without submitting to a dreaded wade through waist high and putrid smelling paddy water.

The fleet of helicopters coming from the south looked like a gaggle of Canadian Geese as their "V" formation approached, the whack-whack-whack of their rotors reviving the lust in us to go find Charlie. The limited high ground surrounded by water forced us to mark the elevated roadway with green smoke for our air transports to use as a landing pad. We had to duck down as the helicopters swooped down to land nearly on top of us.

Instead of the usual covering of dust and grime we took when the rotor blades sucked up the earth's debris during hot and dry conditions, our faces and hands were exfoliated by the blistering spray drawn from the adjacent paddies. My briefly clean fatigues, ruck sack and rifle stock were instantly coated with nasty, slick water.

As always, I positioned myself on the floor in front of

the left side door gunner, my left boot familiarly posted on the runner blade. We took off towards the northeast rapidly gaining altitude until the flight formation turned west over the north end of the twin peaks that formed Liz. We headed due west until we were ten miles or so from the Laotian border when the Cobra attack helicopters suddenly zoomed by us and began to assault the jungle and villages to our front, their forty millimeter cannons and rocket propelled grenades riveting the countryside.

I could see that ahead, among the dust and smoke created by the onslaught, green smoke signaled our landing destination, a welcomed sight that said no enemy contact so far. Our pilot landed us in a clearing surrounded by elephant grass on three sides and the rising slope of a mountain to our western front. I dismounted using the runner to step down from my perch and managed to land on my feet, happy that my heavy pack did not shift or cause me to lose my balance.

Chester Wong took point as first squad assumed the usual duty of being first in line. I was second followed closely by the radio operator. We followed a trail to the southwest that ran along the base of the mountain.

Chester was a much appreciated, cautious and timid leader of our column for our mission from the safety of our base camp. Chester's six-foot-two and two hundred pound physic gave him a formidable appearance. In reality, he was a gentle soul with a teddy bear personality. He was from Quebec, Canada and of French and Chinese descent. His Chinese heritage was revealed by the slight upward turn at the corners of his eyes and the pleasant olive cast to his skin. Chester's stride was smooth and easy, his long legs and size thirteen boots making his movements deceptively faster than they appeared.

Chester was always in the periphery of whatever action we encountered. He was not a coward and did not run or shy away from his duties. He seemed to have an instinct for when to seek the least visible position in our columns and even in selecting night perimeter positions. He never seemed to be the guy who got caught face to face with Charlie or to be pinned down in an ambush.

He had attended college and was clearly more intelligent than most of us. He was first to suggest medals for what he considered to be meritorious or heroic actions. It was Chester who wrote up the recommendations for Zack Rivers and me that scored our Army Commendation medals.

Two clicks down the narrow trail that wound along the base of the mountain with thick brush and elephant grass along the sides, we came upon a large clearing that opened into a cultivated field. An acre of well-tended vegetation and corn covered the expanse of land to our front. Beyond the garden was an elevated row of thatched houses embedded against a tall hill, their back walls appearing to be a dug out part of the hill.

When Chester's big frame stepped into the clearing, a child's voice rang out "Yo, baby san chop-chop." The Viet Cong alarm system had sounded.

Three barefooted, black-pajama clad men darted

toward the left side of the village in a terror stricken retreat. I fired off an automatic burst from my M-16, but they were gone so fast I could not tell if I hit anyone. Following my lead, our guys unleashed a barrage of fire onto the hillside, kicking up pieces of thatched roof and ravaging the peaceful looking village with overwhelming firepower.

When I recognized that we were not getting return fire, I shouted for everyone to cease firing. Chester led as we spread out and moved into position and assaulted the VC village. Growing close, we could see that the grass and mud houses appeared to be brand new, the packed mud was still damp and the grass siding was still green, so it was easy to presume that it was set up by transients, in other words, Viet Cong.

We found only women and children huddled in the courtyard surrounding an old man, wounded and lying on the ground. An M-79 grenade had hit him and severed his lower body below the pelvis. Amazingly, regardless of the intense fire that we unleashed, nobody else was wounded.

Our medic attended to the old man but let me know there was nothing he could do. He lit a filtered cigarette and offered it to him. He took it and dragged, smiling his appreciation for the friendly gesture. It was pitiful to watch as the bearded old guy looked at us and chattered away in Vietnamese for five minutes before he finally died.

We searched the village. We found no sign of the men

or their weapons. We were sure the women were protecting their Viet Cong husbands, brothers and sons. We could not get them to admit anything. Typical of our usual frustration, we would leave this village knowing that our enemies got away, once again.

Since we had revealed our location by setting off the attack, it was important for us to move on to our assigned destination to establish our positions in the safety of the company perimeter. It was disheartening to know that a pitiful old fellow had paid with his life for the young men he tried to protect.

Our mission changed and we were directed to follow a trail to the north along a valley between two grass covered mountains. We were ordered to ascend the mountain to the west and establish a night perimeter. It was an easy climb through hay field grasses that waved side to side in a welcomed breeze.

When we reached the crest of the rounded hilltop, we began the process of digging in and setting out trip flares and claymore mines. The wind on top of the mountain intensified as the afternoon wore on. It reminded me of the way pressure would build before a summer storm back home, the way the air would get heavy with moisture before the sky would unleash explosions of thunder and streaks of lighting.

The storm and the rain did not come. In its place, we got a constant, whistling and westward wind. The tall grasses surrounding us bowed to and fro creating the illusion that the entire hilltop was moving.

Suddenly, we heard automatic weapons fire from the valley below and thought one of our platoons was under attack. We could hear the echo of our soldiers shouting and screaming. I thought at first that they must be getting overrun by the enemy.

"Somebody help us, we're being attacked by bees!" an RTO shouted in a panic into his microphone. "We need Medevac's now!"

I had witnessed the aggressive black bees in the past as they swarmed like a cloud overhead in the process of relocating their nests. We had learned to hit the ground and remain real still to avoid attracting their attention. It sounded like third platoon was not so lucky.

We listened to the terrified radio chatter until we saw four Huey's swoop into the valley, land and quickly take back off again. The entire platoon had to be evacuated. Some of the men were declared to be in serious condition from allergic reactions to the stings.

Once that excitement was over, we got back to the business of securing our night encampment. After that racket, if Charlie had not realized we were here before, he would certainly know our whereabouts now. I called in a request to end the mission and evacuate us along with the remaining platoons in the company. But, it was too late in the day and we would have to wait until morning.

In my experience, wind typically eased off as daylight faded into darkness. The gusts, instead, intensified to near gale force. A trip flare popped off to the west, then another and another until the entire hilltop was aglow. As the flares dropped sparks into the blowing hay, it caught fire and suddenly we were caught in the middle of a grass fire fueled by the high winds.

"Keep your rifles and ammo belts away from the fire," someone shouted. So we all gathered up our munitions and ran around trying to stomp out the rapidly spreading flames. The fire was moving too fast to gain much heat intensity, so we were able to run through lines of it as it burned across the mountain. Our boots were charred from our futile efforts to stomp out the flames. Fortunately nobody was injured other than minor burns on hands and arms.

Our pleasant mountain perch had become a charred and smoldering acre by the time the fire burned itself out. As I walked around to inspect what remained of our camp, I realized that we had claymore mines facing out around the perimeter with blasting caps and detonators still attached. So, I passed word for everyone to stay away from them until we could decide what to do.

I asked the squad leaders to gather on the hilltop. None of us were quite sure what affect the fire and heat would have had on the mines and their wiring, so we arrived at the consensus that it would be best to detonate them all rather than take chances of accidental explosions.

We found twelve detonators among the four squad positions. I counted explosions as they were detonated one at a time. There were only nine blasts.

We carefully searched and located the remaining three claymores. Their detonator wires were burned by the wildfire but all three were still nested where they were placed. That meant their firing pins remained. The claymores were definitely armed and dangerous.

I decided that if the blasting caps had not blown from all the heat and melted wires, it would probably be safe to carefully remove the pins. So, I asked everyone to move a safe distance away and carefully approached the first mine from the side. A claymore explodes outward to the front and also sends a strong blast backwards, so I guessed it would be best to keep to the sides.

I crawled to within reach of the mine and carefully removed the firing pin. No big deal, I thought. Still, I was just as cautious when I went to service the other two units. I breathed a terrific sigh of relief as I joined the guys back on top of the charred hill.

After I returned, Lenny made the wise decision to blow the fire damaged mines with hand grenades. We could not leave them behind for Charlie and could not take them with us.

Chapter 24

With all that had happened during this brief mission, the battalion commander rewarded us with a three-day stand down. It would give the guys in third platoon a chance to heal from their bee attack.

While we were gathered on top of the hill awaiting our Huey's, my RTO had heard the battalion Executive Officer tell our company commander to instruct me to report to brigade headquarters as soon as we landed. The brigade chaplain wanted to meet with me about my adoption request.

When I got back to Bronco, I reported to the brigade clerk's office. I was surprised to see that someone had brought Quang in from Liz. The chaplain was talking calmly with him as they sat in folding chairs. Quang looked like he thought he had done something wrong when his eyes met mine. He jumped up and hugged me, wordlessly.

"You must be Sergeant Christopher," the chaplain assumed. "Sorry to spring this meeting on you with no notice. I thought it would be the opportune time to pursue your adoption request since you were coming in for stand down anyway."

He went on to explain that he had assembled a board of

brigade officers who would consider my request and make a recommendation to division whether or not to approve the adoption. He said he believed division would go along with whatever the brigade panel recommended.

"You need to know, though," he explained, "that the Vietnamese government has final approval regardless what we decide."

With Quang sitting calmly beside me, I thought that the interview was going well. At one point, an interpreter aggressively questioned Quang and, to my surprise, he spat back with attitude. When I saw this, I scolded him and made it clear he was not to get smart with people who were trying to help him. Quang immediately backed down, sheepishly, and said he was sorry as I had instructed him to do.

The chaplain declared the interview ended and informed me that he would be in touch with any news. He said he would make sure Quang got back to Liz safely and I should join my company for the much deserved stand down. I was excited that they were taking my adoption request seriously.

This would be my first time on Bronco as an acting platoon leader. In the spring I was promoted to Specialist Four and given the job of acting squad leader. By summer I was promoted to Sergeant in pay grade level five and in August, when Duke was wounded and sent home, I was asked to become acting platoon sergeant. The normal pay grade for that job was level seven, Master Sergeant. Before the end of that week, I was asked to assume the duties of acting platoon leader, normally a First Lieutenant position. My pay grade, however, remained at level five.

I did not have the experience or self-confidence to try to negotiate for an actual promotion or higher pay. I was just willing to do whatever my superiors believed I could handle. I knew I was not really qualified or formally trained to merit the actual ranks of the positions I was filling, although I guessed there was something to be said for on-the-job-training and I certainly had a gut full of that.

I felt that most of the guys in first platoon believed in me enough to be comfortable with having me fill the acting roles. On the other hand, I was very aware that I had created a lot of resentment by showing I cared greatly for the Vietnamese people and that I had also stopped a lot of guys from doing things they shouldn't do. Everyone came to expect that I would jump in when I saw something inappropriate about to happen regardless of the impact it may have.

The more that I thought about it, I realized that I would face a lot of challenges. They did not like my relationships with Quang, Dam and her friends, and the nuns and workers at the orphanage in Đức Phổ. They also did not like that I went into the villages and shared meals with the farmers and their families. They often called me "Gook Lover."

I was hanging out at the Red Dog Saloon with Lenny and the guys in his squad. *Wooly Bully* was playing loudly on the reel-to-reel stereo that Felix King had acquired for the saloon. We were knocking back a few cold beers after enjoying another steak feast courtesy of the battalion commander. Beer, especially when it's icy cold, causes me to pee like a bandit. So I excused myself and headed for the latrine.

I was still positioned over the six-inch steel pipe in the ground that served as our urinal when the second platoon leader, a young lieutenant new to the company, bellied up to the piss tube next to me. I finished my mission and buttoned up my fatigue pants, then turned to walk back to join my friends.

"Hang on a second, I want to talk to you," the lieutenant summoned.

I waited for him to finish his business and we quickly walked away, wanting to get clear of the unpleasant odors from the latrine area.

"It's a good thing they pay the old men from the village to burn this crap," he laughed. "I would hate to be in charge of assigning troops to that duty."

"Yes sir," I agreed. "I think they take real pride in their work."

I had watched the old men performing their duties of pouring kerosene into the half barrels and lighting them. The putrid smelling black and billowing smoke could be seen all over Bronco from the various latrine locations. To the old villagers, it was regular employment that gave them status among their peers from Đức Phổ.

"I couldn't help but notice you were spending a lot of

time in the troop saloon," he continued. "Do you think that's a good idea while you are the platoon leader?"

"Those are my friends who I have been beside all along," I answered defensively. "Besides, I am just an acting officer, really only a buck sergeant."

"The other platoon leaders and I think you should move into the officers' barracks with us," he persisted. "You need to be involved in our discussions about strategy and our reviews of the daily company reports and plans. Let's go now and get your gear while the troops are busy celebrating their temporary freedom."

We moved my ruck sack and meager belongings to the officers' tent and the lieutenant found an empty cot towards the back for me. I felt awkward and a little out of place yet knew his points about being involved with the other platoon leaders made sense.

"I was just finishing up a letter to my wife before the beer sent me on a nature call," the lieutenant smiled. "I guess I'll get back to it since I like to write her as often as I can."

The rest of the tent was empty. I guessed the other officers were at the officers club or off somewhere else spending time with their peers. I resisted the urge to go back over to the Red Dog Saloon. Now I really did not know where I belonged so I just sat on my cot feeling surprisingly alone. I removed my rifle cleaning kit from the side pocket of my pack and began to take my M-16 apart. I spread the parts out on the cot in the order that I took them apart to make sure I put them back together correctly.

"What is that racket out there?" I heard the lieutenant ask from over by the entrance where his cot was located.

"I didn't hear anything, sir," I answered.

He was close to the barracks doorway and stood to peer out when I heard the ruckus get louder.

"Hey Gook Lover, Christopher, come on out here," someone shouted. I slowly tiptoed over to stand beside the officer who looked as perplexed as I felt at the events that were unfolding.

A group of six or eight guys had apparently gotten boozed up throughout the afternoon and got started bitching about my Vietnamese relationships. The complaining had escalated as the day became the night and I had become the focus of their ire at being stuck in Vietnam, seeing their friends killed by "gooks" and being the one who always stuck my nose in when they had a chance to take out their vengeance on someone. One of them had noticed when I moved into the officers' barracks and that made things worse.

I did not know what else to do so I stepped out of the barracks to face my accusers. I was surprised at the anger I saw and noticed several of the guys had their rifles pointed skyward threateningly. I was relieved to see that Lenny and my other close friends were not participants in this drunken mob.

The group started to move aggressively towards me and the shouting intensified to a fever pitch. I just stood, not knowing what to say or do, hoping they would calm down and come to their senses. They did not seem intent on stopping and appeared to have some sort of vigilante violence in mind. Thank goodness, they did not seem too well organized and were more intent on shouting and yelling than acting.

Fortunately for me, the three other platoon leaders appeared in a group from the direction of the battalion headquarters building. They walked up and surrounded me. The second platoon leader had gone to get the other two when I left the safety of the officers' barracks.

"How many of you have more kills and captures to their credit than Sergeant Christopher?" my lieutenant savior demanded. "Who among you has ever seen him fail to offer help when you needed it? What you are doing is wrong and you know it, so just go on back to your barracks and sleep it off before I have you all arrested," he finished.

The rowdy group began to disperse as they slinked away grumbling. I was beginning to appreciate the acceptance I was getting from my fellow platoon leaders even though I knew I was still only "acting".

The three officers went back to whatever they were doing before coming to my rescue. I went to my bunk at the far end of the tent and nervously resumed reassembling my rifle, needing to feel the comfort of having it for protection, although I knew circumstances would have to be extreme for me to use it against my fellow soldiers.

"I heard what happened," Lenny offered as he entered

the end of the tent nearest my cot. He had come looking for me and saw that I was alone.

"Yeah," I responded. "I guess they just needed to blow off some steam."

"But you didn't do anything to deserve that." I could see he was truly bothered by it.

"The thing is, Lenny, I understand," I reasoned. "I'm sitting here in an officer's tent where I don't belong, trying to fit into a command situation among officers who are trained to command and I don't even know what to say to defend myself when they come to confront me."

"I don't think any of us would handle it any better," Lenny consoled.

"What should I be doing differently?" I asked. "I only took the job because we didn't have any officers, same as when you and I accepted when they asked us to take over as squad leaders and then you as acting platoon sergeant. I know I am not trained to be an officer. Hell, I'm not even trained to be a sergeant."

"Look around," Lenny suggested. "Who else are they going to ask if they don't ask us? I have accepted that we are just here to do a job and do it the best we can, and I don't think anybody else would do any better or try any harder than you have. How many guys have you lost since you took over the platoon?"

Lenny's words of encouragement helped. He was right, we had not lost anyone in the platoon since he and I took on the leadership responsibilities we shared.

Lenny had proved to be a true comrade and friend.

Lenny did not talk a lot unless he had something worth saying. He attributed his quiet demeanor to growing up among his Inuit native Alaskan friends.

Lenny carried himself with the dignity that comes from being reared in a respectful and religious family. He was clean cut and paid close attention to his grooming. He always seemed to have clean fatigues and socks, kept his hair a proper military length and tried to avoid the nasty skin abrasions and rashes many of the guys experienced. There was one period, though, when he got chastised by the brigade medic for letting his feet get a severe case of jungle rot that came from continually wearing wet socks.

"How could you let your feet get in such bad shape?" the medic had pressed him.

"No dry socks for a month walking around in rice paddy water," he countered. "You should try it sometime."

Lenny and I enjoyed each other's company and could sit and talk for hours about life, death and all of the consequences. It was helpful to have him beside me this night when it seemed the world was crashing down around me.

We decided that our job to "fight communism" was a farce. Maybe these farmers would be better off in a communistic society where the rice could be distributed evenly and fewer people would be starving. Perhaps then they could get medical care out in the boonies. We had seen no evidence of any kind of care available to the rural villages which made up most of the population of

Vietnam.

We talked about what we would do when we got home. We both knew we would return to college and take advantage of the G.I. Bill as payback for our service. We daydreamed about someday opening up a real estate company together, even though neither of us knew the first thing about the business.

We agreed that living on the ground had given us a heightened appreciation for mother earth, and her brightly shining moon and stars on dark and frightening nights. We discussed the admiration and appreciation we had acquired for the plight of the farmer, who inherited his small plot of land that his ancestors had used since the 1400's, to grow enough rice to feed his family while enduring every hardship imaginable.

The VC requisitioned his rice, took the little money he had in midnight tax collections and made examples of anyone who did not cooperate or assist their cause. They recruited their young men and boys for soldiers. They forced their women to carry supplies in long death marches up and down the Ho Chi Minh trail that crisscrossed back and forth between Vietnam, Laos and Cambodia.

Their government tried to force them to move into compounds for their protection, leaving their ancestral land and source of survival behind while offering work at menial jobs to feed and clothe their families. The Americans marched their infantry, armored personnel carriers and tanks across the land destroying rice and other limited crops. From the air the Americans rained terror onto their villages and rice paddies with our bombs and artillery, forcing them to sleep under ground in dirt bunkers they constructed next to their thatched roof homes.

Lenny and I provided each other support and encouragement. I was glad he went to the trouble to seek me out tonight. I needed to know I still had a friend. We agreed that we would not allow the grumbling we heard from the drunken troops to sway our conviction to require the guys in our command to act honorably when we went back to the field.

The officers filed into the tent so Lenny beat a quick exit back to the Red Dog Saloon. I laid back on my cot trying to sort out the night's events. I knew I was walking on eggs trying to fill officer's shoes. I questioned my own willingness to take on the responsibility. I was too inexperienced to even attempt to negotiate a promotion or seek a temporary higher pay grade. I was careful not to give orders. Instead I would explain that we were instructed from above, always giving credit to my superiors for the orders I did pass on.

There were times under fire or during intense enemy contact that I was quick to take command. To the extent possible, I would try to demonstrate how things needed to be by my actions rather than by telling people what to do. I could not imagine how to approach my duties any differently.

The fact remained, I decided, that we had not lost

anyone killed or wounded while Lenny and I were in charge. I resolved to stay the course and make getting our guys out of this place alive my number one priority.

Chapter 25

With less than two months remaining, my time as acting platoon leader was coming to an end as was my time in country. I was becoming a "short timer" and every day in the field was another opportunity to get wounded or killed. Being short tended to make you question your responses and reaction times. I had caught myself hesitating before firing when my reactions would normally have been instantaneous.

I was increasingly short tempered, and that was starting to bother me. We walked into a village northwest of Liz one afternoon and the people seemed unusually agitated to me. So, I started questioning the villagers, asking where the VC were hiding and where they hid their weapons. My probing got the villagers more excited and everyone started talking at once. They gathered up in a tight group, the way villagers typically did, when they thought we were going to search them and their homes.

The commotion all this created caused the guys in the platoon to react and start searching and pressing the villagers, now believing something was truly amiss. I noticed the people were particularly watchful when our guys started to search one house that the village occupants seemed to be avoiding. The guys were banging things around, turning over furniture and dropping pots and pans when a young boy, perhaps six and a girl, maybe three, ran crying and screaming from the bunker attached to the side of the house.

Too many times I had seen this sort of alarmed reaction prove that Charlie was either close by or had been recently, often leaving behind one or more booby traps as souvenirs. My instincts led me to caution everyone to be extra watchful for mines or booby traps.

The children ran to the huddled group and that escalated all of their sobbing and wailing, making me even more certain that something was not right. So, I went back into the hooch and shouted for anyone in the bunker to come out now. I shouted over and over, "di-di, di-di mau" telling whoever I was now convinced was there, to get out.

There was no response and the other villagers had quieted down now, all watching intently as the events in their village unfolded. I heard someone yell "torch it". Whoever was on the back side of the hooch decided burning the grass house was a good idea and lit the grass roof with his Zippo.

The fire quickly engulfed the grass roof of the hooch. It burned, heaving a black plume of smoke into the sweltering afternoon heat. Two women, one young with streaming long black hair and one old with betel nut teeth, ran to the village from the adjoining rice paddy, screaming and crying unintelligibly. They went straight for the gathered villagers and found the boy and girl who we had scared out of the now burning house. They picked them up, holding and kissing them in grieved relief.

Their kids were okay, but their house was destroyed. And I felt shamefully and disgracefully wrong. What began as a knee jerk and suspicious reaction escalated into a confrontation between the villagers, who we had no proof were Viet Cong sympathizers, and the American soldiers.

Where was the father of these young children? Why were there no men in the village other than bearded old grandfathers? Once again, we were trapped by the impossible dilemma that was this war. We knew the whole Quảng Ngãi province was enemy infested. The elusive proof left us relentlessly guilt ridden for making decisions that were questioning and doubtful.

It could have been worse, I realized. This could have gotten completely out of hand and turned into a massacre like the two carried out by Korean soldiers within only a few miles of this village. Our guys were hungry for some payback for Franny, Gerry, Duke and the others from that fateful day back in August. Thank God the soldiers in our platoon knew the sergeants who led their squads and now controlled the platoon would not condone murder of civilians, innocent or not.

Chapter 26

A few weeks after my interview about Quang's adoption, the brigade chaplain sent word that my adoption request was approved by division, and so the Army. My imagination went wild with visions of introducing him to America, and all it offered. My first order of business would be to get him that Schwinn bicycle.

The surprise came when we were out on daily patrols and my RTO listened in on a call from brigade to our company commander. "They're offering you a promotion to Master Sergeant and want you to take over brigade S-5, civilian liaison, on Bronco."

I was taken completely off guard. I knew the interview with Quang had gone well and the officers were impressed with the way he responded to me. It would really be something if I got promoted and assigned to Bronco because of my relationship with Quang. Imagine being able to spend my remaining time in country with him at my side as my interpreter. My mind was racing.

The RTO came back to me with bad news. The company commander had denied the request stating that he needed me in the field.

It was every soldier's dream to get a rear echelon position to take him out of combat. The prospect of being turned down because I knew too much about my company commander, or knew he feared I would tell people what he thought I knew, was more disappointing to me than the fact of being denied the opportunity. His guilty conscience was costing me a move that might sway my interest in staying in the army and even continuing my service in Vietnam.

It amazed me that the interview with Quang had aroused enough interest by the brigade officers to offer me control over all of the Vietnamese civilians who worked on Bronco. What did I know about managing such a substantial number of people whose language I did not speak? Maybe they would offer me training to take on the task. It didn't matter. It had been turned down.

I wondered about the captain's motivation. Why was he so paranoid? Guilt was a powerful motivator. I remembered that he had fragged a bunker without warning, in what appeared to be a friendly village, and an injured child emerged. I had carried the child two clicks until our resupply choppers came in. The captain said he could not call in a Medevac because it would interrupt his mission.

I knew he had been involved, or at the worst condoned, the rape of my detainee. And I call her a detainee because I don't want to call her prisoner. I don't know for sure what happened that night, but I know there are people who will suffer from their knowledge for the rest of their lives.

Chapter 27

Captain Fuller, who preceded our current leader, was an excellent company commander who left the field in June and was assigned to a rear echelon job at battalion. He was level headed and put the safety of his troops above everything else, even if he had to work hard to convince his superiors to amend missions when he could see that we were being placed uselessly in harm's way. He kept us all well informed about what we were doing and why, and shared all of the information he was allowed to pass along. He also often asked for and heeded our suggestions and opinions.

He learned that I knew how to play bridge and would summon me to come to his tent for "meetings" when it appeared that we were safe within our perimeters. I was pleased to learn that he was promoted from company commander to battalion executive officer when he called me on the field radio to inform me that he was sending a young lieutenant fresh out of Officer Candidate School to take over the platoon.

Lieutenant Billy Kinder came in on the evening resupply chopper. He was twenty-five and looked all of seventeen. Although older than me he addressed me with respect and was careful to avoid pulling rank or putting me in my place in any way. My job was to acquaint him with our normal routines and teach him what I had learned about our job fighting Charlie. He was eager to learn and take over control of the platoon. But unlike some of the officers sent to command us, he was not scary gung ho.

He made it his first order of business to inform me that I was promoted to Staff Sergeant. He also said that my superiors at battalion wanted to discuss my plans when he released me from field duty.

The unexpected news was that Captain Fuller planned to take me out of the field. He decided that eleven months in the boonies was enough. As soon as the new lieutenant got comfortable to operate without me, he was authorized to send me back to Bronco.

Tonight it was my turn in the rotation to take a squad to set up a night ambush. My acting status as platoon leader did not change the fact that I was not an officer and held the same rank as the other sergeants who were our squad leaders. So we worked out a way to lead by consensus. We took the orders from our superiors and decided among us the best way to carry them out. The other guys recognized that when one of us had to make a final decision we might not all agree on, I was the one who had to take the responsibility. However, we shared the hazardous assignments of leading night patrols and ambushes equally.

I explained this to Billy Kinder, careful to point out that since we had been managing our platoon this way, we had not lost anyone killed or wounded. I knew it was largely due to luck like everything else that happened here, but I truly believed that we had the ability to increase our odds by keeping everyone concentrating on the one most important objective, keeping each other alive.

I was pleased that the new lieutenant appeared interested enough in our unconventional methods to want to know more about how we were conducting our daily business, staying alive while still killing Charlie. It was not really complicated, though, just not how the military normally operated. We still maintained a reasonable level of discipline, just not dictatorially so.

"As you work to accomplish the goals you just defined, are you carrying out your orders as assigned?" the lieutenant asked.

"Look at our record, sir," I responded. "We get the kills. We get the captures. We keep the pressure on Charlie. We may bend the rules when it comes to deciding the little things. Let me tell you a story about the night of the scorpion," I offered.

I proceeded to tell him the experience as best I could remember: It was my turn to take the squad out on night ambush in the valley west of Liz. We had to start out while it was still light because the intended ambush sight was too far out to wait until there was protection of darkness. We knew it was never a good idea to venture too far away from the safety of numbers, but this mission was going to take us more than a thousand meters distance.

I was not feeling good about continuing the mission. But our options were limited. The night was so completely black that the trail to our front and rear was totally obscured. It would be a hard process to make any distance in either direction because we would have to feel our way along the narrow path.

The tiger roared again. I stopped and listened intently. It sounded really close this time, but seemed to be off to our south and that gave me some comfort that it might not be coming down our trail after all.

I realized I had held our column back now for too long, although time seemed irrelevant to the circumstance. We were past the time when we could have properly set up and executed an effective ambush. And the likelihood we would be successful was slim.

So, I passed word back for everyone to get off to the right side of the trail and settle in until daylight. We set claymore mines out facing in both directions on the trail. With all of us on one side of the path we would have a clear field of fire and could still execute an ambush if anyone came along.

I felt my way into the elephant grass, used my back to force a bedlike mat from the heavy grasses, and laid back to test the comfort of what I had created. I went to set my rifle by my right side wanting to keep it at the ready when a terrible stinging sensation hit my right hand. I wanted to scream out. I managed to hold it in. I slapped and hammered at whatever had bitten or stung me. I felt something slither under my attack, but had no idea what it was or if I had killed it.

My hand stung worse than the hornet stings I got when I bumped into a big grey ball of a nest while hiking in the mountains in North Carolina. The stinging and numbing sensation was moving up my arm. I was losing feeling in my fingers and I started feeling nauseous. I felt disoriented and was close to passing out.

I whispered to my RTO that I had been stung or bitten by something and was in serious pain and feeling sick. I told him I knew we could not really do anything about it. I asked that he just check on me through the night and pass the word to the others not to depend on me for guard duty.

I was fortunate. The nausea passed without a vomiting episode. That would have been noisy and almost certainly given away our position if our enemies were as close by as I thought they were. The nausea was soon replaced by high fever and delirium like I used to get as a kid. I would lie in bed thinking the ceiling was caving in on me. Right now I felt like the dense jungle was pressing down on me and I was seeing white spots, a side effect of the fever and delirious state I was in.

My body responded by shutting down and I slipped into an exhausted sleep. I vaguely remember waking up the next morning and was still in a stupor during the walk back to Liz. The guys said I managed okay and was able to walk on my own. They found the scorpion, they told me, and were happy to report it was not the deadly kind. I had killed it with my flailing around.

We never reported our failure to complete our assigned mission. We never reached the intersection of trails. I was so disoriented in the dark that I was not sure how far we had to go but was bothered that we did not get there.

"You had a good reason," Billy Kinder declared. "You were injured and disabled by a scorpion."

"But I scrapped the mission before the scorpion got me," I admitted.

Chapter 28

The new lieutenant wanted to take the ambush out and told me I needed to remain with the platoon in the company perimeter. At first, I was relieved at the opportunity to avoid another risky ambush, now that I knew I was about to leave the jungle for good. But I was worried about the fresh leader being in control of our guys in such a critical situation on his first night in the field. At the same time, I did not want to appear to question his authority or alienate him either towards me or our guys.

"Sir, since I am assigned to familiarize you with the platoon and the jungle, I think this would be a perfect chance to show you how we normally do stuff. You could come along in more of an observer role this first night." I could not believe what I was trying to talk myself into but knew it was the right thing to do.

Billy Kinder seemed a little perplexed, not quite sure how to respond to me. His six-foot slender frame stiffened as if he were about to come to attention. He looked beyond me appearing to scan the area, then turned and walked in a circle, chin in hand. I guessed that he weighed more than me, maybe one hundred and fifty pounds. There were other similarities like his light beard and the way the steel helmet looked too big for his head.

But he did not yet have the thousand yard stare, that soulless and glassy eyed gaze from seeing too much pain, death and the ugliness of war. Sadly, I knew that would come with time if he lived long enough.

"I agree," he finally replied. "I think this will be a valuable learning opportunity. When do you want to get started?"

We set out at dusk. Buddy took point with me second in line. I always walked behind the point man on ambush assignments determined to use my experience to try to keep anyone from being wounded or killed. It was a little bit of a controversial method since Charlie was known to target our radio operators who they could identify by their field radio antennas. The first person walking in front of the RTO would normally be either the officer or sergeant. The enemy would target the antenna wanting to eliminate our leaders along with our ability to communicate and call for help.

On occasion our ambush patrols were caught by surprise when we intended to catch the Viet Cong off guard. There was no sure way to avoid this, but I believed persistent diligence could avoid a lot of pain and suffering. It was easy to get tired or lackadaisical and lower our guard. I had seen times when guys smoked a little weed in the field and got caught off guard by numbed senses.

It was hard to keep the troops on their toes all of the time, and I wanted to make sure Billy Kinder knew how important it was to try. I had spent the afternoon talking to him at length about the difficulty and importance of that responsibility. I wanted him to know that hour after hour, day after day, Charlie's tactic was to beat us down, lower our morale and make us vulnerable. He did that by popping up in a hedge row and firing off a few rounds, often finding a target. More importantly, just constantly reminding us that he was there and waiting. He did that by planting booby traps in advance of our movements, most often by watching our progress and predicting where we would enter a village or cross a rice paddy. He was crafty at figuring out our plans and staying just a few meters ahead of us. And when he was right it could be devastating.

The harassment was brutal, so much so that it made guys lose control with hate and do things that they would regret when they got home. You could only take so much of seeing your friends maimed and killed and still maintain reasonable sanity.

That was the most important message I wanted Billy Kinder to get. Keep it under control at any price. They'll resent you for it. They'll try to make you feel you are wrong if you refuse to allow them to take things too far. Keep your conviction. If you once drop it, you will lose them and terrible things can happen.

I wanted him to know the signs. I explained how one very good soldier took his frustration out by rapping villagers on the head with a cut off pool cue he brought back from R&R. Another time he was harassing people from a village by having them do pushups in the village common. They were small punishments, his way of getting back at the Vietnamese. I was able to step in and prevent those things from going further just by reminding the soldier that things that happened in Vietnam would need to stay in Vietnam when he finished his tour. That could only happen if he could leave the guilt behind.

That was easy for me to say. I knew I was going home with too much baggage. I knew I would feel guilty and responsible for the rest of my life and wondered how I would come to deal with it.

I came upon that same soldier another time, with two others, taking photos of a dead Viet Cong soldier. They were taking turns holding his head for pictures and I saw that they were about to cut off his ears. I stopped them and pointed out the gravity of their actions, again emphasizing that they needed to think about how they would feel when they were "back in the real world." One of the guys, Sergeant Jeff Greene who was my original squad leader, came to see me when his tour was ending. He said he just wanted to tell me he realized I was right. That was all he said. It was enough.

"You're going to get tired", I told him, "more exhausted than you can imagine. If you are tired they are too. So that is when you need to be most diligent, since you are most vulnerable when you let your guard down." I needed Billy Kinder to know that it could get much worse. And it all came down to the leadership.

I told him about the young woman who I believed was raped by our company commander and the guys in his CQ section. I told him about the guilt I felt for bringing her into the night perimeter and seeing her stripped and bathed while I was dispatched by the captain, whom I did not trust, to conduct a night ambush.

"Did you report this incident?" Billy Kinder asked.

"I wanted to," I responded. "I had no proof and since she was dead and there was no body, I had no idea what could be done."

I could tell that the shock of this last story elicited an amazed reaction from a still innocent Billy Kinder. He needed to know the extreme consequences any lapses in his leadership could bring, and the weighty responsibility that could come with them.

The new platoon leader walked behind me followed by our RTO and the other four troops in first squad. The night was hot and humid with little air stirring in this mountain river valley. The sky filled with stars as we set out, the moon not yet clearing the horizon. The night was so clear I could already make out the Southern Cross, the four stars that formed the American Division insignia, the patch on the left shoulder of my fatigue shirt.

Five hundred meters to the south the narrow path dipped as it approached the shallow water of the river ford. I noticed a path that ran off to the north, no more than a few feet parallel from the water's edge, that would conceal us from view from the terrain above. I moved forward and touched Buddy on the shoulder to stop him from entering the river.

"Let's take that path and see if we can find a spot out

of sight where we can see anybody crossing the ford," I suggested.

Buddy was one of the good guys. You could depend on him to always do the right thing. He was short and stocky, a studious looking young man who could not see a thing without his black framed glasses. Buddy was the guy you would envision sitting in the front row of the class, anxious to please the teacher, but too shy to ask a girl to the prom.

As Buddy picked his way, leading us along the riverside, Russell, who was last in line, passed word forward that he heard noise coming from the far side of the river, beyond the ford. Once again I moved forward and tapped Buddy's shoulder, and whispered that I thought we might be about to make enemy contact. I passed word back through the line for everyone to hunker down off to the side of the path.

As if on cue, the moon peaked over the mountain to our east and shone a gray-white line of light across the river ford. There, entering nature's spotlight, was a line of soldiers making the river crossing from the west, what appeared to be at least platoon strength.

Lieutenant Kinder whispered to me that we should be attacking. I pointed out that we were badly outnumbered and that he needed to call in an artillery strike. I normally would have made the call but I wanted him to take the responsibility. The lieutenant would get credit for kills just for calling in the strike on the basis of having made contact with twenty or more NVA soldiers. Before he made the artillery request, I suggested that we needed to move further north along the river. The enemy would realize that somebody was close enough to know their position for artillery to pinpoint them. They would surely come looking for us if we hung around.

So we moved a hundred meters up river and found a wide spot next to the path. I asked the RTO to get a message to the company commander that a platoon sized enemy force was headed in their direction and to report the change in our location. We studied our map, agreed on coordinates, taking into consideration their likely progress along the trail, and Billy Kinder called in the artillery strike. He ordered white phosphorous artillery rounds, affectionately called willy-peter, with the command to fire for effect.

As our barrage began to explode to the south, we hurried to select a northern route that would lead us back to the company. Our new commander displayed his training and leadership skills by quickly selecting a reasonable trail that should get us back safely. An hour later, we radioed our entry back into the company perimeter. I hoped from what I had seen so far that our platoon would be in good hands with Billy Kinder.

I spent countless nights on night ambushes, some successfully executed and many more nervously anticipating contact that never came. I was always disappointed when we didn't accomplish our mission of catching the Viet Cong or NVA by surprise. Anytime we did blow an ambush, our six to eight man teams were vulnerable to being overpowered by whoever might be supporting the soldiers we attacked. It was always a terrific relief to get back to the company when the mission was over.

I expected this night to be my last ambush assignment. It carried extra meaning to me since my first and last nights in the boonies of Vietnam would, hopefully, have been spent taking the war to Charlie, making contact and living to tell about it.

I had a bad feeling about the area we were in. I did not think it was just short timer nerves. I had developed good instincts in my year chasing and dodging Charlie. We were encountering too many booby traps, bungee pits and even tree slung bamboo spear racks, multiple pointed stakes mounted on a sling made by using a small tree as a bow tied to a ground level trip wire or rope. Charlie would dip the bungee stakes and spears in water buffalo dung so that if the initial impact did not kill you, the infection that followed would take you out of action. This was definitely Viet Cong territory.

We had no way of knowing if our artillery strike was on target. We knew that we would be credited with kills based on the intelligence we provided for the strike. We also knew the numbers were just speculation because we saw an NVA patrol. We had no way of knowing how many were still out there or whether they intended to attack. They had to know our location by now.

We had no time to relax just because we were back in the company area. We went about digging our fox holes deeper without needing to be told. Charlie was here and we all knew it.

Chapter 29

The night passed without event. The company started out at daylight moving north along the river in a column until we reached a confluence with a wider stream flowing from the east. The conjoined stream created class one white water that made a pleasant sound as it poured across rocky fords that broke its flow.

The company commander decided this would be a suitable bivouac site. He announced that we would establish our perimeter on the east side of the river and conduct day patrols from there. First platoon would, thankfully, have responsibility for securing the company perimeter during the day.

As the other platoons started out on their patrols, I saw Billy Kinder walking towards me from the company commander's CQ area. His posture seemed down, not his usual erect and positive nature.

"Is something wrong?" I asked, as he approached.

"I'm afraid so," he confirmed. "I just got word from the CO that the Vietnamese government turned down your adoption request. They said Quang would be turning thirteen before your ETS in January and they would not allow boys who were becoming military age to be taken from the country."

I was flabbergasted. I could not think of anything worth saying, so I just put extra effort into digging my fox hole, feeling exposed by the hills that looked down on us from both sides of the river. The sand was filled with river pebbles smoothed by ages of wear from the flowing Sông Ve River. An hour of using my shovel as a spade yielded only a foot deep hole three feet long and two feet wide. As I wrestled with the stubborn river bed, I thought of all of the sacrifices I had made for Vietnam and found myself incredibly angry over their ridiculous denial. How would I break this terrible news to Quang who now had his hopes up to go home with me to America?

I saw that the other guys were busy gathering large rocks and piling them around their shallow holes. They had given up on boring deeper into the river bed. The sun was settling over the western hills toward Laos so I scrambled around, gathering stones to get my rock fort in place before I lost the precious remaining daylight.

My night position was in the center of the platoon, fifteen meters back from the edge of the perimeter. Billy Kinder had taken over command of the platoon fully now but still wanted me next to him and his RTO during the night. I was sweating profusely as I scrambled to finish my miniature fortress when I spotted the lieutenant coming in my direction again, his ruck sack slung over his right shoulder as he lugged it by one strap.

"You've built me a first class castle," he smiled as he removed his pack and laid it against the wall of rocks I had gathered and stacked. "I wanted you to know that I radioed Captain Fuller and asked him to appeal the ruling by the Vietnamese. He promised it would be done today. And, by the way, you need to grab your gear and head up to the landing zone. The resupply chopper will be here in five minutes, and you need to be on it."

And just like that my time was up. There was no ceremony or opportunity to say goodbye and wish everyone farewell. There was no final tipping of beers, no patting each other on the back, no time for congratulations for living through the year and saving each other along the way.

I hesitated, filled with mixed emotions of feeling guilty for desperately wanting to leave against fear for the safety of the close friends I was leaving behind. Would they need me and get in trouble if I was not there with them, I wondered. I realized I did not really have a choice. To stay with them I would have to extend my time in the military, and I did not consider that to be an option.

I took the ten full metal jackets from my ammo pouches and handed them to the lieutenant. I removed the four hand grenades and laid them on the rocks in front of him. I opened my rucksack and dumped out all of my cache of food and beer, including the six cans of Campbell's soup I got in my last goody box from home.

"Keep the soup, it's better than any rations," I suggested to Billy Kinder. "Give the rest to the guys for me. And thanks. I know you will take good care of them," I added, as I lifted my pack and walked away.

The soldiers, my soldiers, of first platoon were so busy

struggling to prepare their night positions of rocks and sand that nobody seemed to notice as I left the perimeter area and headed for the green smoke that marked the helicopter landing area. I kept turning back to look but couldn't seem to get anyone's attention. I hated leaving without some kind of acknowledgement. The truth was, I just hated leaving them.

The Huey flew low over the LZ then did a tight one eighty and swooped in to land dead on top of the green smoke grenade, and that created a swirling haze of smoke. Out of habit, I dropped my pack on the ground, laid my rifle on it and climbed on board to help speed the process of unloading supplies of C-rations, cases of beer, soda and wooden boxes of hand grenades and ammo. I tossed out two bags of mail and wondered in the process if there was anything in them for me. I jumped down, grabbed my gear and rifle and tossed them on board, then stepped on the railing and signaled all clear for the pilot to take off.

As the helicopter rotor accelerated to gain lift for takeoff I heard someone yell out "hey, sergeant, where are you going?"

"Home," I shouted in reply. I felt my voice cracking and realized, embarrassed, that I was almost crying. I quickly regained my composure and waved hello to the door gunner behind my usual left side seat. On this flight I decided to keep my legs and feet inside although my rifle was locked and loaded, just in case.

The pilot took off to the west then abruptly circled back and flew low over the company perimeter and the first platoon position to the north. Lieutenant Billy Kinder and all of the guys were looking up and waving enthusiastically. I hung my left leg out the door and perched myself on the runner. I smiled broadly and gave a long and symbolic solute, then waved one final farewell as they disappeared from sight. I had gotten my ceremony after all.

I had the cargo compartment all to myself and chose to sit in the center of the canvas bench seat. I didn't want to press my luck by sitting exposed by the open doors on what, I expected, would be my last Huey flight.

The pilot leveled out at about three thousand feet. I could see Quảng Ngãi to the east and the vast expanse of rice paddies beyond reaching to the South China Sea. The mountains of Laos and Cambodia were just a silhouette as the sun eased behind them to the west. Highway one, beneath us, was void of traffic to comply with the sundown curfew.

To my surprise, we made an abrupt turn over Mai's little store at Mộ Đức and headed directly for Liz. Someone popped green smoke and we landed on the helipad up the hill from the mess hall tent and next to the artillery battery.

The pilot leaned between the seats he and the copilot occupied, and told me to go get any personal gear I had stowed in my bunker, and double time back.

I jumped out the door and heard him yell behind me, "and I'm instructed to tell you to bring the little boy with you."

I could not believe my ears. I did not think I would have a chance to see Quang again, much less get to take him back to Bronco to spend some time with me.

The cooks were super to look after him when we were away in the field. They didn't seem to mind and had taken a real liking to him. So, I made a detour and hurried to the mess tent where I found Quang playing cards with some of the guys from B Company. He was wearing the green military shirt and pants I had given him. His combat boots were brightly polished. He was proud of his boots and kept them in better shape than any of us.

"Hey, kiddo, want to go ride in a helicopter?" I said before he knew I was there.

He leaped from the table bench and gave me his usual bear hug, a homecoming I always looked forward to with each return from the boonies.

"When you come back?" he asked. "Where other soldiers?" he looked around, confused.

"Let's go get our stuff from the bunker," I suggested. "We're going to ride a helicopter to Bronco."

There wasn't much to get. Quang shared our bunker when we were on Liz. Others used it when we were away. He bunked with the cooks during those periods but left his belongings tucked away in our wooden ammo boxes we kept hidden under the bunks. There was not much, his boot polishing kit, a rifle cleaning kit that he used to keep my M-16 in perfect condition, a second set of size small fatigue shirt and pants, and sodas and snacks he "requisitioned" when the opportunity presented itself.

I stuck my head in the door opening and said hello to the first squad leader from the first platoon of Bravo Company. We picked up our two wood cases of belongings and hurried up the winding path. It was almost dark and the pilot made it clear he wanted to be airborne while there was still light.

We were both so excited we hardly noticed how hard we were breathing as we climbed aboard the Huey. I was still grungy from my efforts digging in back at the company perimeter. A shower was top on my list when we arrived at brigade. The thought of being able to get clean and stay clean made me smile.

"Why you smile?" Quang asked, perplexed.

"Because I'm happy to see you and I'm going to wash, wash, wash," I laughed.

Quang held his nose in mock protest and declared, "Jared stinky number ten!"

Quang could not hide his excitement as the helicopter accelerated, lifted then pitched forward down the east side of Liz. After the initial descent from the hill to gain speed, the pilot quickly assumed a nose high attitude and rapidly climbed as high as he could get as fast as he could get there. He wanted to be high enough so the bullets from Charlie's rifles could not reach us. Flying after sundown was hazardous. The enemy would be shielded from view of the door gunners by the cover of darkness.

We stopped climbing at the same time we started our descent into Bronco. The base runway was dimly lighted, just enough illumination to allow the pilot to pick it out among the few village fires scattered among the rice paddies.   The farmers would stretch curfew beyond sundown in order to burn their cooking fires so they could feed their families after long days working the rice. The armored soldiers on top of Bronco would fire off a few rounds from their APC mounted fifty caliber machine guns in the general direction of firelight they spotted and bet on how long it took for the fire to go out.

I was used to barely landing before jumping from helicopters, then hurrying to set up a protective perimeter. It felt odd to wait for the rotor engine to grind to a halt to unload and walk away erect. I could already feel the effects of coming away from the hazards of war. I worried that I might relax too much and end up like Felix Queen.

Quang and I said thanks and wished well to our helicopter crew who had gone to special trouble to bring us here. We walked side by side across the tarmac and headed for the battalion area west of the airstrip. I knew it was too late to check in with the headquarters office. So, we headed for the mess hall. I hoped to catch a hot meal before it was too late.

The mess sergeant was closing out for the night when we walked up. I explained that I had just returned from the field for the last time, and we were hoping to have something other than rations for dinner. He told us the guys over at the Red Dog Saloon were cooking grilled hamburgers for a stand down and he was sure they would not mind us getting fed.

I told Quang we needed to go to the barracks and get a place to sleep first. I wanted to keep him out of sight of the soldiers who were in from the boonies, worried that they might resent his being here. So we went straight to the barracks and found two cots next to each other.

I think he understood. He had probably been harassed by some of the guys who replaced us on Liz from time to time. It was important to me to just get our burgers and be left alone.

"You stay here and I'm going to go get our food," I ordered.

"No problem," he answered.

If You're Going To San Francisco by Scott McKenzie resonated from Red Dog Saloon. At that moment it hit me that I really was headed home. I wondered how people the song referred to would feel about returning veterans like me.

I didn't recognize anyone when I retrieved our burgers and sodas and took no more than five minutes to get back to Quang. It really did not matter what we ate anyway. We were just happy to see each other.

I opened my wooden ammo box and found a set of clean fatigue shirt and pants, a tooth brush, razor and small piece of soap. Quang copied my search and pulled his clean fatigues from his box and we headed off to the showers. There was nobody to heat the water for us. It didn't matter. It was still hot and muggy out and the cool shower felt good.

All cleaned and groomed, we headed back to our

bunks. It had been a long day for me and I was ready to sack out, but I knew it would be hard to settle down from the exciting events of the day.

"You take me to America now?" Quang asked. I knew he was going to ask and I was not prepared to answer. I had hoped to report in and inquire about the latest news myself. I did not want to set him up for disappointment since I knew we had already been turned down by the Vietnamese government once.

"I don't know, but I don't think so," I answered reluctantly. "I will find out tomorrow morning first thing."

Quang did not understand all of my English, yet I could see that he got the gist of it. He assumed his best pouting posture, turned away from me, and said good night.

I lay awake staring at the dull green tarp ceiling of the barracks. The reality that the commitment of a year of my life to war was ending was starting to sink in. That tremendous relief was overpowering compared to all of the other emotions that raced through my mind.

I knew I would probably never see most of my comrades again. I had heard lifers, the guys who committed to be career soldiers, talk about how they ran into people they served with as they moved from one duty station or war to another. It was different for draftees who were brought into the military for the sole purpose of populating the manpower needs of the Vietnam War. The hundreds of thousands in our category would process out of this ugliness wanting only to forget, and part of that forgetting would require leaving the memories that went with friendships behind with the war.

We all knew the finality of these ending friendships although we all promised to stay in touch back in the world. The urgency to forget, to try to leave the thousand yard stare behind with the exploding sounds of sniper fire and tripped booby traps, would require that we attempt to blank all of this unwanted experience from memory. There would be no way to selectively forget just the bad stuff. Any attempt at sanity would mean forgetting about trying to make sense of any of it.

How would I be able to just walk away and forget Quang? I had become his hope for a better life. He had grown to believe he could depend on me and I had caused him to let his guard down. I knew that beneath his outward tough demeanor was tremendous fragility. He had been abused by the war and his country.

His family was sacrificed in the power struggle that had no meaning to Quang. He had learned to survive on just his outward and endearing personality, gaining the gifts of trust and affection from transient American soldiers that were here today and gone tomorrow. It kept him fed and clothed but left a void where the love and affection of family belonged. I knew that when I left, he would have to start again, trying to win over those who remained after I was gone. I knew there were many who would not be accepting to him, and serious abuses could await him if I had to abandon him to the whim of whomever I could convince to look after him.

I dreamed of seeing his face the first time I took him into an American grocery store.   I imagined his excitement at being able to browse through the packed shelves and select anything he could imagine wanting to eat or drink.

I fantasized about taking him to a toy store to pick out a Tonka truck or Lionel electric train. I visualized him riding a shiny new Schwinn bicycle on a paved neighborhood street.

I pictured him in a baseball uniform with red cap and leather glove. I craved seeing him in a classroom full of school children his age. I knew his intelligence would yield good marks.

All these things I wanted for Quang were about to come crashing down to reality and I suspected that my last futile efforts on his behalf before I left would fail. My instincts said there was no way the Vietnamese government would reverse their policy of refusing to allow a child of thirteen to be adopted just to satisfy my futile effort. Still, a flicker of hope had been sparked in me when the helicopter pilot told me to go get the little boy and bring him with us.

Exhaustion finally overcame my racing mind and I sank into a restless and fitful sleep. The sun heating the tarpaulin roof of our barracks caused me to wake up in a sweat. I was in the habit of sleeping in my clothes and boots expecting to need to get up and move quickly. I made a mental note to get some boxers from supply before another night so I could strip off my fatigues to sleep. I had not worn underwear since the early days in country after getting sand in my skivvies.

I saw that Quang was sleeping restlessly from the heat as well, so I decided to wake him and get the day started. We visited the latrine then headed to the mess hall for a hot breakfast of pancakes and bacon. Then we hurried over to see the executive officer in his sand bag bunker to check in.

It made me sad not to find Felix Queen at his usual desk. He had been replaced by a young specialist who took his position much too seriously. He instructed me in reporting procedures; knock, be admitted, salute and report my name and rank and state that I was reporting as requested. I was actually relieved that he did that since I had not followed these formalities in months. Officers did not want to be addressed as officers or saluted in the field. It made them easy targets for Charlie.

Major Fuller came out of his office to greet me, guiding me by the hand to a chair in front of his desk. "We'll forgo the military protocol this time, Staff Sergeant," he smiled with special emphasis on the rank in his voice.

I looked back to check on Quang and saw that the clerk had him busy getting a soda from his little office refrigerator.

"He'll be fine," the major assured me, noting my concern.

"Thank you for getting me out of the boonies early sir," I offered. "I can't believe those eleven and a half months are over and I'm still in one piece. Congratulations on your promotion to major and XO," I added.

Major Fuller looked more like a college professor than a military officer. He wore his West Point education well, without being showy about his accomplishments like some officers liked to do. When he was our company commander in the field, he was always clean and pressed. His boots somehow had a newly polished look even after trudging through rice paddy mud and mire. His clear rimmed glasses further accentuated his studious appearance.

"I miss our bridge games," I mused. "I sure hated hearing the news about Felix Queen. He was a good friend to me. Everybody liked him."

"I feel extra bad about it. I authorized him to use my jeep," he explained. "He wanted to make one last trip into the village to get some souvenirs, laundry, and tell everyone goodbye. I cannot imagine what possessed them to go out the gate before the mine clearing team opened the road."

"You said them, sir," I noticed. "I only heard about Felix. Was someone else with him?"

"I'm afraid we lost Sergeant Alias at the same time. I guess you knew that the two of them started the Red Dog Saloon and brought the reel to reel and all that great music to the little club," he added.

"But enough of that, let's get down to business," he directed. "I'm getting on a flight to Chu Lai today and wanted to get you taken care of before I left. My tour is over, too."

"Congratulations, sir," I offered. "I really appreciate what you have done for me. We missed you after you left. Things were not so good for us under your replacement."

"I've been authorized to offer you a direct commission to First Lieutenant," he announced, seeming to want to avoid any discussion about the other company commander. I guessed the army would frown on an officer discussing another officer's performance with a sergeant. "The job you have done as acting platoon leader has not gone unnoticed. You'll be given your own platoon. It comes with a condition, though," he added. "You will have to commit to stay in Vietnam another six months, after a month of leave to go home first, of course."

I was taken aback. I did not know how to respond and just sat there in shock. A thousand thoughts raced through my head. I could have more time with Quang. I could go home really proud to have become an officer. I would have to put off my college education. I could hang around and be with my friends a while longer until it was time for them to leave.

But, I thought, there was so much risk that would go along with the reward. I had felt myself becoming callous, starting to feel less sympathetic towards the villagers and finding it easier to judge people before thinking about the trap they were in between us and the Viet Cong. It was getting harder to live up to my reputation as "gook lover." I found it hard to imagine going back for extended time in combat again. Besides, I would just be prolonging the agony of saying goodbye to Quang and Dam.

"What about Quang, sir," I asked. "Is there some news about my request to adopt him different from before?"

"I'm afraid not," he answered. "I had them run your adoption request back through channels again. The Viets declined like before on the basis of his age. However, I have made arrangements for you to take him to Nha Trang to see if you can find a suitable orphanage for him. That's why I had them stop on Liz, for you to get him on your way in."

Wow, I thought. The major had really gone out of his way to help me. I was feeling overwhelmed. I had not traveled to a big city in Vietnam and didn't know what to expect.

"Don't worry, it's not complicated to travel here," the major pointed out as if reading my mind. "I have travel papers ready for you both and you just have to jump a C-130 flight tomorrow. They run up and down country every day. And I've arranged for you to be issued a forty-five sidearm for the trip since you cannot carry your rifle in the city."

"There's one more thing," he added smiling. "To justify getting you out of the field early to my superiors, I arranged an R&R to Taipei for you, if you will accept it. Today is Sunday, December twenty-second," he noted, referring to his desk calendar. "You'll leave from Đà Nẵng for Taipei on Saturday, the twenty-eighth, so you will need to be back here by Wednesday, Christmas Day. Can you make that work?"

This was amazing. Until now, my movements in the military consisted of getting travel orders and going where and when they sent me. I had no say in it. I felt like I was sitting with a travel agent who was working out my agenda for my approval. I figured there had to be a catch.

"Sir, I really appreciate everything you have done for me," I started. "But if all this is based on my accepting the direct commission and staying longer in Vietnam and the army, I'm just not sure about all of that yet. I need time to process all of the options you have given me."

"It's nothing like that," he defended. "Just think it all over while you are in Nha Trang and let my replacement know your decision when you get back. You'll still have the R&R even if you decide not to take the promotion," he concluded. "I'll warn you though. They will still be after you to take the promotion and stay in when you go to your next duty assignment stateside."

My next duty assignment stateside was something I had not even considered. I wondered where that would take me. The only thing the army had trained me for was being a boot, an infantry soldier, a leg, no special qualifications required. The major's clerk had reminded me just how little I knew about military protocol and correctness, and I worried that my lack of knowledge and experience would make it very hard if I decided to take their offer and become an officer.

I thanked the major, stood to attention and saluted,

giving my best attempt to be militarily proper and respectful. He kindly returned my salute and wished me well. In life's worst circumstances, it was people like him who restored my faith in humanity. I wished there was something I could do to show how deeply he was appreciated. But he was an officer and I was a grunt. The social barrier dividing the ranks prevented either of us from bestowing further emotion to one another, although I knew we shared the same feelings of comradeship.

Chapter 30

I liked the feel of the forty-five pistol when I strapped the green belt on my waist. I knew that if I had one of these, I might have saved Franny from the sniper. The tarmac, heated by the early afternoon sun, burned my feet through my boots as Quang and I waited for the military transport plane to board.

Quang was excited to travel with me to Nha Trang. He had never been on an airplane. I had not told him that my purpose was to try to find Vietnamese people who might be willing to care for him. I was worried that he would run away like he did from the Catholic orphanage in Đức Phổ.

The back end of the utility airplane dropped open exposing the ramp that led to the inside of the wide belly. A row of green canvas seats lined each side so you sat with your back against the fuselage side-by-side with the other passengers. Freight lined the center of the compartment so you could not see the people sitting on the opposite side from you. I was surprised at the number of Vietnamese passengers who boarded with us, mostly wives and family of ARVN soldiers, I guessed.

Back in North Carolina they referred to Piedmont Airlines flights like this as bunny hops. Although I had not flown on any of them, I learned from my job meeting the flights to pick up air freight that they jumped from town to town, picking up and delivering passengers and freight along the way.

Our airplane would take us southwest from Đức Phổ inland to land among the mountains of the Central Highlands at Pleiku. The passengers all filed out and freight, contained in large palletized nets, was unloaded. Then those passengers who were continuing on south boarded and we quickly took off again, the C-130 climbing abruptly over the mountains that surrounded the army base. We flew southeast to make a brief landing on the single runway at the coastal city of Qui Nhơn then on south to the sprawling airbase at Nha Trang.

Quang's wide eyed air travel education was a joy to watch. Observing his pleasure at this experience was almost as gratifying to me as I imagined I would feel as he mounted that Schwinn bike I dreamed I would get for him. Only a year ago I had boarded my first flight. I remembered the excitement I felt and tried to relate to what Quang must be feeling.

Nha Trang airport was a new world to us. Mobs of people were everywhere creating a mass of hustle and bustle. Everyone seemed to know what they were scurrying around about. I just needed to figure out how to get us to the hotel the major had arranged for us.

I looked through the travel papers we were provided by the battalion clerk at Bronco. I saw that I still had the two flight authorization vouchers, except the one with my name still had a ticket on it. On closer inspection I realized that the writing on Quang's ticket authorized only one way travel to Nha Trang compared to mine that included a return ticket for Đức Phổ.

I thought at first there must have been some mistake. Then it hit me. They did not want Quang on the base at Bronco or on Liz if I was not there to take responsibility for him. They were not just doing me a favor by sending me to find Quang a new home. It was my assignment to take him to an orphanage and leave him. It occurred to me, too, that they might be using Quang's destiny as a means of bribing me to take the promotion.

I flipped through the papers attached to the flight vouchers and found official looking orders typed out on battalion letterhead. They told whoever inspected them that I was authorized to travel with Le Van Quang, described as an orphan of the war, for the purpose of seeking out a suitable orphanage in or around the city of Nha Trang. It went on to state that we were to lodge at the Kampong Hotel as recommended by MACV. A voucher for the lodging to be presented to the hotel was attached to the orders. My travel agent had been thorough.

I led Quang out through what appeared to be the main airport exit and saw a line of three wheeled taxi's lined up along the curb. Barefooted, hungry looking street kids intercepted us, all desperately trying to get our attention and wanting to sell us "number one souvenirs." This is the life I feared would face Quang if I was not successful getting him accepted at an orphanage.

The taxi excursion from the airport to the hotel was like a circus ride. The three-wheeled contraption had a single wheel in front steered by the driver perched on what appeared to be a tricycle seat. The passenger compartment was a vinyl bench seat mounted over two rear wheels and covered by a canvas canopy. He rode it like a motorcycle, maneuvering side-to-side and in and out of traffic. Quang and I held on tightly to the little steel handles on each end of the seat, our packs held tightly between our feet. Neither of us wanted to admit we were afraid.

The Kampong Hotel was a two story grey concrete structure, a leftover from the French Indochina architecture. The sign out front read Kampong (Village) Hotel. I asked the taxi driver if we were in Kampong Village. "No, no, Kampong mean village," he answered. It was the Vietnamese way of marketing to Americans.

An old Mama Son welcomed us to the hotel, carefully inspected my hotel voucher and informed me that I should pay a hotel tax of five dollars for each day. I had the feeling I was being taken but there was really nothing to be done about it. So I forked over the money in MPC, not wanting to give up the little American currency I had with me.

"You no take gun outside hotel," she instructed, eyeing my sidearm suspiciously.

I showed her my orders that included my authorization to wear the weapon while in Nha Trang. She just grunted her disapproval, handed me our room key and disappeared through the beaded curtain behind the hotel desk.

Our second floor room overlooked the noisy street below. The single window was open allowing a humid breeze to circulate through the room. I closed the window, curious to see if the room would be bearable without air conditioning or a fan. I went into the hall to find the communal bathroom and returned to find Quang sitting on the sill in the open window.

"Too hot," he announced.

The room was sparsely furnished. The bed, smaller than a typical double, was a slat of bamboo covered by a thin down mattress. A three drawer chest was centered on the wall opposite the window, the paint peeled away from years of use. A bamboo mat covered the concrete floor between the door and bed.

"It's not much but it sure beats the bunker on Liz," I announced to Quang.

"This number one hotel, A-Okay," Quang declared. "I hungry. We eat soon?"

I checked my Seiko watch and was surprised to see that it was after three. We had not eaten since breakfast at the mess hall early this morning.

"Let's stow our gear and go find something to eat," I responded.

Quang announced he needed to go to the bathroom so I stowed our rucksacks under the bed as best as I could squeeze them under. The supply clerk had outfitted Quang with a brand new rucksack and filled it with fatigue shirt, pants, boxer shorts, towel, a bar of soap and a bush hat. A poncho and poncho liner were rolled up and tied to the rucksack frame beneath the pack. The size small clothes were all too big, but Quang was excited to have them anyway. He had stuffed all of his belongings from his wooden ammo box into the backpack. He strained under the weight, too proud to consent when I offered to help carry it. He reminded me of a soldier loaded up for an extended field operation as he lugged the pack around. What he carried on his back was every possession he owned. That realization made me sad.

"Close the window and let's go get some food," I suggested when Quang returned from the bathroom. "I think maybe that is a restaurant across the street so we can try to go there."

On the street people stared at us and pointed us out to their friends while whispering to each other. I considered our appearance and realized for the first time that we must, sure enough, seem like a strange pair. Quang wore his green military clothes and I was still wearing my camouflage covered steel pot. That, along with the sidearm, would probably be enough to attract attention since most other Americans we had seen wore civilian clothes, and even sandals.

We crossed the street, dodging bicycles and motor scooters as we went. The open air restaurant had multiple folding doors that were all swung open to reveal cloth covered tables neatly arranged inside. When we started to enter, an elderly man with thin grey beard stopped us.

"You no come here with this," he said emphatically,

pointing to my pistol.

"But I'm authorized to carry it," I informed him as I unfolded my orders to show him I was permitted.

"No, no, no, no good," he nearly shouted as he tried to usher us from the restaurant.

I had spotted a plastic table and four chairs by the street in front of the establishment on the way in so I suggested to the old gentleman that perhaps he could serve us some food out there. That seemed to satisfy him, so I asked Quang to order us some food.

"What you want to eat?" Quang asked.

"I eat what you eat, just order me a cold beer, too," I pleaded.

While he negotiated our food and drink order with the old man, I surveyed the neighborhood. Umbrella covered stands offered all sorts of trinkets; beads, leather goods, black sandals made from tires like the VC wore, and pyramid shaped mu la hats that hung in bunches.

While I was still standing at the curb peering up and down the crowded street, a nice looking man approached me with his hand extended. "I bet you're not from around here," he offered, smiling.

He wore blue jeans and a lightweight white sports jacket. His Weejuns, my favorite loafers that he wore without socks, caught my attention. He looked to be in his early thirties, was about an inch taller than me, and he had sandy blonde hair accentuated by sparkling blue eyes. What was this cool looking civilian doing in Vietnam, I wondered?

"You don't exactly look like you're from around here either," I laughed as I shook his hand.

"My name is Frank Byers," he introduced.

"I'm Jared Christopher and that is my sidekick, Quang, over there trying to get us some food," I answered, pointing.

"You look as though you just came from the field, steel pot and all," he smiled. "It's very unusual to see a soldier traveling with a Vietnamese kid. What are you guys doing in Nha Trang?"

I looked to verify that Quang was still occupied with the old man. I wanted to answer Frank honestly, but I was not ready to alert Quang as to my true assignment for being here.

"Quang is an orphan I have looked after as a Kit Carson kid for some months now," I offered. "My tour of duty is about over so they sent me here to find an orphanage to take him in. I tried to adopt him. The Vietnamese government turned me down even though the Americans gave their approval. I haven't told him why we are here."

I could see that Frank was taken with my story. He stared at Quang thoughtfully without saying anything more.

"I order chicken, one Coke for me and one beer for you," Quang announced as he came towards us.

"They wouldn't let us in the restaurant because of this," I explained, pointing to my forty-five. "By the way, this is Frank and Frank this is Quang."

They acknowledged one another with a nod as Quang pulled a plastic chair from under the table and sat.

"Mind if I join you?" Frank asked. "I might be able to offer some advice or help on your quest," he added secretively, carefully choosing his words. "I know the city pretty well. I'm in my third year here and get around a good bit. I'm an American paid independent contractor working for the South Vietnamese government. What do you do in the army?"

"Infantry," I answered. "I just got out of the field after eleven and a half months and am about to process out."

Frank pulled out one of the dirty white chairs and sat. I took five dollars from the side pocket of my fatigue pants and handed it to Quang. A broad grin creased his face since he seldom had his own money.

"You go buy sandals," I suggested, pointing to the umbrella covered vendors down the street. "You not wear boots all the time," I added, pointing to his shiny black and green jungle boots. I wanted to pick Frank's brain since I was at a total loss how to go about my mission. I waited for Quang to get out of earshot and turned my attention back to Frank.

"You're the first American civilian I've met in Vietnam," I began. "What do you do for the South Vietnamese?"

"I'm trying to help them increase their rice production capability," he answered. "Their primary commodity is rice, but they have not been able to export much because of the war. There is not enough to feed their people much less help their economy by exporting. What we don't destroy with our war machine the Viet Cong take from the villagers, leaving their families to starve."

"I had some initial success bringing in machinery to help with irrigating, planting and harvesting," he added. "Before we could begin to see an impact on production, the VC got wind of what we were up to and sabotaged us. They followed the tractors and harvesters to where we stored them and blew them up during the night. We learned that they used the same people we were trying to teach to farm more efficiently to disable the expensive equipment. We found rubber tree sap in fuel, for example. That has the same effect on an engine as pouring sugar in a car's gas tank."

"We're pretty much confining our efforts to improving irrigation now," he said. "Even that is a challenge. We build dams and tributaries to convert dry paddies to productive rice fields and Charlie comes behind us and blows them up. Sometimes it just all seems so futile. But, maybe I can help you. I need to feel like I have accomplished something now and then."

I showed Frank the list of orphanages Major Fuller sent with me. He studied the list carefully, mostly shaking his head discouragingly.

"This first one is run by the Vietnamese and is very poor," he explained. "It gets what funding is available from the government because it is primarily a leper colony. The kids they take on are there mainly to provide cheap labor to help run the place."

"I could never put Quang in a place like that," I declared.

Referring to the list again, he announced that there was only one orphanage he would ever consider taking a child to and it was supported by the Catholics. "We could go there today if you like," he proposed.

"You would go there with us?" I was getting excited now.

"I have a jeep and would be happy to drive you," he offered. "And I know the mother superior. I go visit and take them stuff I don't need. It makes me feel better about being in this God forsaken country."

I saw Quang headed our way, proudly carrying his newly bought tire-tread sandals. His timing was perfect. The old restaurant owner brought our chicken-on-a-stick and drinks as Quang plopped into his chair.

"How much you pay?" I asked, pointing to the sandals.

"Man say ten dollar, I say five," Quang answered. "Man say eight dollar, I say five," he continued. "I say xin lỗi (which I knew meant sorry), only have five. Man say okay, five," he bragged, proud that he had bartered and won.

We gobbled our chicken sticks. The spicy meat made the beer go down too fast so I ordered another. Frank decided to have one too. When the old man returned, Frank spoke to him in Vietnamese, pulled out a leather wallet and handed him a crisp new American twenty-dollar bill. I saw him gesture toward Quang and instruct the old man to bring him another Coke.

"I can pay my bill," I said, defensively.

"Not on a sergeant's salary," he laughed. "I'm making pretty good money from being here and I hope you will not be offended if I buy."

Frank drove the jeep through the winding and pothole filled streets of Nha Trang displaying his experience and confidence of having done it many times before. He knew where the worst sections of road were located, and wove in and out of traffic and took back roads and side streets to avoid them. From a partially paved, one-lane, side street, he suddenly pulled the jeep to a stop in front of a walled courtyard with a lattice woven and steel gated entrance.

When Frank silenced the engine, we could hear the happy shouts and squeals of children playing within the walls. A boy passed by the gate in front of us taking aim with a round white ball, evidently engaged in a game of dodge ball.

"What this place?" Quang asked, his face a mask of concern.

"It's a very nice boys' and girls' school," Frank answered, before I could figure out how to handle it. "I suggested to Sergeant Jared that you might like to visit. Wait here a minute," he added turning his attention to me as he dismounted the open drivers side.

Frank walked through the gate and disappeared inside the compound. Just like that, he had worked out how to introduce Quang to the orphanage, so I would not have to give him a chance to think too much about it and set his mind against the idea.

Frank appeared back at the gate accompanied by a nun in habit. They spoke and smiled pleasantly to one another as they walked in our direction. Their demeanor was that of two old friends pleased to have the opportunity to spend time together.

"This is Sergeant Jared and his buddy Quang," he introduced as soon as they reached the side of the jeep. "And, this is Sister Le. She is principal of the school."

Frank was astute at his diplomacy in the way he chose his words to describe the orphanage and the Mother Superior. I wasn't sure if Quang understood his description of her as school principal, but he seemed to grasp that this was a school.

Sister Le invited us for a tour, so we followed as she led us into the courtyard. The children had all filed back into a large open- air classroom adjacent to the playground and resumed their lessons. A Vietnamese girl dressed in the traditional white ao dai, flowing tunic over silk trousers, stood at the front of the class leading a reading lesson in Vietnamese. She appeared to be in her middle teens with long, groomed black hair and lovely unblemished white skin. She interrupted the lesson, walked directly to Quang and put her hand on his shoulder.

She carried on a conversation with him at length, ignoring the two Americans by his side. There was a lot of smiling and amicable conversation between them. Quang seemed comfortable in her presence and perhaps a little bit taken by her beauty. I had not seen him blush around a girl before. I thought I detected a hint of adolescent infatuation going on.

Quang turned and pulled up his shirt. He pointed to the two-inch shrapnel scar on his back.

"Can you tell what they are saying?" I asked Frank.

"She's asking him questions about where he is from, where his parents are and what he is doing here with us," he said. "He just told her about his family getting attacked by the Viet Cong near Quảng Ngãi, and that his mother and sister were killed. He just showed her the scar where he was wounded in the back. He told her he has been with you a long time and he wants to go with you to America."

Sister Le motioned for us to follow so she could continue to show us her school and orphanage. She displayed a lot of pride as she pointed out the shiny terra cotta floored cafeteria furnished with benches and narrow tables arranged in neat rows the length of the thirty-foot room. Down a narrow corridor that opened into a washed out concrete floored workroom, we were introduced to a bustling, commercial laundry resembling the one at the Đức Phổ orphanage, only much larger. It was staffed by barefooted old women proudly moving about from one work station to another in a production line of washing, rinsing, ironing and packaging.

We passed through the laundry down a wider corridor that led to the east side of the complex, and into the boys and girls sleeping quarters, rows of wooden beds covered with bamboo sleeping mats and white sheets. The kids all slept in one big room, so I guessed it was not an issue for girls and boys to sleep in the same quarters here as it would be in America. It was probably a privilege just to have a safe place to sleep, I thought.

"This not school, this orphanage," Quang announced, upset at seeing the sleeping room and neatly arranged beds.

"We do not think of ourselves as orphans here," Sister Le piped in. "You can see all of our children are very happy. We think of ourselves as a big family." She turned her attention to Quang and repeated what she told us in his language.

Quang looked as though he had been scolded and had nothing more to say. His expression said he was not happy though.

Frank gestured that the tour was over and suggested that Quang and I go on out to the jeep. He and the sister huddled in quiet conversation on the raised veranda by the courtyard. After a few minutes he trotted to the jeep, cranked the engine and turned back down the same narrow road going the opposite direction from before. I wondered if this was a one-way street, thinking it would be impossible for two vehicles to pass in opposite directions. Luckily no cars came the other way.

Back at the hotel, Quang jumped from the back seat and ran in the front entryway. He had been silent during the entire ride back and was still pouting. He had decided we were conspiring against him.

"That didn't go as well as I hoped," Frank offered.

"What did you think of the place?"

"It was terrific," I answered sincerely. "I don't know how to thank you, for me and for Quang. This is the right place for him if I can just convince him and get the sister to accept him."

"Sister Le told me she would gladly take him in, if that is what you want," he assured me. "That is what she was talking to me about at the end. She said you could bring him with his belongings tomorrow and they would get him oriented to his new home. I'll come take you and Quang in the morning, if you like, then drop you at the airport if you're planning to leave right away."

We agreed to meet at ten in the morning. As Frank drove away it occurred to me that tomorrow was December 24th, Christmas Eve. I felt bad to be ruining his holiday.

Quang was sitting in the window sill when I entered our room, tears streaming down his cheeks. I went to him and found myself starting to well up. I put my arm around his shoulder. We sat perched awkwardly on the window sill and just held onto each other for a while. When I started to talk, my voice was breaking, but I made up my mind this was too important to let emotions get in the way.

"They told me I can't take you to America," my voice broke the silence. "I tried, but they said no again. You can't stay with the soldiers anymore on Bronco or on Liz. That is why they let me bring you here, to find a new home and school with people who will take care of you."

Quang just sat with a blank stare on his face and the tears started again. I could feel my heart hammering away in my chest and my throat felt constricted.

"Okay, I try," Quang finally spoke up. "I no like, I try."

Frank pulled his jeep to the curb in front of Kampong Hotel precisely at ten. Quang and I had packed our ruck sacks and were sitting out front waiting. It needed to get done and putting it off would just make things harder.

Sister Le was waiting for us when we arrived. Frank had presumed what our plan needed to be, so he had arranged a schedule with the sister before we left yesterday. When he pulled to a stop at the orphanage, Quang leaped from the back, shouldered his ruck sack and bravely walked toward the gate, not looking back.

He was braver about it than I was. I ran up behind him and gave him the biggest bear hug I could muster.

"I love you, Quang," I pronounced. "I will miss you, and I am sorry to leave without you."

He gave me one wordless, long hug, then turned and walked to the sister and pretty teacher who were waiting for him with open arms. I watched as they walked arm-in-arm into Quang's new home without another backward glance.

Chapter 31

I returned from Taipei rested and anxious to leave Vietnam for the last time. Before I left for R&R, I had informed the battalion commander that I would not be remaining in the military. I thanked them for the offer of a promotion, but I had decided I needed to go home and finish college. Now that Quang was settled in his new home, I felt better about my decision, even though it meant I would never see him again.

My orders were waiting for me at the battalion clerk's desk. I was so excited my hand was trembling when the clerk handed them to me. This was the real deal, the last process before going to get on that freedom bird we all fantasized about that would take us back to the world.

The new executive officer emerged from his office and I came to attention and saluted, trying my best to be militarily proper. He returned the salute and invited me into his office.

"I have some disturbing news for you, Sergeant," he began. "I'm afraid the boy ran away from the orphanage in Nha Trang and managed to get back here somehow. He and his little friend, Dam, begged us to let them see you before you leave, so we allowed them on post just for today. They're waiting for you up at the mess tent."

I thanked the major, excused myself while fumbling to find the right words, and hurried out the door. I had to go back in to retrieve my rucksack that I forgot in my haste.

I felt completely deflated, my emotions turning from the excitement of getting away, to the awful disappointment of learning Quang had just destroyed my only shot at peace of mind. And why was Dam on post with him, I wondered. The orphanage and school seemed so perfect. I could not imagine what got into his head to make him run away.

The two of them were waiting expectantly. They started to wave, laugh and cry all at the same time, as they called out my name and ran to me. It was like a planned homecoming to a family I had not seen in months.

"What are you guys doing here?" I yelled, trying to be heard above their celebration.

"Quang come Đức Phổ, tell me he no like orphanage," Dam explained. "He say orphanage Catholic, him Buddha. No like Catholic."

"This is no good," I replied, giving Quang the most disgusted look I could muster. "There's nothing more they will let me do for you. They no let you stay on Bronco any more. I can't do anything to help you now. I have to leave today," I tried to explain.

Quang's little body seemed to shrink into itself as tears welled and streaked his dust coated cheeks. That caused me to turn my attention to his appearance. His clothes were coated with dust and grime. Even his normally shiny boots were red with road muck.

"Why did you run away from the school? How did you get here?" I needed an explanation.

"Not school, orphanage," he whined. "I not Catholic, I Buddha. I not stay there, I run away in one day. Get rides. Get Đức Phổ today and see Dam. Dam say we go find Jared."

"How did you get on Bronco," I asked Dam.

"See G.I. I know, tell him we need go find Jared," she explained. "He bring us to Bronco, see XO," she added, matter-of-factly. "XO tell us wait here, he send Jared."

"Who is going to take care of Quang now?" I asked myself aloud, completely exasperated that all of my efforts and plans had fallen apart.

"I wifer you, go America, you, me, Quang," Dam declared. "No sweat, I take care Quang."

How sadly preposterous, I thought. This terrific fourteen-year-old girl, my language teacher, advisor and friend the entire time I had been here, had it all figured out in her mind how she wanted this to get worked out. She had consistently acted more adult than the boys and girls who were always gathered around her and looked to her for guidance. I viewed her much as I would a little sister. Never in my wildest imagination would I have thought she perceived me as a possible mate. I was only twenty-one but felt light years older than Dam.

"I love you like a sister," I tried to explain. "I'm too old, you're too young. No can do wife."

"Okay, no sweat, you take Quang, go America" she stated emphatically, tears belying her intended brevity.

"No can do," was all I could muster, the words slicing my throat as they escaped my lips. "You take care of each other for me," I added as I picked up my rucksack and started walking away, the dirt roadway to the airfield blurred by the salty tears now filling my eyes.

"Tôi biết Jared, tôi biết Jared," Dam shouted as they trotted along behind me.

I hastened my pace, needing to leave them behind and hating myself for that knowledge. There was just nothing more I could do that would not just cause more pain.

"I take care Quang, no sweat," Dam yelled in her most confident voice as I boarded the C-130 that would take me to Chu Lai and out of their lives forever.

I looked out through the fuselage and could see Quang and Dam silhouetted as the ramp started to close like a turtle shell. They were both waving frantically, desperate for one last glimpse and a final farewell.

"Dam," I shouted, my voice crackling. "You'll forever be my Đức Phổ girlfriend!"

Chapter 32

The division base at Chu Lai was a radical change from the brigade headquarters in Đức Phổ. Officers wore their rank insignia in silver and gold clearly visible on their shirt lapels, and they expected you to salute when you passed by. I got dressed down a couple of times for failing to salute, until I could get back into the habit of checking people around me to pick out the officers.

The base was a sprawling menagerie of wooden buildings, heavily fortified with sand bags around the exterior walls and covering the roofs. I managed to find my way to the personnel office, once a kindly lieutenant saw that I was confused and needed directions. I needed to report in so I knew where to go and what to do to check out.

The office was manned by several clerk typists who mechanically processed soldiers of every rank in and out. When my turn came, I sat in front of the young PFC and handed him my travel voucher. When he saw my name he said he had a message to hold me. Someone from the chaplain's office wanted to talk to me.

I sat across from the PFC and watched as a line of soldiers reported and received their orders that would authorize them to fly to various places for R&R or to ETS,

End Tour of Service, and go home. In about a half hour, a soldier wearing crisply starched fatigues with a chaplain's cross on one lapel and captain's silver twin bars on the other, entered the office. I presumed that he would be looking for me so I approached him, saluted and introduced myself.

He said he thought I would want to know that one of my platoon members was wounded and at the division hospital. He did not know the circumstances except that the soldier's name was Buddy. He offered to walk with me to the hospital. I carefully stowed my travel orders into my pack and followed as he led me out the door.

Familiar hospital odors permeated the humid air once I was inside the vestibule entrance. It struck me that I tasted the smells, a combination of sterile cleansers, rubbing alcohol and ether, the same as when I visited people in hospitals back home. I found the experience somehow reassuring since I assumed all medical facilities in Vietnam would be like the simple evacuation unit on Bronco.

Buddy was in a ward room, where single hospital beds lined the walls on both sides of an isle wide enough to roll beds in and out, and maneuver them into their orderly positions. I found him sitting up in bed and that was encouraging. His left leg was heavily bandaged so he rested on his left elbow, unable to sit up straight.

"Wow, what a surprise," he greeted me as I approached his bed. "I thought you left a couple of weeks ago. How did you find me?"

I was pleased to see that he was completely lucid and did not appear to be in any serious pain. I hoped this was a sign that he was not badly wounded.

I explained my movements since I left them in the field, including the regrettably failed story of trying to get Quang situated, and then taking an R&R to Taipei. I explained how I was held up at division personnel so a chaplain could bring me to the hospital.

"Tell me what happened to you." I was concerned.

Buddy adjusted his black rimmed glasses. It was a familiar gesture. He always seemed to have trouble keeping his glasses in place on the broad bridge of his nose.

"After you left we kept making contact, a sniper here and there, and we discovered some well-placed mines on trails," he began, anxious to fill me in. "Luckily, we didn't trip any of them, and the snipers just fired off a few rounds and disappeared. Sound familiar?" he smiled.

I nodded my understanding.

"The patrol we ran into when I was walking point the night before you left disappeared, too, so that never turned into a conflict," he continued. "But on new-year's day I was not so lucky. One of the other guys tripped a wire and I got the shrapnel from it."

"How bad is it," I asked, anxious that he would fully recover.

"Not bad enough, I'm afraid," he complained. "They had to pick several pieces of shrapnel out of my thigh but they tell me I'll be back with my unit within a couple of weeks. I was hoping it would be my ticket out of here."

"Was anybody else hit?" I asked, anxious about the others.

"I think I was the only one, I'm not sure," he replied. "You know how crazy it gets with the Medevac coming in and people carrying you to get you out of there as fast as they can. I do know that I was the only casualty on the chopper, so hopefully it was just me."

"How is the new platoon leader working out?" I needed to know the guys were being looked after.

"He's great," Buddy declared. "I worry that he wants to walk point himself all the time, though. As officers go, he's the best we could hope for and not so gung ho."

I explained to Buddy that I had to be on a flight to Đà Nẵng today and needed to get to the airport. I hugged him and shook his hand all at the same time in a sort of awkward embrace.

"Please tell the guys I miss them and hope they all get to go home in one piece," I added, as I left Buddy, knowing I was about to mist up.

Chapter 33

The Chu Lai airport terminal was an open air facility covered by a metal roof. A combination of soldiers and civilians filled the waiting area, moving in waves, either to board their assigned flights when called or to score a place to sit when the travelers vacated the rows of slatted wooden benches that served as seating.

Phantom jets created a constant roar as they departed the single runway in squadrons, spraying off in all directions. They were heading off on missions to provide support to troops making enemy contact. I hoped my guys were not one of the units needing them today.

I was finding it hard to get my head around the fact that I was really leaving this place for good. That knowledge brought with it the pain of lost dependency on close allies. I realized I felt more alone than I had ever been, even though I was surrounded by dozens of people.

I could easily distinguish between the cleaned and pressed rear echelon soldiers and the battle worn grunts recently returned from the field. I was in fraternity with those who appeared severely fatigued and disheveled; the privates, specialists and sergeants with wrinkled fatigues and filthy boots, even though I was issued all new gear before I left Bronco.

I managed to score a seat vacated when a flight south was called. A Vietnamese boy in pressed white shirt and navy blue slacks walked over and sat near me. He had a cold soda and it looked awfully appealing in the stifling midday heat.

"Where did you get the Coke?" I asked, pointing to his soda. He pointed to a little red cart next to the check-in booth.

"You buy me one, I give you money," I requested, not wanting to leave my pack unattended or lose my seat. I unbuttoned the pocket of my fatigue shirt, took out the pocket Bible that had found its home there for the last year, and retrieved a crumpled dollar bill. I held it out to him. He looked puzzled so I pointed to his drink, then to my money and motioned towards the drink cart.

He smiled his understanding, grasped the money between his thumb and forefinger and went to the cart. He returned, handed over my Coke and tried to give me change in Vietnamese piasters.

"You keep," I offered, motioning for him to put the money in his pocket. There was no difficulty with that communication as the money quickly disappeared into his clothes. Although younger and smaller, he had the same short cropped hair and long thin face as Quang. From his clothing and well groomed appearance, I guessed that he was the child of a well-to-do officer or businessman. He sat down on the bench next to me and continued to watch me as I popped the top on my drink can and took a long swig.

"I'm Jared, what's your name?" I offered. He continued to stare at me without response so I took it that he spoke no English.

He pointed to my shirt pocket, then reached into his nap sack and removed a black pocket sized book. He held the book out to me and motioned to my shirt pocket once again. I thought I understood that he wanted to see my Bible so I took it out and handed it over. In exchange, he pressed his little book into my right hand.

I could see from the cross on the cover of his book that his was also a Bible. I flipped through the pages and saw that it was written in Vietnamese. He carefully inserted my Bible into his pack and signaled for me to put his Bible into my pocket. He had decided to trade with me, so I tucked his book into my shirt pocket. I reached out and shook his hand, which he didn't quite understand. Then he nodded his head and said "okay."

"Christopher, is that you?" someone interrupted, slapping my back.

It took me a minute to recognize Bobby Dow, who I had not seen since we split company to join our respective units this time last year. I identified him from his stance more than his face. His toes were still pointed outward and his shoulders swayed even more than the last time I had seen him, I thought.

"Man, I can't believe it is really you," I nearly shouted, jumping up to give him a hug. He was really stiff, not responding well to my display of affection.

"You're on the next flight to Đà Nẵng, I guess," he

assumed. His expression was grim and unemotional. His demeanor caused me to inspect his appearance more closely. His heavy beard was unshaven. He still wore his dirty fatigues and boots tarnished from months of wear. He had not bothered to clean up on return from the field, or maybe he just had not had the chance yet. His face and hands were grey with unwashed grime that gave me the impression he had not bathed for some time. I knew the look and the smell that went with it. Extended missions in the boonies without an opportunity to clean up left you in this condition. I guessed he must have arrived here directly from his last combat assault.

"It's going to be crazy if we're on the same flight home after all this time," I observed.

He glared at the boy on the bench where I was sitting. The hateful look made the boy get up and scamper to the other side of the terminal in search of another place to sit.

"I hate every one of these slant-eyed dinks," he declared. "I'd kill them all, men, women and children, if I could. I almost re-upped just to have the chance to take out some more of these slopes. They killed too many of my friends, and I'll live the rest of my life wishing I could have killed all of the bastards who did them."

I could barely distinguish these last words as they were drowned out by more fighter jets taking off, although I figured I had caught the gist of it. I had seen some of our guys consumed by hate and anger, but nothing like what I was witnessing with Bobby Dow. I wondered what ugliness had happened to change the shy and studious young man I left a year earlier.

"I'm having a hard time hearing you," I shouted, trying to be heard above the roar of jet engines.

He leaned into my right shoulder and yelled in my ear that he thought there was a place across from the airport to get a beer. He suggested we should go over there and wait for our flight. It made sense to me. We would be able to see when a C-130 landed and could come back to check whether it was ours.

I hoisted my pack over my shoulder and followed Bobby as he started walking through the rows of benches and throngs of travelers. I glanced back across the pavilion and caught sight of the boy who now had my pocket Bible in his nap sack. I saw that he was watching me so I waved and patted my shirt pocket then smiled to show my appreciation for his trade. He waved back with a big grin creasing his face. I had made a friend and knew I would remember him pleasantly.

It hit me that the little book he now possessed was the only remnant of me I would leave in this country. The realization that I had left nothing of me with Dam or Quang saddened me. I could have left the Bible with Quang, I thought. But he had made it clear that he was Buddhist so he may not have appreciated the gift of a Christian Bible.

That thought brought with it an unaddressed awareness that I no longer held high regard for my southern Baptist upbringing. I had seen and done too much, too many things that would make me a violator of the beliefs of my church back home. I guess I still considered myself to be a Christian. I questioned what gave me, or others of the faith, the right to consider our religion superior to Quang's Buddha or the intense religious rites I had seen practiced by poor villagers and farmers, whether Hindu, Muslim or pagan? I think my religious feelings had evolved into more of a private consciousness. I knew and practiced the differences between right and wrong and that, to me, was what mattered most.

I wondered where all of that heavy thinking came from. I guessed I would probably question myself a lot in the days ahead since most every attitude or belief I had before Vietnam seemed like childhood folly now.

Fortunately, I had taken lots of pictures of Quang and Dam, so I would have those precious remnants. I had sent the film home to be developed and just hoped the rolls had survived the military mail service. The only thing I left with them was a much wounded part of my heart. I knew I carried theirs with me as well.

The intense sunlight reflecting off of the hard packed white sand attacked my eyes when I was out from under the protection of the terminal canopy. I observed that Bobby's pace was that of an old man. He walked slump shouldered, more so than I remembered, and his face was fixed down upon the roadway. His steps were short and timid, like he was being careful not to step on a mine. It was still comical to me the way his toes pointed outward. His boots seemed too large for his body, but that was a memory I had of him from the training camp that now seemed so long ago.

The beer hooch turned out to be a small enclosure with a lean-to porch attached to the front. It offered comfort only to the Vietnamese girl inside. She provided service through a sliding glass window. When she slid the window open, a gust of cool air escaped offering a brief sampling of the air inside, cooled by a window air conditioner. The Ballantine beer she extracted from the cooler was frosty cold and that made the walk from the airfield worthwhile.

We sat with our beers at the one round table. It was a wooden cable spool turned on its side. The makeshift chairs were stacked wooden ammo boxes. We were shaded from the sun, and the airport noise was now down a few decibels, so we could hear each other better.

"I see that you made Sergeant," I observed from the three stripes on his shoulder.

"Yeah, but I'm no leader and sure as hell not gung ho Army," he replied. "I got the rank because I was the platoon leader's RTO and ended up staying in the platoon headquarters section after that. They probably gave me the rank more to get me to keep my mouth shut than anything," he added with a sarcastic tone.

I thought to myself that maybe that's why I got my last stripe. I quickly put that out of my mind since I knew the promotion came from battalion and not our terrible company commander who would, in fact, like me to keep my mouth shut.

Our conversation rambled back and forth awkwardly

for a while as we traded stories about trips for R&R to places like Hong Kong, Taipei and Bangkok, news from home, and our plans once we got home and out of the service. Bobby's desire to return to college seemed to have waned some. I tried to be encouraging by espousing the need to use the benefits of the G.I. Bill we had earned. At the same time, I was not sure I saw the A-student in him that was once there.

Bobby had become truly cynical towards his role in society. He wanted it to be clear that he did not care what anyone thought of him or his actions. He felt betrayed by his country for requiring him to be here in the first place, then not supporting his cause once he was thrown into it.

"We have not accomplished anything by being in this country," he said. "We captured no real estate, we freed no people, we improved no lives and we did nothing to change the country's future. We will not win this war, and I cannot see any way to get out of it since our politicians and generals are too politically influenced to do what needs to be done."

There was a lot of intelligent thought reflected by his comments, yet they were laced with tremendous resentment and negativism.

"Don't you have any good memories of your time here, Bobby?"

"I got to see Bob Hope and Ann Margaret at the USO Show in Chu Lai when I came back from R&R," he declared. "That was pretty cool."

"What do you think needs to be done?" I asked.

"Nuke them, all of them," he declared. "Start with the north, and then clean out all of the provinces like Quảng Ngãi that are thick like a cancer with enemy sympathizers."

"But how would you distinguish between killing the enemy and the innocent civilians?" I wondered, not liking the turn our exchange was taking.

"They're all enemy," he demanded. "Kids are the alarm system with their 'souvenir baby san chop-chop' crap. Mama san tries to look innocent sitting in the village after hiding the men and their weapons. And we have smoked a lot of armed women who killed and wounded our guys with AK-47's and booby traps. Papa san works for the ARVN by day and the Viet Cong at night. How many men older than fifteen have you ever found in a village in Quảng Ngãi Province? There are none," he added, answering his own question.

"There is only one answer," he finished. "Kill them all."

I did not know how to respond or add to Bobby's ranting. He could tell from my reactions that I did not agree with him, but I could see no future in trying to reason with him. After all, we were finished here and nothing I could say would change anything. I did wonder, though, what caused him to be this engulfed in such bile wrenching hatred.

"What happened, Bobby?" I attempted. "Did you guys get into something really awful that makes you hate these people so completely?"

"Did you ever hear of a place called Pinkville?" he started. Without waiting for my response he continued. "Not long after you and I left each other, we combat assaulted into the rice paddies adjacent to this place out near the South China Sea. It was colored pink on the map since so much American blood was shed there."

I didn't interrupt him. I knew that the map coloring indicated an area of dense population, as Lenny learned from our company commander, when we tried to assault there back in the summer.

"Our whole platoon had walked into the wooded area when the men started stepping on land mines. We tried to retreat back to the rice paddy where we landed, but the guys just kept detonating more mines. Only four of us walked out; me, the lieutenant and two others."

"The four of us stayed together until they could get our platoon back up to strength with replacements and transfers," he continued. "By March, we were fully manned and ready for some payback. That's when the assault on the Mỹ Lai villages was planned and we were told to shoot anything that moved. And that's what we did. We gathered up everyone in Mỹ Lai and blew them all away."

I remembered the house we burned when the villagers got excited because of the terrified boy and girl and knew that incident could have gone down the same way. That could have potentially cost the lives of a dozen or more villagers if you counted old people and children. I despised what I was hearing. I had to ask how many people were there.

"Hundreds," he answered matter-of-factly.

We sat speechless as we finished our beers. I was relieved to see a C-130 landing so I could suggest that we needed to get back to the airport. I was enraged and disappointed. I had heard all I could stand to hear, and I think Bobby had said much more than he meant to say.

I had heard stories that something bad happened in Mỹ Lai. I had no comprehension that it could have been as awful as Bobby described. The story of mass murder was just more than I was equipped to handle.

It occurred to me that the stroke of a pen or a switched place in line could easily have sent me to Bobby's battalion and him to mine. I knew I did not want to follow through on where that line of thinking could take me. I guessed I had a reason to feel lucky.

Walking back to the airfield, I wondered if Bobby and the other soldiers involved would be prosecuted. I guessed that, like most things in Vietnam, it would probably be swept under the rug as if it never happened. Nonetheless, I was anxious to get away. It was despicable to me that people like him made us all look like ugly Americans. I was ashamed to know what he told me when there was nothing I could do about it.

There was no doubt he would face a terrible fate having to live with the crimes he committed against humanity. I imagined he would be allowed to simply meld back into society as a college student, boyfriend, employee and even parent. I wondered how many more like him I would meet in my lifetime without ever suspecting their lurid pasts.

Just as we were entering the terminal pavilion, a C-130 departed into the wind to the south. I ran to the boarding podium and asked if that was the flight to Đà Nẵng. The specialist informed me that it was, indeed, our flight. We had become so engrossed in the story of Mỹ Lai that we missed our scheduled departure.

"Don't worry," the specialist assured me. "There is another flight leaving for Đà Nẵng in a couple of hours."

Relieved, I turned away from the podium and heard a thundering explosion to the south. The airplane, filled with soldiers going home, exploded a few miles from the end of the airfield.

I looked at Bobby and saw the shock that rocked me reflected in his gaze. I felt a silent acknowledgement from him that we were still standing here only because we ran into each other. I was taken by the irony that we were alive only because he was telling me about killing hundreds of people.

I waited anxiously for news of survivors. There were none. Neither was there any indication what caused the explosion other than speculation it might have been an RPG or perhaps a bomb planted on the aircraft.

I suddenly remembered the little boy and searched through the terminal hoping he did not get on the flight. I returned to the podium and asked the specialist. He confirmed that the boy did board.

I felt ashamed that I was more devastated by the loss of

the Vietnamese boy than my American comrades, even though I was not acquainted with any of them. The boy carrying my Bible represented all of my feelings of failure for deserting Quang and Dam. My thoughts turned to the anxiously waiting families of all those boys who were finally going home. I could not imagine the depth of sorrow, especially after believing they had lived through it all, just to come to such a tragic end.

Chapter 34

I was relieved not to be seated with Bobby on the Northwest Orient flight when we boarded in Đà Nẵng. He represented the ugliness of the war I wanted to leave behind. We had pretty much said all that we had to say to each other.

The airliner was not on the ground long. Upon landing, the captain expeditiously taxied to a stop and the waiting military ground crew maneuvered the mobile steps into place. The unloading soldiers trotted down the steps and ran across the tarmac to the terminal, their faces showing the stress of their fear and uncertainty. It reminded me of my arrival at Cam Ranh Bay a year ago.

A green army gasoline truck with the letters "Jet A" it's only markings pulled alongside. Within twenty minutes we were boarded, all fueled up, the steps were whisked away and we were on our way.

We sped along the taxiway to the south so fast that I thought we were taking off until the pilot reversed jets, bore down on the brakes, and flipped around to get into position to take off into the wind northbound. Without hesitation, the powerful engines roared to full throttle. We raced down the runway and took off, immediately banking right to head east away from land and out over the South

China Sea.

As we soared through the covering of white towering cumulous clouds, I felt the weight of the war lifted from my shoulders. This would be my final view of the Vietnam shoreline. Nothing could hurt me now. They could not shoot at us up here. It was truly over.

You learn to sleep anywhere and in any position in the army. In Vietnam I had lost my ability to sleep more than an hour or two at a time, always afraid to let my guard down, even briefly. Within minutes after we were aloft I was soundly and blessedly asleep, more completely relaxed than I had been since before I entered the military.

I had a recurring dream. In grade school we sang a civil war homecoming song, *When Johnny Comes Marching Home Again*. In my dream, the streets were lined with cheering people and we were in a homecoming parade, marching proudly in formation, our heads held high. The tune kept repeating over and over in my head.

"When Johnny comes marching home again,
Hurrah! Hurrah!
We'll give him a hearty welcome then
Hurrah! Hurrah!
The men will cheer and the boys will shout
The ladies they will all turn out
And we'll all feel gay when Johnny comes marching home."

I slept through most of the twenty-two hour flight,

waking only when the attendant would touch my shoulder to offer me food or beverage service. After each interruption I would drift quickly back into a slumber and the music would pick back up in my head again.

"When Johnny comes marching home again, Hurrah! Hurrah!"

During my brief waking moments I wondered what sort of reception would greet us. Would the army have a marching band waiting? Would there be some sort of ceremony at the airport or on the base when we arrived? Would family members or loved ones be waiting? God, how I wished Quang and Dam could be there.

The long flight across half of the world ended when we landed in Seattle at night on a white, snow covered runway. On touchdown, the pilot welcomed us home and the anxious soldiers sprang to life in an uproarious cheer. Then it was abruptly quiet again as we all wondered what awaited us. Nobody voiced any hope or expectation that something special might happen, but I knew that we all shared a secret wish for some sort of recognition.

We taxied past the main terminal, then past the gate entrances as the pilot drove the airplane to a dark and secluded part of the airport, next to the air freight terminal. We sat silently peering out the portholes into the darkness, tensely waiting for word of what would come next.

We waited for most of an hour before a line of busses appeared out of the night, their headlights reflecting off of falling snowflakes, as they approached our lonely aircraft.

The flight crew lowered the steps at the rear of the airplane and we filed out and into the waiting line of green army troop transports. The line of troops moved slowly. Unlike Vietnam, there was no urgency, no reason to hurry. I think we all felt a little deflated that nobody came to greet us.

The song kept playing in my head, *"When Johnny comes marching home again..."*

There was no reception. There was no band playing. There were no cheering crowds. It appeared to us that the army had intentionally shuttled us to a hidden place, almost as if they were ashamed of our arrival.

The busses took us on an hour-long ride to Fort Lewis and dropped us off in a dimly lit area of wooden walled buildings. The army clerks methodically checked us in, processed our orders and sent us to supply to get our new dress green uniforms that we were required to wear when traveling via commercial transportation.

All the while the music kept playing in my head. *"When Johnny comes marching home..."*

Finally, after several hours of checking in and getting supplied by the quartermaster, we were directed to barracks that looked like they were carried over from World War II. It was reminiscent of the accommodations we were assigned for basic training back at Fort Bragg. The wood floored barracks with steel framed bunk beds lining two sides of a center aisle, while primitive, were a marked improvement over our digs in Vietnam. Sheets, a blanket, pillow and pillow case lay folded neatly at the foot of each bunk.

I opted to sleep in my jungle fatigues, but I did remove my boots. I tucked the neat stack of bedding under my bunk deciding to use only the pillow without the case. I only intended to use the bed until daylight, a few hours away, when I would make my way out of the army base and head to the airport.

I slept intermittently, popping awake every hour or so to the music in my head.

At five-thirty I awoke to a recorded revelry bugle blasting from somewhere on the post. I had not heard the army's wake-up call since leaving stateside. It reminded me that I still belonged to Uncle Sam.

I went to the latrine to shower and saw that Bobby Dow was already in front of a mirror, shaving. I acknowledged him with a nod; he didn't seem to notice. Seeing him showered and mostly shaven, he reminded me more of the young man I remembered from our earlier time together stateside.

I selected a sink, and began my own process of brushing my teeth and shaving. Bobby, evidently finished in the latrine, turned away from his mirror and walked by me. Although he gazed in my direction, there was no recognition or acknowledgement. He seemed to look right through me. His face was fixed in a glazed mural of pain and hatred. Dark circles lined his bloodshot eyes. He looked like he had not slept in a very long time.

I realized, sadly, that Bobby's payback for his deeds in Vietnam had begun. His eyes would see only what had passed. There would be only a dismal future of lost hopes and dreams. I felt sorrow, not for the empty shell of a person I saw now, but for the hopeful young man he had once been. I expected that his face would permanently bear the shell shock look of battle fatigue that we called the "thousand yard stare."

Chapter 35

I was uncomfortable in the new winter dress green uniform. I was not accustomed to the stiff glossy black shoes and thin socks. The last time I had dressed this way, I was as green as the outfit I was wearing. I now viewed myself as an experienced jungle war veteran and thought the army should provide us with clothing to reflect that accomplishment.

I decided I did not want to wait with the others for the free bus ride to the airport. I shouldered my green duffle bag that now contained all the stuff I had carried in my rucksack, and grabbed a taxi parked next to the bus stop.

"Headed for the airport, I guess," the driver presumed. I noticed that he wore a faded green army fatigue jacket with the name tag Jones on his left chest pocket. He did not look much older than I, though his scruffy beard and long hair probably made him look older than he was.

"Just as fast as I can get there," I confirmed.

"Are you just getting back from the Nam?" he asked.

"Yeah, thank God," I answered. "Are you a veteran?"

"Yes," he answered as he left the curb and pulled into traffic. "I was lucky though. I was in Germany for my overseas tour. That was in 1965 before Nam got so bad. What did you do over there?"

"Infantry, the whole year," I announced with pride.

"It's been a bad year here," he offered. "Martin Luther King murdered, Bobby Kennedy assassinated, students organizing against the war on college campuses everywhere. Race riots, war protests; I think you might have been better off in Vietnam. You need to know that people are not going to be nice to you when you get to the airport. The protesters will be there and they want to blame soldiers for the war."

The Seattle Airport's passenger entrance reminded me of the basement level of a parking garage. It was dark, damp and gloomy-looking.

Up ahead, on the right side, the signs announced the entrance to the gate areas. As we got closer, I could see that throngs of people lined the curb and were blocking entry to the doors. The people were shouting and shoving protest signs in people's faces as they got out of cars, taxi cabs and busses.

Seeing the commotion, my cabbie eased past the Northwest Orient entrance where I was supposed to get out. He drove me to an unmarked set of doorways further down the curb, not occupied by the mass of ugliness we passed at the doors to my gate.

"When I stop, grab your gear and try to get inside the doors quick," the driver instructed. I could see that he was experienced at trying to protect the soldiers he delivered.

I thanked him, sincerely, paid my fare with a five-dollar tip, dragged my duffle bag from the curbside door and made a dash for the terminal entry. Once inside, I realized that the airport police were not having much success at trying to control the mob of protestors. I would have to walk through the harrowing and shouting masses to check in at security.

It was like a bad dream. Rows of people, some in jeans or frocks, others in three-piece suits, shook their fists and waved signs. Distraught mothers, with tears in their eyes, desperately screamed in protest of the war taking their sons. Draft aged young men, some probably college students, chanted "hell no, we won't go!" as they held their draft cards for all to see. An attractive young woman holding a toddler waved a sign reading "bring my baby's father home now!"

The worst were the long-haired, hippy-looking people who screamed obscenities and called me "baby killer" as I tried to walk past. The anger and hate I read in their faces made me want to strike back at them. I despised the way they were making me feel.

These are my people. Why are they attacking me so? I put my life on the line for them. I lost my close friends for them. I killed for them. After a year of facing the enemy, I find myself facing a new kind of enemy, at home, where I am supposed to find peace and love. Where are the flowers in the hair like the song talked about?

I've got to get away from this and find some sanity. Surely my whole country has not gone crazy like this, I thought.

I angrily forced my way free of the mob and ran for a

restroom in the brightly lit corridor, dragging my duffle on the polished tile floor as I went. I slammed open the door and went to a white porcelain basin and splashed my face with cold water. I needed relief from the surprise of an unanticipated confrontation, and the new adversaries who ambushed me.

I glanced in the mirror above the sink and was shocked to see the glassy-eyed and soulless mask of the battered soldier who looked back at me. I recognized the look of failure and despair brought on by my fellow Americans … at home! As I gazed in the mirror, I saw a person I didn't know; face drawn, smile gone and eyes that used to glow looking through me with the thousand-yard stare.

I was overwhelmed by a combination of emptiness and confusion, my emotions now fueled by a senseless and misdirected resentment of those of us who ventured into the face of danger for the country we loved. Instead of the euphoria of a rewarding homecoming, I was descending into a red smoke landing zone, once again "flying into the storm."

> *We fought, for what we did not know,*
> *We returned, but the parades forgot to show.*
> *We survived, but the rewards have yet to come,*
> *We lived, denied memories of youth long gone.*

About The Author

Bill Norris lives in Jacksonville, Florida with his wife Sheila and four cats. He is an entrepreneur who, with Sheila, created businesses having operating locations in most states, across Canada and in Mexico. Bill is a decorated veteran of the Vietnam War. He holds a Bachelor of Arts in Business Administration from Lenoir Rhyne College (now University) in his hometown of Hickory, North Carolina. Although not a pilot in the war, he developed a love for flight from dozens of helicopter combat assault missions. He later earned his wings as a private pilot owning airplanes he flew primarily to expand his business interests.